The Unbroken

Alex Caan

hera

First published in the United Kingdom in 2020 by Hera

This edition published in the United Kingdom in 2020 by Hera

Hera Books
28b Cricketfield Road
London, E5 8NS
United Kingdom

A CIP catalogue record for this book is available from the British Library.

Print ISBN 978 1 80032 112 0
Ebook ISBN 978 1 912973 19 4

This book is a work of fiction. Names, characters, businesses, organizations,
places and events are either the product of the author's imagination or are
used fictitiously. Any resemblance to actual persons, living or dead, events
or locales is entirely coincidental.

Printed and bound in Great Britain by Clays Ltd, Elcograf S.p.A.

To the Red Hot Chilli Writers – Amit, Vaseem,
Imran, Abir and especially Ayisha – my hero

Prologue

The sun cracked the sky like lava as it began to set into the black waters of the Bosphorus. Despite the heat Millie Beaumont felt herself shiver. She was wearing a summer dress, a light shawl in her lap, which she had not wrapped over her shoulders. She closed the car window, turning her gaze away from the cliff-edge roads the SUV was hurtling along. The driver didn't even flinch as he took sharp turns and rounded corners with no idea what was coming in the opposite direction. Millie tried to close off the images in her head, some vehicle bearing down on them, knocking them through the flimsy barrier on the side, the SUV hurtling down the sheer mountainside. They would be dead before they got to the water.

She closed her eyes and rested her head against the car seat, not even bothering to look at her husband, Oscar Hayat. She knew he would be engrossed on his phone, lost to her and oblivious to anything around him. How instantly things had changed. For months he had made her the centre of his existence, his every breath for her, he had claimed. There was nothing that would make him feel differently, he had told her. She had let him lead her to the altar, exchange their love in front of everyone. Only to find herself alone and adrift on the night of the wedding itself.

There were some things, then, that *would* make him feel differently.

Millie felt the familiar pounding in her head, the migraines regular since the wedding day, warnings that everything was wrong. How could she have been so blind? How did she let a man do this to her? Of all the clichés, the naivety and the downright stupidity. How could she have let him play her like this? She felt a mixture of rage and despair itching under her bronzed skin, trying to break out and scream.

She wouldn't though. Girls like Millie weren't expected to scream. They were meant to get on with it. Paint their faces, dress their bodies in the finest labels and live the lives that had been bestowed on them like some sort of charity. Millie Beaumont, the poor girl who had strayed into the marquee of the wealthy. She should have been the cocktail waitress or the one serving the starters; instead, she dared to want to be the one giving the toast. Her audacity. She had to be grateful for life.

As her spirit broke inside, she had spent the last week in Bali, the Indian Ocean paradise of white sand and sapphire waters, smiling for the thousand guests and cameras. Her wedding was a buzz online, social media commenting on what she wore, how she looked, trying to gauge her mood. The world watched, hating her and loving her, vicariously wanting what she had.

It was the same lie the world got told over and over. That wealth was the key to happiness. Money would solve your problems, pay your bills, let you live a life of luxury and escape.

Millie wanted to laugh. She had seen through the façade, seen the dead eyes, people living lives of quiet

3

desperation, masking their cracks with designer handbags and Kensington flats. Money might buy them everything, but not happiness. Oscar had hidden this side of his world so well.

As she played her part in the marriage of the century, Millie had felt her life ebbing. The secrets in her head squeezing her from the inside, crushing the breath from her brittle bones and tight skin. The fake laughter around her hammering at her, mocking her Vera Wang dress and her Louboutin shoes. Sixty different dishes were served; as the wedding banquet lasted from breakfast to afterparty, the guests fed on tables laid out on the beach, served by exotic-looking men and women with model bodies. It was grotesque in its opulence, the groom arriving on a flotilla from his father's yacht which was parked a mile off the island. They were married under a canopy erected on the beach, and when she had looked out across the waters, Millie pretended it was just the two of them and the officiator. Only they were not alone: the applause from the thousand people behind them after they kissed was oppressive.

Millie opened her eyes and looked at her husband. He was tapping and swiping on his phone, far enough for her not to see what he was so interested in. Whatever it was, it wasn't Millie.

She studied his profile, thinking again how beautiful he was. Not pretty, but a man displaying the confidence that came with his lot in life. He had his father's dark eyes, his mother's facial structure and jaw; he looked Italian. She often joked with him about that. Back when they were pretending to be young people in love. Both pretending.

Millie, at first, had thought she could carry on the pretence through their marriage. She knew what she was fighting for, what she wanted from him. But he didn't want the same; she had served her purpose posing for the pictures that were being sent around the world. His wife. The greatest sham. Done. He didn't need her beyond the altar and the kiss, was now willing to spend their lives apart in the same sphere. They had enough houses and interests to go months without having to be in each other's company. Millie's happily ever after, dead, as soon as she had agreed to it. She felt hurt and cheated: despite herself she had loved him. She knew no-one would ever be able to silence the demons inside, or give her the sort of peace she wanted. Still, she wanted him to try, thought he would. Except, he didn't, the promises and declarations of months trampled as he walked down the aisle, his arm linked in hers, but his eyes looking ahead, to the future. His future.

Millie felt tears stinging her eyes. He hadn't even made love to her since the marriage ceremony, the honeymoon villa wasted on them. She had tried, reminding him of the passion they had shared in the months before, but he hadn't even made an excuse. Just grabbed her hands, hard, and pushed them off him, as though her touch disgusted him. As though what she had done was infectious, and he didn't want to be poisoned by her. Millie had cried herself to sleep that night, and every night since. And then told him she wouldn't do it. She wouldn't play this role. Whatever it cost her.

Now they were in Istanbul, the city she had dreamed of visiting one day, the place her own mother and father had met years ago, falling in love while exploring the domes of the Blue Mosque and the cavernous awe of Hagia Sophia. Millie had wanted to do the same, take her husband around this city that spoke of the love of her parents, and feel something similar.

But Oscar had destroyed any chance of that happening. She studied him again, a frown on his face as he typed something furiously into his phone. His mood shifted, and he looked up and straight at her.

'Forgive me if you can,' he said.

She didn't understand, forgiveness for what? His coldness, the way he had used her and discarded her? She didn't have time to think on, as the car suddenly slid to a halt. She was knocked out of her seat, as was Oscar. They righted themselves, and she looked at the driver for understanding. A shot fired through the windscreen, shattering it. Her heart hit her ribcage. The driver's head lolled to the side. Blood poured back over his ear.

She looked at Oscar, who looked back at her hard. He didn't seem concerned or scared, just cold. As though…

Millie didn't get time to think. The car door was pulled open and she was dragged out, her screams loud and raw, as she kicked and fought. She called out for Oscar, again and again, screaming for help. But he never came.

Chapter One

Detective Inspector Sarah Heaton checked her phone again. It still felt too early at five in the morning and she knew her team would not be awake yet. This case was going to be hard, they deserved a bit of rest. She could handle this part. She would ring the alarm later on, when they would be alert and ready to give her what she needed. She had messaged DI Scott Blake, her boss, who was acting up while they filled his vacancy permanently. That meant he felt the pressure to perform, as he angled for the top job. Pressure he applied to Sarah and which she tried to hold back from her team. She thought about messaging her detective sergeant but then stopped. Sarah would start this off. She had worked enough cases as part of her role in the Serious Crimes Unit of the Met Police, she took confidence not from arrogance or ego, but from experience and results. Their unit specialised in cases that the powers that be didn't trust detectives in local stations to investigate, namely because they involved some sort of sensitive or important or connected individual.

This case was bigger than any she had headed up before though. She felt a chill go through her, not just from the sunless morning, but from the shitstorm she knew this case would throw up. Was she strong enough to handle it?

Sarah knew better than to get in the way of forensics as they carried out their meticulous work. There was nothing she would bring to the search.. The CSIs had enough equipment and experience in their arsenal to make sure anything that needed to be found was.

They had already marked out the search perimeter in this section of Hampstead Heath and begun collecting evidence. Faceless bodies in sky-blue plastic outfits, as though they had invaded the earth from some strange scientific base.

Sarah tried to work out which faceless CSI might be hiding the form of Doctor Marcello Ramone, the forensic pathologist normally assigned to their cases. Although there was nothing normal about murder. For Sarah, it was the worst: the proximity of death and a life gone. Her job was now to logically dismantle what had happened, make sense of the why and find out the who. She owed that to the deceased. To be their final voice. An echo of their existence to try and make sense of the end.

A young man on his daily morning run had discovered the body and dialled 999; PC Riz Hussain had been the first responder, confirmed it was a murder scene and started the process that eventually got herself drawn in. She would question him later, or get one of her team to.

A flash of black hair and Sarah spotted Doctor Ramone. He waved at her as he made his way towards her. He always looked so out of place in a crime scene, his Mediterranean looks more suited to a soap opera. The accent just added to his exoticism.

'My favourite officer,' he said, ungloving to shake her hand, his nails manicured, as usual.

'I know for a fact you say that to them all.'

'Who has been talking?'

'All of them.'

The smile vanished from his face, dramatic and sudden, as though he was an actor and it was time for his shot. Serious medical professional she kept reminding herself. She also felt twice as bad. She was judging him for his appearance and accent, the way people had judged her over the years for her gender and her own unpolished accent – in fact those people were still judging her for her new choices in life.

'The serious part. I did a reading of her body temperature. I think she died around midnight. The weather has been consistent and we are using the new kit which correlates against algorithms for external influences to get us a pretty accurate reading. Cause of death seems to be a bullet wound to the front of the head. Close range pistol of some sort from experience, clean entry and no exit wound. Lack of blood in the surrounding area suggests she wasn't killed here. I'll do a more thorough investigation back at the lab and we can facetime for the results later.'

Sarah nodded, her mind reeling with the information that he had just given her.

'ID?'

'The police officer first at the scene knew from all the media coverage, and confirmation is being done by the father based on images from the scene I believe.'

Not how she would have done it, but with technology being the way it was, it was better to get these things done quickly. Especially a case like this. Last thing you wanted was a journalist finding out and breaking the news for you. She wondered at the lack of media presence though.

'Word will get out. Luckily, we are in a secluded spot. There's no reason for anyone to be here; it's not particularly near the Lido or the Pagoda or Golders Hill. It's just a rather depressing raw part of the heath.'

'Probably chosen for being just that,' she said.

Sarah looked around and Marcello was right. There was grass that had lost its colour, trees without leaves and nothing but the wild heath in every direction. You could almost forget you were in London. The ground rose into hills in all directions. She had only been able to find it because of the vehicles that had been parked nearby from the teams responding. You would have to know this spot. It wasn't random: it was chosen because no one would see you access it or leave. You would have to walk for miles before you got to where the main roads around the heath were, where the body might have been transported. Yet someone had to have carried it to where it ended up.

Sarah caught herself. It. Wrong word. She. They knew who this was. It was Millie Beaumont. A young woman cut from the very essence of her life. But Sarah couldn't help thinking, just how did she get from Istanbul to London alive and then end up dying here?

'Do you want to have a look at the body?' he asked.

'Want? No. Need? Yes.'

Sarah put on the shoe covers and gloves that he gave her, then followed him through the thick muddy grounds. The forensics team ignored her. She never understood that level of attention to detail, how they were wired. It always made her appreciate that everyone had their purpose and their strengths. She didn't have the patience for the job yet some people could think of nothing better.

Marcello looked over at her, nodding, preparing her for the moment she would see Millie. Until you were up close you wouldn't really see the body; it wasn't visible from a distance. Sarah felt the silence deepen as she looked at Millie. That first actual interaction. The image that would carry her through the case, keep her focused on why she was doing this.

She recognised the face from the pictures she had seen. They weren't front page news, they weren't celebrities, but the wedding had made headlines for the money spent on it. If you were interested, pictures were available, although surprisingly, not many of the wedding itself. They had signed an exclusive deal with *Hello!* according to reports. They didn't think it was appropriate to publish after Millie and Oscar had gone missing. The pictures online seemed to be taken from social media and older pictures that might have come off phones and cameras. Still, she felt as though she knew what alive Millie looked like. The healthy perfect skin, neat hair, minimal make-up but the invisible kind that enhanced her features, rather than the all too familiar caked on look the next generation seemed to be going for. Even on the wedding day everything about her was understated, as though she was flicking a finger at the Instagram generation. Sarah admired that in her. This woman who could have gone *Drag Race* crazy because she had the platform to do so, chose instead to keep it simple. There was determination in that, a young woman who had purpose, who knew what she wanted from life. A young woman aware of what the world had to offer. It might have been her mixed heritage, but there was just something about Millie that made her stand out surrounded by the vacuous Tamaras and Binkies that probably inhabited the world she had married into. And in death, the young woman was already losing that aura. Her skin had tinges of blue in it, her eyes hidden behind closed lids. Resting face. Only the gaping black wound on her forehead giving away something was wrong. She had been laid down with care, not thrown at an angle. Sarah imagined the father seeing Millie. How his daughter had gone from being his world to this.

There was no point prolonging Millie's journey, her carcass would be dissected by the vicious tabloids for weeks no doubt. The girl with brown skin that had dared to marry into the establishment, then paid a price for it. The pressure built inside Sarah, as she became more and more aware of just how much focus would be directed towards her team. She told Marcello he was free to take the body. But Sarah wouldn't allow her just to be another case number. She was determined to find out what had happened to her. It was time to call in the back-up.

Chapter Two

'Don't fucking come near me, I've got mace!'

Moomy was looking for her keys, on her knees, scrabbling around in pebbles and bits of weed. It was 3 a.m., the Edgware Road traffic at an unusual lull. She kept looking at the entrance to her mansion block, hoping someone from one of the flats would go for a late-night walk, or come home. She couldn't be the only person out so late. Maybe she was. Stuffy old twats.

When she saw him for the first time she thought he was going to mug her. She was pissed, tired, shoeless (how did that happen?) and technically homeless and he was a random black guy who had come out of nowhere. Hey, she was allowed to be prejudiced – she was technically an ethnic.

But where were her shoes?

She saw the shock on his face after she had screamed at him.

'Get the fuck away from me!' She needed a lock on her mouth. It didn't help he stayed silent.

Until he jangled some keys and then she guessed he lived here. He opened the communal entrance. He would have been right to slam it after himself. Luckily for her he didn't. She tried to stagger to the door, but tripped over herself, as she was still sprawled on the floor and didn't realise it.

'Fuck it.' She hurried in, the warmth of their block hitting her exposed flesh.

The red strapless number had seemed like a good idea at 7 p.m., to make an entrance to the hottest Chelsea bars and clubs where she was meeting her girls; not so good when she was fuzzy headed. Maybe someone had given her Rohypnol. She couldn't remember.

She didn't see where the man went. She lived in the basement, so she rode the stairs down to her flat, like she used to ride the stairs back home. Hump hump hump. She got to her front door by crawling and then passed out.

Her last thought was: 'Where are my fucking shoes?'

–

It was still dark when she woke up. No, that wasn't true. She was woken up, the man's face looming in at her.

'Are you okay?' he was saying. American accent. He looked quite cute from this angle. Fuck, she was a mess. He must think she was a lush. He might be her neighbour but he might still be a rapist or murderer or something. No, they had CCTV. He wouldn't get away with it.

'Yes,' she muttered.

'Do you live alone?'

Why did he want to know? The adrenaline of fight always came before flight in Moomy's case.

'Fuck,' she said.

'You look pretty… ill. You got anyone to look after you tonight?'

Fuck, he looked like Will Smith. She was becoming lucid, could feel her limbs again, feel them bent out of shape.

'I'm fine,' she managed. It sounded distant.

'Okay. If you say so. The Super ain't here, so if you get stuck you can sleep on my couch. In case your keys are…' He gestured out behind and above him. 'Apartment 305, third floor. I'll be up for a while. Third floor.'

'I'm fine,' she said.

'Okay. Like I said…'

He went away. Moomy slumped against her front door and went to sleep again.

–

It was breaking dawn when she woke up. She tried banging on the building manager's door but no one answered. She had no keys. Her spare set was in the office. There was no way she was getting an Uber down to Vauxhall. Actually, Sarah had a set too. Moomy texted her, asked her to drop them off in the morning.

Moomy decided she needed a slash. What was that guy's apartment? Shit. Third floor: she could remember that much at least. Where were her shoes? How could she lose her shoes? What had gotten into her tonight? Well, last night. Was that right?

Harry. Bastard. Even now, the thought of him brought tears to her eyes.

She hated him. Yes, she did.

She wanted her mum. No, she didn't.

Mumtaz wanted her mum. And Mumtaz was dead and fucking buried. Moomy was who she was now. And Moomy didn't want anything to do with that cow.

The elevator pinged when she got to the third floor. She was trembling now, the morning cold affecting her limbs even inside the building. The doors to the different apartments all looked the same. The velvet carpet felt good though. Where would she start? She leaned against each apartment door listening in, seeing if some background noise like TV or music would give him away.

She got a mad dog barking at her behind one door. Fuck, she nearly jumped out of her skin. So she kicked that door. That was clever. He lived a couple of doors down and opened his front door at the commotion.

'Found it then?'

'Yes. Can I use your facilities?'

'Sure.'

She looked around wearily in his sparse modernist flat, trying to plan an escape route, identify weapons. His toilet was in the same location as hers. She caught sight of her face in his bathroom mirror after she was done, recoiled, decided a freshly scrubbed look would be better than The Joker look she had acquired. She pinched her nipples before she left the bathroom.

He was chatting on MSN when she found him. She had used his toothpaste and even dabbed on his cologne. Her feet didn't bear thinking about, collecting debris like they were. Where were her shoes? Maybe she shouldn't stand on his carpet. She felt more awake though.

'Thanks,' she said.

'No problem,' he said, turning away from his chat windows.

'I'm Moomy.'

'Jake,' he said. He held out his hand. It felt cool and strong as she shook it.

'You're American,' she said, feeling dumb straight away. He knew he was. 'Which part?' Desperate to redeem herself.

'I'm from LA.'

'No one's from LA. People just move there to be movie stars.'

'I really am. Grew up around Crenshaw.'

'Thought that was Korean?'

'You been? Then how would you know? I'm from LA. And you?'

'I don't think you are.'

'You're quite opinionated for a drunk lady,' he said.

'I sober up fast when I'm in a strange man's apartment.'

'I'll make you some coffee.'

'You got any brandy for that coffee?'

He didn't answer. She texted Sarah, told her she was okay, at a friend's, keys could wait.

'I think the coffee might be better black,' he said. 'I think there's enough alcohol in your system probably.'

'Sorry. Who died and made you my dad?'

He ignored her, got her straight coffee.

'How old are you?' she said.

'Twenty-eight. Yourself?'

'Twenty-seven. The unlucky number.'

'What do you mean?'

'Janice Joplin. Amy Winehouse. Although I think most of my life has been pretty shitty.'

He didn't reply. He wasn't her therapist. She sucked in the coffee.

–

Moomy wasn't sure who made the first move. She liked to think it wasn't her. She knew this was a lie though.

One moment they were talking about post-Trump America and then she was asking him about high school, girlfriends, sex, then they were exchanging saliva and looking for condoms.

He warmed her croissants while she showered. She was light-headed and sober when they ate together on the sofa in his room, awkwardly. This was why you didn't stay after the shag.

Her phone rang as she had a croissant halfway to her mouth. Encrypted number showing on her screen. Work.

'Detective Sergeant Moomy Khan,' she said seriously.

The look on Jake's face.

'Moomy, it's me,' said Detective Inspector Sarah Heaton on the phone.

'I told you to drop the keys off in the morning. I'm at a friend's.'

'Friend? What sort of friend?'

'You're so fucking judgemental. I wish I'd known you before you changed. I bet you were a right goer.'

'You need to get dressed. I'm picking you up in fifteen minutes,' said Sarah, ignoring her.

'It's seven a.m.,' Moomy said.

'And?'

'I hate you sometimes.'

'Just sometimes?'

'You know, I left my parents' home for a reason.'

'It's important.'

Moomy looked at the still shocked Jake, winked at him and made her way to her flat.

'Go on spoil my day. What have we got?'

18

'Are you alone?'

Moomy stayed quiet until she was outside Jake's flat.

'Yes, I am now. Also I'm locked out, so I don't have clean clothes. What's going on, Sarah?'

'Millie Beaumont. You know the case?'

'Yeah the newly married one? Went missing with her husband in Istanbul a week ago?'

'Yes. They found her.'

'I don't get it. What's that got to do with us?'

'They just found her body.'

'In Istanbul?'

'No. Hampstead Heath. I'm on my way from there now.'

'Are you shitting me?'

'No.'

'Someone kidnapped her in Istanbul, killed her and dumped her body in London? What the actual fuck, Sarah? Am I drunk?'

'Probably, but I don't have time to question that.'

'And what about the husband? Oscar?'

Sarah didn't reply for a beat. Then: 'He's still missing.'

Chapter Three

Victor felt the buzz of the night before him as he sat at his kitchen table inhaling another line of coke. He had perfected the art of pretence, letting others around him think he was out of it, when he really wasn't. He had laid out two lines: one harmless placebo powder, the other the dirtiest-probably-cut-with-spice he could find. That was for Spencer, who had readily inhaled it. Victor laughed at Spencer thinking he was enjoying the experience. In reality Victor saw another defeat for his brother, another day he had managed to take golden boy and show him off for the incompetent fool he was.

They had just spent a tough week together, holed up on some ass wank island for their brother's wedding to that shaggable Millie Beaumont. Millie Hayat now. Trust Oscar to pick an outsider to marry: no one in their circle was stupid enough to go for him. And then the nightmare of them being kidnapped. Fucking useless. From Bali to Istanbul via gangster's paradise. Trust fucking Oscar.

Spencer's head hit the glass of the kitchen table; Victor's eyes flickered, a moment of hoping he was dead. Spencer lifted his head, grinning, blood pouring out of his nose. Great. Victor helped him up, took him to the bathroom, got him cleaned up; his shirt was stained though. He could have helped him change, but no, Victor wanted golden boy to go home and show his parents exactly what he was.

Spencer was running around the flat now, dancing to songs in his head, taking off his clothes. Off his fucking face. Victor filmed it on his phone. It would be useful one day. Maybe this day. Victor poured himself some champagne, his first actual drink of the night. As Spencer had guzzled his way through bottles, grinding against every desperate girl in the King's Road, some of them titled, all of them entitled, Victor had stuck to tonic water. Spencer thought it was vodka.

'Yes Spenny loving life, mate,' he said now, cheering his brother and sipping at the ice-cold drink. 'Totally loving life.'

—

'How?' Lara's eyes were sore, red. 'What about Oscar?'

She was lying in the Marie Antoinette four poster in their Knightsbridge townhouse, to where she'd decamped after the wedding. They needed the downtime, it had been a full-on week. It had been a full-on two months. Oscar insisting he wanted to get married quickly. But Lara knew it was Millie. She knew it was Millie pressuring her precious son to do this. Eager to get her hands on his money no doubt.

'They don't know the details yet. Bill identified the body; she's been shot.' Her husband, John, so composed, so unaffected. He was so cold, not displaying emotion even as their son was lost to them. And now Millie was dead, what did it mean for Oscar?

'Let me speak to him, to Bill,' said Lara. 'He must have made a mistake. He's not in his right mind, he's never in his right mind. His wife… well, you know the situation.'

John stared at his wife. She seemed to be in the middle of a parallel drama, making this all about her.

'Bill is her father. He knows it's Millie,' he said softly.

'If she's dead then what does that mean for Oscar?' Lara said, hysteria in her voice. She pulled back the sheets and tried to get up, but slumped back into the bed.

'They don't know, my love. He isn't with Millie. So there is hope.'

'What do you mean? Our son has been missing for over a week. Why aren't you there looking for him still?'

'I spent a week looking for him. We searched every inch of Turkey. My people are still searching for him. He wasn't with Millie. That's something, there is still a chance.'

Lara closed her eyes.

'That bitch. She did this to him. If it wasn't for her… you know I hope they find she was tortured to death. It's what she deserves for what she did to this family.'

John stood, shocked, staring at his wife, at the hatred she had for Millie. He didn't understand what it was. And all the while he was worried sick for his son. Scared that Oscar was paying the same price as Millie.

Chapter Four

Sarah knew Moomy was irritated. It was too early for her, and more than that she hated being in Sarah's Toyota. Her fingers drummed on the dashboard; she was lowering and raising the car window. Then lit up, blowing smoke purposefully into Sarah's face. Sarah had brought her spare keys, so Moomy had changed into a black dress, finished off with tights and boots to ward off the cold. She had managed to put on a full face of make-up though. Sarah could see past the mask, most people couldn't.

'What is that?' Moomy said, eyeing up Sarah's own dark pants and grey shirt. 'Primani again?'

'I don't shop there anymore, you know that.'

'Oh yeah, I forgot. Fucking save the planet organic clothes shop now.'

'Nothing wrong with buying from charity shops and places that sell ethically produced clothes.'

'Nothing right about it,' Moomy muttered, flicking invisible tobacco off her tongue. It was a tick she had when she was thinking. 'I know you live on a fucking council estate, and grew up on a fucking council estate, but honestly. Do you have to push your sanctimonious poverty into everyone's face all the time?'

'Okay, fine I'll stop here, get your paracetamol, deal with your hangover and please get yourself together before we get to the office.'

Moomy grinned, kissing Sarah on the cheek as the car came to a halt. She bounced out, half running. She looked like she was going to a Goth club.

Sarah sighed, remembering why she was so lenient with Moomy. Why she was the only one who could work with her. It wasn't just Sarah, at forty-three, being over a decade older than Moomy. Moomy had spent a drunken night at Sarah's soon after they had started working together in the Met, just a year ago, where she had opened up to her, where she had told Sarah what life and her family had done to her. Although Moomy did have a point, Sarah thought. Sarah was proud of her background. She came from less than nothing, didn't even go to university, and still she had carved an important career for herself in the Met police. Moomy wasn't so different. She might live in Chelsea bars and rent a flat on the border of Little Venice and St John's Wood, but it was all paid for by credit cards. A manic breakdown had fuelled her spending spree for years.

'Here, got you some cheapo value chocolate, I know label-less food is the only one you enjoy. Swallowing your poverty with each bite.'

'I only eat...'

'Yeah, yeah, ethically sourced. It is. You should use cooking oil in your car too, don't know how you manage to deal with the petrol you're pouring out into the world.'

They drove in silence as Moomy washed down her tablets with Red Bull.

'So, come on, before Sexy Scotty gives us the lowdown, what do we know so far?'

'Millie Beaumont, twenty-two...'

'Fucking hell...'

'You saw the wedding?'

'Yes, of course, you know I dig that shit. Instagram explosion. Her husband's a social media freak. And then the kidnapping, on their honeymoon. Fucking crazy.'

Moomy had her phone out, tapping away and then thrust it into Sarah's face.

'Can you not do that while I'm driving?'

'Soz.'

'They were on their way to a private mansion his family own in the Istanbul hills. It was the first leg of their month-long trip, only their car was hijacked on its way. The driver, a local man, was shot dead. Millie and Oscar disappeared, no trace whatsoever. It was a mountain pass where they were taken, very little traffic and no witnesses to what happened.'

Moomy went back to her phone. Sarah knew what she would see. Lara Hayat (nee Wickham) was from a family that were heirs to vast property portfolios, her family tracing their ascension back to Henry VIII, surviving wars and revolutions. They owned a number of exclusive addresses across the capital. When Lara had married John Hayat their combined interests created a monstrous business empire.

'They own houses all over the fucking Monopoly board, only in reality,' Moomy quipped. 'They have three kids it says, three boys.'

Oscar was heir apparent to the business, with Victor and Spencer, the younger sons, also involved. Like most of these families they were not in the press, preferring anonymity to protect themselves. Apart from Oscar.

'It says John Hayat struck it rich through a string of successful fast-food restaurants and supermarkets across America, before expanding to gas and steel. Big player on the world market and richer than Lara's family even. Dodgy as hell probably. No one is that rich and self-made and not. Hayat doesn't sound very American. Met Lara when she was walking for New York Fashion Week, when she was twenty. A decade separates them. He looks hot though, I can understand why she would fall for him. She didn't need his money anyway. No ransom demands yet?'

'None that we're aware of. Unless the family are hiding them from us,' said Sarah.

'Maybe knocking off Millie is the threat they needed. They'll be willing to pay a lot more knowing what happened to her. What might happen to their son?'

Sarah drove on, the traffic thin as they wound their way through north-west London.

'I can see Oscar Hayat being a target. Millie though? Anything in her background?'

'She's the only child of William and Angelica Beaumont. The father used to work as a civil servant, as did his wife. Until she got early-onset Alzheimer's. Gave up work to look after his wife. Modest family from what I can tell.'

'But Millie met Oscar at Oxford. How modest can they really be? Compared to the Hayats, sure.'

'She was a scholarship student from the bits I read online.'

'Trust you to do your research before you even got to me,' said Moomy. 'Scott will be impressed.'

Sarah didn't reply. The relationship between DI Blake and DS Khan was not an easy one and she usually ended up playing referee between them.

'So who found the body?'

'A PC Riz Hussain. Works out of Hampstead police station, I need you to go and speak to him. See if we missed anything.'

Moomy gave Sarah a look.

'I'm sure he's lovely. Be nice.'

'I'll try.' Which was code for she probably wouldn't. Sara just hoped Moomy didn't let her personal feelings get in the way of this case. It was too big to mess up.

Chapter Five

Victor saw the look on his mother's face, the brief glance over his shoulder, the registering of disappointment. She looked a mess, her face puffy and aged from the crying. Propped up in bed like some invalid, instead of prancing around like the show pony socialite she was. Looking over his shoulder for her fucking golden boy. Who wouldn't be coming.

'I tried to get hold of Spencer, but he's not picking up.'

Lies. Spencer was stoned out of his brain and feeling the effects of the sleeping tablets Victor had given him on top. He probably wouldn't wake up for a good twenty hours, snoring away in Victor's spare room. Victor couldn't help feeling good about that. Another plan working his way.

'You came,' John said. He placed his hands on Victor's shoulders, squeezing them for comfort and support. Shoulders his father knew were strong enough to carry the family forward. And now it was his chance to convince his mother, the one who would champion Spencer's cause. Her second born, blond and blue-eyed Spencer who looked like a mirror image of her. Victor had his father's darker colouring, and his father's rougher nature. Clever but not the best with people. Unlike party boy Spencer. Heir apparent with Oscar gone. Heir transparent more like, a cliché of what money could do.

'Are they sure?' Victor asked. Dutiful son, dutiful brother. When he had heard he had been devastated for Millie's family. Whatever he thought of his own, the Beaumonts seemed like decent people. His sadness had evaporated as Spencer had laughed like a maniac at the news. It had turned into hatred for his brother instead. And he remembered why he did what he did.

'Yes,' his father said assertively. His mother began sobbing.

'What do we do? Who did this? And where is Oscar? What do you need me to do?' Victor said.

'No sign of Oscar yet,' John said. 'I need you here since your useless brother seems to be MIA. Look after your mother while I deal with the police.'

Victor gave his best martyr look; his father hugged him.

'Why don't I help you? We can find Spencer to look after her?'

The words sounded harsh and he saw his father flinch slightly. Victor was asserting himself at an inopportune time. Then again, Spencer wasn't around.

'Maybe you should wait for Spencer?' his mother said hesitantly.

'I don't have time,' his father muttered.

'You can rely on me,' Victor said, holding his mother now.

Strong, reliable Victor. The future. The dependable future. A future now where he only had to deal with Spencer. Oscar was gone surely, no longer a problem for his dreams?

'Wait for your brother. When he bothers to show, I want you in the office. There are people who need us.

It will be a big help, allow me to focus on finding your brother.'

Victor nodded, his ambition blazing.

—

William Beaumont's voice broke as he said it. He let out an animalistic sob, and then swallowed it back. Bill wouldn't break. Not yet. He was too strong, he had to be. He held Angie's hand, feeling her dark skin, always so soft and papery, frozen in position because she couldn't move it anymore. He looked into her eyes, the black eyes that he had fallen in love with so many years before. Eyes that still lit up when he was in front of them. Eyes that probably had little idea of who he was.

The Alzheimer's had been sudden, early, devastating. Within months Angie had gone from wife to patient to stranger. As her mind gave in so did her body, until she needed to be under medical supervision in a care home. They pumped her full of liquid food, vitamins, medicines. All trying to keep her alive. The look on their faces always the same: let her go she's not here anyway. But Bill couldn't do it. Not to his wife. Not to Millie's mother. As she breathed there was life, there was hope.

Only now, there was none.

He gripped his wife's hand, hoping today she would feel the torment in him. The need in him. Their precious baby was gone. Missing for days and then gone. Someone had ripped her from the world. They had all thought Angie would go first. Instead, life had taken Millie from him. His future, her future. He had imagined grandchildren, the look on Angie's face when she tried to place them. Would they trigger something in her? Bring her back to him in some moment?

And now? Seeing his precious daughter laid out like that. Cold and gone. The bullet wound through her forehead.

'Is this Millie?'

God please no, it's not her, make it not be her, let there be some sort of mistake, a universal mix-up. A miracle, anything. And then realisation that it was real, his everything was gone. His life plans empty, finished. Millie and Angie both taken from him. His precious girls, the loves of his life.

He felt the tears fall and brushed them away quickly. Angie looked distressed, confused. He didn't want her to worry, to pick up on his grief. He smiled at her, kissed the back of her hand, stroked her cheek.

'Everything is just grand,' he said.

She nodded. Not believing him or not understanding. Just agreeing to his voice because somewhere she recognised it.

Bill closed his eyes, the silence of the room suffocating and placating him at the same time. Everything taken from him. It wasn't an understatement; he was at a place where he was questioning everything. And what he needed most of all was someone to blame. And someone to take out his revenge on.

Chapter Six

PC Riz Hussain looked like he was the same age as Moomy, probably slightly younger. He was the new breed, fresh graduate encouraged into the Met to improve its diversity and bolster its dwindling numbers. She tried not to hate Pakistani men on introduction. Really tried. She knew it was never about them, they just reminded her of her past. And none of the men from that past had been good to her. Still, she shouldn't demonise a whole race, that's what fuckhead Nazis and right wing nutjobs did.

Riz was based at the local Hampstead Police Station, not a far walk from the heath. It was an odd location to put someone like him. Moomy didn't think Hampstead was particularly diverse. In her head it was rich white people mixed with a few Arabs and Indians. She asked him as much. He looked bemused.

'Are you only there to make up the equality and diversity numbers?' he asked back. There was none of the rudeboi attitude she hated, the one that reminded her of the people she had grown up with, so she decided to give him a chance. Maybe he was like her? On the outside? She knew what it would mean, him joining the police.

'What time did you get the call?'

'It was around six thirty in the morning, just before I alerted you guys.'

'You guys' being her and Sarah via New Scotland Yard HQ in St James's Park.

'Jogger by the name of Craig Hughes, twenty-three. He found the body.'

'That's early. Did you ask the guy what he was doing jogging in the dark at that hour?'

'The sun was rising in the sky by then, there was a weak light. He works for Goldman Sachs, does his runs early, works hard, parties at night.'

Moomy knew the type well. They littered the sort of bars she went to. Burnt out by thirty.

'How did he find it? It's not an easy place.'

'It's his route as no one uses it. He's terrified of dogs, so tends to go places dog walkers wouldn't. Said he's mapped it out carefully. Said he nearly stumbled over it, didn't see it until he was practically standing on top of it.'

That fit with what Moomy had seen and what Sarah had reported as well. It wasn't meant to be discovered this early.

'He said he recognised the body, thought it might be the missing girl. He knew friends in common with friends of her husband. Six degrees of separation sort of thing.'

'And when you saw the body? Did you touch it?'

'She was shot in the head, it was clear to see. No one survives that, so I did a cursory check. Just for a pulse, just in case.'

'How was she laid out?'

Riz took out his phone and showed Moomy the pictures. Millie was on her back, eyes closed, bullet hole visible, but the blood had been cleared. Sarah would be seeing this live. Moomy did not envy her that.

'Obviously, someone shot her, cleaned her up, drove her across London and then left her,' Riz said.

'What did you do after that?'

'Usual protocol. Called forensics and the boss and your lot. Running a check on vehicles that might have accessed the area. There's a dearth of CCTV though around here. Most of it points to people's houses; they're worried about what might happen to their sofas rather than random strangers on the street.'

'Anything of interest?'

'Nothing yet, way too early.' Moomy knew the tech team back in HQ would look for the licence plate on traffic cams and let her know if they found anything.

'Anything else unusual?'

'Nothing. Obviously, I knew the victim from the press reports, so we locked the case down quickly to avoid media leaks. It's going to get out though.'

'If it does, I'll blame you. Who else knows about it?'

For a moment he looked scared. Only a moment. Moomy smirked at him. They knew it was impossible to control information these days.

'One thing though,' he added as an afterthought. 'The case was assigned straight to your team. Normally we would investigate this out of our station, but this one was flagged top priority.'

'That's the power of money,' Moomy said.

Moomy messaged Sarah as Riz spoke, just to alert her the case had been escalated to their team. It would mean DI Blake would be under pressure, so they would have to put on their best show for him. She didn't think she'd get anything of interest from Riz, so decided to head off to her next appointment. It was with Millie's parents.

She had hoped Sarah would deal with that side. Moomy hated family situations. They were always reminders of the mess that her own was. Still, she had to do it, see what secrets Millie and her family held that might have got their daughter killed.

Chapter Seven

Bill Beaumont was a tragedy, a man in his late fifties whose face was reflecting the pain he was in. Moomy couldn't even begin to imagine what he was feeling. What possibly could anyone say to him? And here she was digging it all up for him, not even letting the wounds heal.

'My beautiful, clever, brave daughter. She was so amazing. I know all parents think this. She really was though. I can't believe this...'

He couldn't control the tears, covering his face to stop Moomy seeing him at his lowest. Moomy put a hand on his shoulder. Fuck protocol, she wasn't a robot. This man was in pain.

Moomy stared at the pictures of Millie around the room. The mixture of her parents evident in her; she had her mother's colouring and her father's features. She wondered at the relationship between them though. Millie, for anyone looking at her, would be classed as black. They would assume some sort of Afro-Caribbean background anyway. Bill was white as they came. Still, loving someone wasn't about that. Her own parents were as brown as her and yet they hadn't loved her. Fuck them. This wasn't about her or them it was about Bill and his daughter.

'It's fucking shit, I know. I can't even say sorry because what good is that. This stuff shouldn't happen to anyone. There is no way I can take away what you're going through or what you're going to go through. What I can do is help catch the bastards that did this and fuck them up for you.'

He laughed through his tears at her earnestness.

'Thank you. I believe it. The officers who called to tell me she had… they were a lot more polite. But you're right. I can't be magnanimous and forgiving today.'

Moomy squeezed his shoulder and sat back. She needed a fag. She hardly smoked these days, who needed cancer on top of all the other crap life gave you, but sometimes it was the only thing that worked. Especially since getting mind numbed from vodka shots was for some reason frowned on while on duty.

They were meeting in the house Bill shared with Millie. She hadn't had time to move in with Oscar, he told her. After university she had come home, a final push at helping him out. Even though things had changed now that Angie was in a medical facility. It was a small terraced house on the Surrey borders, the zone between Croydon and where the really expensive estates had been built. He told Moomy he had sold everything to pay for his wife's care. That really he had nothing left, Millie was helping financially as well as emotionally.

Moomy hadn't asked him to give her a tour of Millie's room yet. She would go up later herself. There were pictures of Millie with her parents all over the lounge they were in. Always stopping when Millie was a teenager. The time her mother became ill.

'Did you let your wife know?'

Bill shook his head.

'There's no point. She wouldn't understand. She doesn't recognise me or Millie. I'm scared she might have her one lucid second in years when I tell her, that this will be so devastating it will get through and it will be the one thing she understands. Abnormal thinking.'

'There is no normal for this. Seriously you don't owe anyone any excuses or explanations. No one can understand.'

'It doesn't make any sense. This should have been the beginning of her life. She just found the man she loved, they had this surreal wedding, she was supposed to be starting her happily ever after. After years of us dealing with her mother's illness, I thought, finally, Millie had found her happiness. The sacrifices she made for us being paid back to her multiple times. Instead…'

Moomy allowed the silence to sit between them. She couldn't work out why anyone would want to harm this family. They seemed so innocuous. Too innocuous.

'What did you do before your wife was taken ill?'

'I worked for the Foreign Office. As an accountant. I still do tax returns for people, from home; it brings in some money. I just couldn't work full time when my wife became ill; and when we moved her to the home, I stayed with the work from home. Increased my client base, did some more tax returns for the Foreign and Common-wealth Office as well.'

'Did you get to travel at all?'

'Yes, just a couple of postings. Me and Angie met while I was posted to Istanbul the first time. My second posting was to Madrid.'

'What was Angie doing in Istanbul? When you met?'

'She was on a gap year after university. She had just studied biochemistry. It was a hopeful time. Before Millie, probably the happiest times we spent. Angie cut short her travels and ended up staying six months in Istanbul with me.'

'That's why Millie went there?'

He nodded, his eyes taking on a brightness of happier times.

'What did your wife work as? Before she became ill?'

'She was a lecturer for Imperial College, in biochemistry.'

'She never did any work for a commercial firm?'

'Nothing like that. Hated corporations. She was a free spirit in a way, enjoyed interacting with her students, fulfilling their potential.'

'And Millie? What did she do?'

'She was always bright. We didn't have a lot of money as she was growing up, but it was more than enough compared to others. We were normal.'

Moomy imagined that on their civil service and lecturer salaries they probably had a comfortable life. Until his wife got ill.

'When Angie got ill, Millie was only fifteen. It was her GCSE year and within months things just went from normal to bad. It really became a hand-to-mouth existence while she did her A levels, so when she ended up at Oxford to study PPE, it was an amazing day. My wife was too far gone to properly understand but she still had some semblance of recognition. I remember the smile on her face as Millie told her.'

'PPE?'

'Philosophy, Politics and Economics. It's the course that runs the country. Its alumni are in every sphere of influence. And there was Millie. My daughter.'

What a waste, Moomy thought. Here was a girl who wasn't born with a silver spoon up her ass and could have made a real change. She could probably count on two hands the number of black or mixed-race women at Oxford and probably on one finger those doing PPE. And now that was it, all that change and potential. Gone.

Bill got up, offering to make Moomy some tea, his memories clearly too painful. Moomy declined his offer but waited while he made himself some. Distraction time to get his head in order she supposed.

Moomy took a closer look at the small house, the signs of make do evident. Nothing was in bad shape but everything was dated. When you had care bills to pay buying new furniture or replacing carpets were probably low on your priority.

Bill seemed calmer when he came back. Stoic. The dams people build to stem their grief. Moomy knew how that worked. But it always found its way through the cracks when you least expected it. Even now, twelve years later, it had the ability to wind her severely. Her body ached in a familiar rage and devastation. She bit it back. She would save dealing with her own demons for another day. Today was about Millie and finding the bastards that had murdered her.

Chapter Eight

Sarah was feeling disquiet back at HQ in Vauxhall, as she waited to catch up with DI Scott Blake. She didn't believe in gut feelings but couldn't shake her doubts about this case. Already it was more complicated than she'd ever had to deal with in the past. How do you get a kidnap victim across Europe alive and then end up killing them and dumping them in London? And where exactly was the husband while all of this was going on?

Scott was on the phone when she entered his office, rolling his eyes as he gave perfunctory answers to whoever was on the line.

'Foreign Secretary,' he said when he was finished. 'They are concerned.'

'I can't imagine they care much about Millie Beaumont,' Sarah said. 'The pressure must be from Oscar's family.'

'Of course. Still, Jane Haslam is a nasty piece of work at the best of times, we don't need her sniffing around getting in the way of this.' The Foreign Secretary, Jane Haslam, was notoriously rude, patronising, borderline racist and had a mouth that didn't think before it engaged. She was constantly in the press for her blunders, yet her closeness to the PM kept her safe from being shifted around. She was being touted as a possible leader of the party, which was more frightening.

'Noted,' Sarah said softly. 'What about the Hayats?'

'John Hayat is on his way here. He asked to speak to us himself. Wants to be as helpful as he can. He believes Oscar is still alive and wants to do anything he can to keep him that way.'

'Why is he so convinced?'

'Lack of a body. Why wouldn't he be?'

Scott was wearing the lack of sleep and stress on his face. It was 10 a.m. but felt a lot earlier, Sarah's body craving rest. She had been awake all night again after a blazing row with her father. He had called her, drunk. She should have ended the call as soon as she realised. Still, she hoped he might have some news. He didn't. Just his regular dose of abuse and accusation, a hollow bag of hatred.

'We have contact lists with family and friends. They were already being questioned about Millie and Oscar's disappearance at the request of Turkish police and the Foreign Office. So in one respect we have a head start. Only now it's picked up a gear. Do you have any contacts over there?'

'Yes because all Muslims worldwide know each other.'

Scott turned red, finally embarrassed by something. Sarah laughed because she had meant it as a joke. Her conversion to Islam had been something she did when life had taken a particularly dark turn three years previously. It had got worse since in some respects. She sometimes wondered why she had done it. She was already fighting the system being a working-class woman who hadn't gone to university, without adding membership to one of the most profiled and bashed clubs as well. Scott wasn't like so many people she had met, the people that couldn't comprehend why a woman, a British woman at that, would convert. And then they thought she was joking because she didn't wear the headscarf. It was probably why she and Moomy got on. Moomy judged her for everything equally, the Muslim part wasn't picked on more than anything else.

'No I mean from your time over there,' Scott said.

Sarah had spent three months in Istanbul and Turkey. The reasons were personal, not work related, she reminded Scott of that.

'You think his family could be involved?' Sarah said, but Scott didn't give his opinion.

'The powers that be are shifting the entire case to us. It's high profile and a mess with Millie dead and Oscar still missing. I have a liaison with Turkish police somewhere in the file I'm sending you, he can help with what they know from the kidnapping.'

'I don't understand how they could smuggle a grown woman into London and do this. That takes planning.'

'Yes, the whole thing has been executed to perfection. The vehicle that Millie was dropped off from is being traced as we speak but nothing so far. The officers dealing with the kidnapping are sending everything over to us for us to pick up the trail.'

'Why can't they carry on investigating?'

'John Hayat is an economic attaché for the American Embassy and does some work for the UN. He's pulling strings to get us involved. He doesn't want the overworked departments to investigate this; he specifically asked for one of the best units. You can imagine the sort of offices involved in this already. The security services for a start, the Foreign Office. John Hayat is a friend of the President.'

Great. Sarah was going to be faced with dealing with those sorts of people. People who thought their money got them a free pass. Or special treatment.

'It still doesn't make sense. There is no ransom request, no threat, nothing that might explain why this is happening. It appears on the surface to be senseless. Yet... there's a message here. One we don't understand. The location, the way Millie and Oscar were taken, the way she was dumped. A message is being sent to someone, and I think that person has to be someone in Oscar's family.'

'I agree. The question is who and what, and how will this end?'

Sarah didn't know yet.

'How are you otherwise? I need you to stay focussed. You need to pull back from the other side.'

Sarah didn't trust herself to reply. They both knew what he was referring to.

'I owe it to her,' Sarah said quietly.

'It wasn't your fault,' Scott said. 'None of it was your fault.'

'Tell my father that.'

'Your father is a... he's just from a different place that's all.'

'It doesn't make it easier to listen to what he has to say. And it's true, isn't it? The things he accuses me of. What I brought into their lives. It was my fault.'

'She already had problems. We both know that.'

'Yes.' Sarah remembered the early days of them working together. They had been colleagues back then. She had been crumbling and had told him candidly about what was happening in her life. Before he became her boss and she got his job. She had started her career before him, but watched as he was fast tracked over her. She didn't resent him, he didn't belittle her either; instead, she worked harder. And here they were. Both of them nearly at the same place. Although he was still the one giving orders.

'We need to know who did this. Who killed Millie and who has Oscar. This is your focus, Sarah. Don't let yourself down.'

'Can you be any more patronising?'

'It's not meant to be. I care, that's all.'

Sarah didn't like the direction this was going in.

'I'll be fine. Plus I have Moomy with me.'

Scott snorted. 'That does not fill me with confidence.'

His phone buzzed. 'John Hayat's here. Let's see what secrets he has, shall we?'

Chapter Nine

Moomy was still with Bill, trying to piece together Millie's life. She had grown up in an ordinary world it seemed, thrown into extraordinary circumstances by her mother's illness. Overnight her life plunged into something else. Moomy got that, she had suffered the same herself.

'How did Millie meet Oscar?'

'It was a party in university. They were both at Trinity College, both on the same course. I didn't like to think of Millie with anyone, tried to close my mind to the idea my little girl was now all grown up. After the very first term though, she started to talk more and more about her friends at Oxford, and his name kept popping up. Whatever she was doing, he was usually there.'

He stopped as his thoughts told him something else.

'I was surprised though. Just in that she seemed to be more friendly with another boy. Someone called Declan. She was much more animated about him I remember. Still, she wouldn't tell me what was going on. And she always kept that part of her life hidden. As though she felt guilty she was having fun when things at home were so tough. She hated being away at weekends, always made the trip to help me. I felt for her, so encouraged her to stay over in Oxford occasionally. Even go away with her friends. She rarely did but when she did, Oscar was always there. In her words and pictures. I think she kept her boyfriends from me because she didn't feel she had the right to be happy. Silly girl, didn't she realise we both only wanted the best for her?'

'When did things become more than just friends?' Moomy asked.

'I honestly can't say. She said it was a few months before they got married. She would go for a lot of walks when she was home for the summer, to make phone calls in secret. It broke my heart to think she was feeling like that, that she couldn't be happy or have a relationship with someone because of her mother or me. I never knew.'

'She hadn't been in a relationship before?'

'Not that I know of. She was quite a studious girl, never shy, but always focused. And she was only fifteen when her mother first got ill. There wasn't time for boys.'

'So Oscar was her first boyfriend?'

'You know, it's embarrassing but I can't even be sure.'

'So when did she tell you about Oscar and her?'

'It wasn't until much later. She had finished studying by then, had landed herself a job at HSBC. She told me that she had met someone and that they wanted to get married.'

'How did you feel about that?'

'I thought she was too young. She was only just beginning her career. Yet she was adamant that Oscar was the right man for her.'

First love. Harry. Moomy felt the searing pain of her own past again.

'I met him a couple of days later. He seemed nice enough. Very polished, a Hooray Henry accent, but polite and respectful.'

'Did he say anything about his family?'

'Just that his father was a businessman and his mother was in property.' Bill laughed bitterly. 'He failed to mention it was a billion-dollar business and the homes his mother owned were some of the most exclusive across the capital.'

'How many times did you meet Oscar?'

'After that first meeting he came by every week almost. He even visited Angie in the home. He didn't have any pretentions. He was crazy about Millie. That much I could tell.'

'How?'

'The way he would look at her, watching her every move while she was in the room, as though he was obsessed with her. The world disappeared for him when she was around.'

Moomy wondered at the choice of word 'obsessed'. Being in love with someone and obsessing over them were two different things.

'I did argue with them on occasion though. Told them they were rushing into things. They wanted to be married within three months. It was overwhelming if I'm honest. I did ask them to wait, but they insisted; it was what they both wanted.'

He shook his head. Wishing he had stalled things? Maybe Millie would still be here today? Moomy didn't want to dwell on the doubts that might plague Bill Beaumont for the rest of his life. She felt sadness for him at the prospective lonely life he was going to live. She hoped that he had a support network, or a therapist. Someone who would be there for him. Family was meant to be your safety blanket at a time like this. What happened when their loss was the thing you were mourning?

'Did they say why?'

'No. At first I thought Millie was pregnant. She denied it and there was no sign of a pregnancy in the months that followed. I never really understood it. Oscar said Millie was his soul mate and he wanted to make her his as quickly as he could.'

'And Millie?'

'She was just as convinced it was the right thing to do.'

'What about Oscar's family?'

'I met them a week before the wedding. There was a dinner at their Knightsbridge home. It was another world. The money they had became obvious to me and it made me like Oscar even more. Despite this mansion he grew up in, and I realised soon after there were much bigger estates in America and other parts of the world that he called home, he was still reasonably down to earth. I think that came from his father though.'

'How so?'

'John wasn't born into money. He immigrated to America when he was younger, with his family, was a self-made man from all accounts. He didn't really care for the wealth he had accumulated. Ate very little during the dinner, didn't drink, wasn't ostentatious. He was very subdued. The people around him, their close friends, family, they were loud and very posh. Everything was about their lives, where they had been, where they were going. Oscar's mother seemed more at ease with that side. She was born into her money though. Inherited her fortune. Still, she was incredibly warm, was very sympathetic about Angie. They both came to see Angie,

49

you know. The day before we flew off to Bali. Turned up in a chauffeur driven Rolls, setting the staff in the home off with excitement. It meant a lot they made the effort.'

Moomy was surprised they had. She was also curious as to why they had accepted Millie so readily. Maybe John Hayat had a different attitude, although his choice of wife in the billionaire Lara didn't fit easily with that theory. Still, Lara would have had dreams and ambitions for who her eldest son would marry. Millie knew the uber rich liked to play arranged marriages the way European royalty once had. Although there were enough ex-hookers playing billionaire wives in her experience already. Millie was clever and attractive. Not model beautiful but she definitely had a refined beauty that would cause heads to turn in any room. And did it matter to Lara that her daughter-in-law and grandchildren would be mixed race?

It all just seemed too easy though. Why had they accepted Millie so quickly and agreed to the shotgun-pace wedding? Moomy didn't think Bill would know. Possibly the only people who might know the truth were Oscar and Millie themselves. But Millie was dead, and Oscar was missing. Their secrets buried deep in their absence.

Chapter Ten

John Hayat claimed he was only sixty-five, but he looked much older when Sarah met him. His face was lined with too much sun and hard living, his hair all white with tufts of black over his ears and in his salt-and-pepper beard. His eyes were dark and she didn't know if the stress circles around them were from this last week or before. Still, despite the stresses on the surface, she felt his energy, the easy confidence with which he carried himself.

Space was an issue while the HQ was developed; they did have one decent living room converted into an informal interview space though. Interrogations were always done at local police stations or in the state-of-the-art interview room they had set up. She didn't want to speak to a father with a missing son in that closed-off environment. The cornices, gilt-edged finishes, high Georgian ceilings and polished floor of the breakout room in HQ were all lost on John. He was wearing a tan coat, dark suit and shoes. The price clear from the cut. Yet Sarah got the impression he was dressed by someone else rather than being the one who had chosen what to wear. He was too casual in the way he threw his coat aside, and she saw the creases in his clothes. There was nothing vain about him.

He refused a drink; his voice was throaty and confused. He had a strong accent from wherever he was born – she was guessing an Arab country, but it had twangs of American and British all through it. As though he had tried to copy the worlds he was inhabiting now.

'There is no doubt? That it is Millie?' Feeble hope grasping. She was used to that.

'I'm sorry, John, it is definitely her. Bill identified her body this morning. We are, of course, carrying out standard DNA checks to corroborate.'

'How did she die?'

'At the moment we are thinking gunshot to the head. A full autopsy is being carried out which will give us more details.'

'My God,' he said. 'Poor Bill.'

Sarah let the silence settle. What was there to add? Bill was on the dead end of this whole thing.

'And Oscar? There is still no idea where he is?'

'I'm sorry. There is a strong possibility he was brought into the country at the same time as Millie, it's just an angle, so an alert has been sent to check airports, ports and rail terminals. Anyone matching Millie's and Oscar's descriptions. It takes time but it is a priority I can assure you.'

John seemed to accept this. More calmly than she anticipated anyway. She had assumed he would be throwing around the weight of his money and status. Then again, the Foreign Secretary, Jane Haslam, was doing that already.

'How can I help?' he said. Obviously, a no–nonsense man who knew there was a time for emotion and this wasn't it. Sarah could work with that.

'With Millie's death, we are now leading a murder investigation. Trying to understand who is behind her death and potentially who might have Oscar.'

John nodded, only the briefest tremor in his eye at the mention of his son.

'If I knew this, I would tell you. I want nothing more than my son back. I had wanted Millie back too. Now for her it is too late. I only want those who did this found.'

'How well did you know Millie?'

'We met a number of times over the last few months. Oscar had brought her home after he graduated and told us he wanted to marry her.'

'You hadn't met her before then?'

'No. I had no idea who she was. Maybe my wife knew, I can't be sure. I have so many demands on my life, and I've three sons. I care for their education, their health and wellbeing. Making sure they have a future plan. Who they fall in love with is not my main concern, unless the relationship becomes permanent.'

'Are any of your other sons married?'

'None.'

'And Oscar is the eldest?'

'Yes. He is my heir. He didn't go to university until much later than he was meant to because he wanted to join the business and learn it. From eighteen until he was twenty-three he worked with me. Then I asked him to go to Oxford, to get the education he was capable of. The world we are in hold those things up, give value to them. I never went to university.'

'You went to America as a child?'

'Yes. I was a refugee from Iraq. My family were Iraqi Christians, my father an outspoken opponent of the

53

Ba'ath Party at the time and we were targets for them. My father and mother were both doctors; we lived in Baghdad, but they often did humanitarian work in poorer villages. They would take me with them. When things got bad for them, they got me safe passage to America with a relative of my father's. I grew up with this man and his family, but they had even less in Queens than we had in Iraq. They treated me with kindness and as their own, but I wanted to make my own life.'

'And your parents?'

'They didn't make it. They were casualties of Saddam before they could escape his regime.'

'I'm sorry to hear that,' she said.

'It is life. When you lose your parents, you learn quickly that nothing is permanent or real. It hurts when you lose loved ones, but you also know it is something you cannot control. My sorrow for them is still in me; every day I wish they were here to see what became of me, how I fulfilled their promise. Only it remains a hope.'

Sarah knew about hope. She had her own desire for reunion. Not with her mother, the woman who had died after a hard battle with cancer, whose loss she felt acutely in the face of her own father's coldness. It was the loss of someone else, the hope of someone else. Scott had warned her to keep her focus though, and so she would.

'Did you approve of Millie? For Oscar?'

'Completely,' John said emphatically, moving his head as spoke. 'His mother was disappointed. She wanted him to marry someone like her. You see, my wife, Lara, I know loves me. Yet I feel sometimes she thinks she may have had an easier life if she had married from within her own people. She doesn't see that her people are dwindling though. That her city is now full of Arabs, Russians, Chinese and Indians. They are the super-rich now. The world she grew up in, the English wealthy, they have moved out of the capital. They prefer their country estates to the stickiness of London. Still, she threw every suitable girl Oscar's way. All those pretty little girls with their posh voices.' He said posh like Porsche. 'None of them made it for Oscar. And for me I was scared. My children are so different from me in so many ways. They grew up with their mother's finishing, her manners. I felt rough around them. Millie, though, she was different to the girls my wife had wanted for Oscar. She was real. Impossibly clever but real. I liked her immediately.'

'You didn't have any concerns about her? About her motives?'

'You see the rich girls my wife wanted, they were more after Oscar's money than Millie was. Those girls wanted Oscar to keep them in the same life that their fathers had kept them in.'

'You don't think that amount of wealth made Oscar more susceptible to girls like Millie though?'

'Girls like Millie? She wasn't that type. She wasn't brainless, spending her time focusing on her looks, trying to trap a rich man. Also…' John couldn't look directly at her as he spoke, 'I had her checked out.'

'Checked out?'

'Money does make my family targets. I can't deny that. I have to employ security, keep our properties protected, make sure we are not taking unnecessary risks. I don't tend to vet my children's friends, they are usually from families like ours, but if I think there is a need to… then I do.'

'With Millie you felt a need?'

'Not her. It was more the situation. They wanted to marry so quickly, three months. It was crazy. I didn't care but it made me anxious. I wanted to know why the rush. So I had Millie investigated.'

'By who?'

'There is a man I use, he is very good. Works as a private investigator. I usually get him to look into the people I do business with. Sometimes he does personal investigations for me. I wanted to just check there was nothing in Millie's background, in her life, that meant she was targeting Oscar.'

It seemed natural enough to Sarah. Unusual but she might be tempted to do the same if she could afford it. She had thought about it when her police contacts had failed to deliver. PIs were not cheap though. Not an issue for John.

'He gave me a report on Millie and her family. There was nothing there to worry me. I'm not proud of doing this; I am, however, not ashamed either. It is needed.'

'I understand. There were no red flags at all?'

'None. Her family are very clean, normal.'

'Clean how?'

'Nothing underhand about them. They are just normal, working. No criminal connections, nothing odd. Millie didn't target Oscar from what we can tell. They were just part of the same circle, thrown together by fate. Fell in love.' He stopped here, measuring his words. 'Being honest, I was very happy with the match. I wanted Millie in the family. My children didn't know the poverty I did. They feel entitled. The world is theirs. It is dangerous to think so. It makes you weak, unable to deal with the darkness that exists. Millie had been through so much with her mother's situation. I wanted that strength for Oscar. It was me who quieted my wife, who told her, no, this was the right thing to do. Even at the end she wasn't happy about it. She went along with it, for me.'

'Your wife didn't accept Millie?'

'No. If I am honest she didn't. She did only for me and because Oscar loves her.'

Sarah wondered about Lara Hayat and what exactly she was capable of. Then again she doubted she would put her own son at risk, even if the idea of him marrying an unsuitable girl was hard for her to take.

'This file that was given to you on Millie, can you give me details of who did the search for you?'

'No, I'm sorry, that is not possible,' he said with almost aggression. 'It was done on the insistence I kept his identity secret. And I cannot betray it for anyone.'

Sarah didn't like secrets that meant she couldn't do her job, and however much John might block her, she needed to know who his source was. They might have information on other things that might help. The question was how she was going to break through John Hayat's misplaced sense of loyalty.

Chapter Eleven

Moomy was exhausted by the time she got back to Central London. Maybe she should go home. Have a nap. See if Jake was free. She messaged him. He didn't respond. Probably asleep still. He was on night duty at the hospital. She remembered that he was a doctor, so probably not some immature little plaything she had stumbled on. She checked her watch, it was only 2 p.m. but felt a lot later. She also realised she was being too needy. It hadn't been twelve hours since she had met Jake. Fuck that. She wasn't going to be one of those girls. No way.

She parked her borrowed police car in an unassuming street in Kilburn. From the outside, the building looked like it needed a good wash. The sort of mansion block she lived in, only crummier. She called Emma Works and told her she was downstairs.

'I'll buzz you up,' she said.

The one-bedroom flat Emma shared with her boyfriend was on the first floor. It was a lot nicer than the front of the building would have you believe, with matching dark wood furniture in the lounge, occasional screens in the room separating the adjoining kitchen area and a small desk space.

'Ben's at work, so we have the place to ourselves.'

'You're not working today?'

Moomy saw the blanket on the sofa, the scrunched-up tissues, the empty glass of wine.

'I couldn't. When I found out about Millie…'

Emma was the same age as Millie, different colouring though. Where Millie was dark-haired and dark eyes, Emma was fair with blue eyes. She sat down on her couch, wrapping the blanket around her. Moomy took the small single seater next to her.

'I'm sorry,' Moomy said. She'd been given Emma's details by Bill Beaumont. He said if anyone knew Millie it was Emma, although he didn't know how it could help. 'Must be devastating.'

'It's more than that. We've been together in the same school since we were eleven. Became friends since the first day, kept that going. Even when we were at different unis – I ended up at Cambridge – we stayed close.'

'You were at the wedding I take it?'

'I was bridesmaid. The only one she had. Millie was a bit taken aback by the whole thing, tried her best to keep things simple when she could, you know? Insisted on only one bridesmaid, that the wedding be a location wedding, that they get married under a simple canopy on the beach.'

Moomy didn't think it looked very simple from the pictures she had seen on social media. It was like someone had puked money all over the proceedings. Emma blew her nose loudly.

'She was like a sister. I have two brothers. Millie was an only child. I feel like someone's ripped off a limb. I don't know how I'm going to get through this.'

Moomy knew all about that. Losing your family in an instant. Moomy was alone. At least Emma had others. Bill

59

was alone now too. Moomy ran her fingers through her hair, keeping her ghosts at bay.

'What was Millie like?'

'I'm probably the wrong person to ask. I loved her completely. We were both so nerdy at school, but we found solace in each other and that gave us the confidence to get through high school. We weren't outcasts or weird because we gave each other worth. We wanted to make it, academically. Millie went into overdrive when Angie became ill. She was obsessed, determined to get to Oxbridge, make Angie proud. As though she believed Angie might come to if she did. I rode on her coattails and got into Cambridge because I worked hard with her.' Emma wiped away warm fresh tears, wrapping her blanket tighter. 'It's so unfair. Millie got me here. She deserved this future more than I did.'

'What do you do?'

'I work as a research analyst for a hedge fund. I know, sold my soul. Ben works for an investment bank.'

'Money was important for you and Millie?'

'Yes. Not like that. Not gold-digging style. Millie wanted to earn money to help her father, pay for her mother's care. I want to build a future with Ben. There is no bank of Mum and Dad for us.'

'You met Ben at uni?'

'Yes. We both captained the rugby teams.'

'There's a nice symmetry to your lives. Millie and you finding love in university at the same time.'

'Yes, it was so weird. That first term we both came home at Christmas and had something to tell each other. We both confessed it then, we had boyfriends.'

Moomy could picture it. The academic girls had suddenly become women. Moomy had been forced to confront those ghosts far too soon.

Emma's face softened as she remembered.

'Did she introduce you to Oscar soon after?' Moomy said.

Emma looked confused, then laughed.

'Oscar? No it wasn't Oscar. Millie met someone else that first term in Oxford. Oscar didn't happen until the end. Until all that was over. In fact, I think it came to an end because of Oscar.'

'Who are you talking about?'

'I'm talking about Declan. Millie fell hard for him as soon as she got to uni and met him.'

Declan. The boy that Bill suspected at first. So his instincts were right. Yet Moomy didn't understand. If Millie was in love with someone else, why did she end up rushing into a marriage with Oscar? What happened in those three years that made Millie change so much?

'Tell me about Declan,' Moomy said.

'Declan was a star. You could imagine him being the lead in one of those BBC costume dramas. He was big in amateur dramatics, Irish heritage, all brooding dark good looks. Millie was really into him. From what I could tell, he felt the same.'

'How often did you meet him?'

'We met for New Year's, after our first term at uni ended. The four of us rented an apartment in London. Ben, Millie, Declan and me. It was an amazing time. We did the Thames and the fireworks. Midnight kisses, resolutions. We stayed up all night. Then in early Jan we got a last-minute deal and headed to Turkey for a long weekend. We all got on really well.'

'Sounds idyllic. Where in Turkey?'

'Bodrum.'

Moomy knew it was notorious for the airbase, but actually was a major summer tourist destination.

'Did you visit Istanbul at all?'

'No. Millie was always adamant about that. It would be her honeymoon destination. Her parents met there, did you know?'

'Yes. Her father told me.'

'So romantic. So she was keeping that for something else. We were just in an all-expenses-style villa on the coast.'

'Did anything happen while on that holiday? Something that might have put Millie at risk?'

'Nothing at all. We didn't leave the villa for two weeks. We sat by the indoor heated pool, drank a lot, slept late, read. It was perfect. We were so relieved, you know? That Ben and Declan got on so well. It felt so perfect.'

'How long was Millie with Declan?'

'They were together for most of her time at Oxford.'

Emma bit her lip, unsure if she should betray the confidences of her best friend. In a way Emma and Millie were each other's soul mates.

'The thing is when Millie told me she going to marry Oscar, well, I was shocked. She had never mentioned him in that capacity ever. I knew of him, he was one of her friend circle. Boyfriend though? That came as a shock.'

'And Declan? What happened to him?'

'One day he was with her, then she was marrying Oscar. He disappeared. I didn't have any contact with him.

I even messaged him but with no response. Ben tried as well. I asked Millie. She said it didn't matter, things didn't work out.'

'What do you think happened?'

'Honestly? I think Oscar happened. He wanted Millie and no one was going to stop that happening. Not even Millie herself.'

'You never heard from Declan again?'

Emma looked unsure before she spoke.

'He called me, just before the wedding. Said Millie was making a mistake, and that I should stop it.'

Chapter Twelve

John Hayat was not the sort of man to be pushed or pressured, that much Sarah knew. He didn't want to share the details of his private investigator. That was the wrong word though, from how he described him. He sounded more like special security, someone John used for those awkward things that others just couldn't do for him. Sarah did ask to see the file on Millie though, just in case anything in there helped.

'I can have that sent to you. There is nothing in there.'

'I believe you, John. I'm just thorough. What about Oscar? Was there anything else in his life that might make him a target? You said you were worried about your wealth attracting the wrong person? Have you had any threats directed towards you or your family?'

John looked furtive, sitting forward, his physique imposing in his clothes that didn't sit right on him. He had an authority from somewhere, not his money, a confidence probably from his past. Losing your parents probably made you self-sufficient by force. She already understood that, losing her mother and, in the process, losing her father in a way too. It made you insecure and in need of standing on your own merits.

'There are always threats to the money. Always. Direct threats? Hatred or personal threats? No. Oscar was nothing extraordinary. He was a boy born to a rich family. There was nothing in his life that would mean this would happen. If I knew what this might be, where this danger was coming from, I would do whatever I could to end it. I don't. I have my man looking into everything, every link.'

The mysterious man again.

'John, I understand your need for privacy, but if Oscar is in the UK, and we have to believe there is a chance he is, any help you can give would only benefit your son. This man of yours, maybe he can save us time, stop us repeating what he's already done. We can focus on things he might not be able to do.'

John scoffed, the idea that the police could possibly match what his money could buy. His eyes became thoughtful; she had dropped a carrot. How much was his son's safety worth?

'I will liaise with him. Part of his allure to people like me is that he stays under the radar.'

Outside the law probably, Sarah thought.

'And there's nothing in Oscar's personal life that might have put him at risk?'

'I really can't think of anything.'

'What about your own past? You said your family were in conflict with Saddam Hussein. Do you think the remnants of his regime could be interested in you?'

John flinched as she spoke, uncomfortable at the reminder of his past. He had buried that deep, Sarah was digging it up. She had to though. The location of the kidnapping, his work for the American Embassy, his past. There was a pattern she needed to explore. He shook his head though, convinced or convincing himself? He seemed confident then, sure of his answer as he spoke.

'It's not something to worry on. I was a child when I left, my parents both died. There is no reason for anyone to come after my son and his wife. It was so long ago and I have had nothing to do with Iraq since I left. Even during the second war, I didn't get involved. Saddam was not even in power when I left for America. Some things are too painful to go back to. There is no one to make the link between my past and me. I changed my name when I came to America, when I was older. Not many people know this; you won't find it anywhere. No one is interested in Nabeel Shams. I chose John because of John Wayne. My father loved him. And Hayat means life in Arabic. That is what it felt like coming to America. And I didn't want to carry my parents' name with me. It felt like a burden, like pain.'

Sarah wondered at that. She had been told to change her name when she chose her new life. When her mother died, when she found another way of being, of surviving. She didn't though. Sarah Heaton was the name that she was raised with and the name that she had kept for over forty years. She wasn't going to change that.

'I'm struggling, John, to understand then. Why was your son taken? Why was Millie killed? What about your wife? Is there anything in her life that might have led to this?' He shook his head. 'Then what do you think this is?'

He looked at her, something was desperate to leak out of his mouth but he kept it closed. Sarah knew then that he was hiding something.

—

Sarah Skyped with Marcello after her meeting with John Hayat. She didn't feel any clearer after speaking to him: there didn't seem to be any reason Oscar would be taken or Millie killed. Sarah knew John hadn't been honest though. Somewhere there were secrets that she didn't know yet, which could give her the answers she needed. Maybe John was relying on his own people to track down Oscar. But they had failed Millie, so why did he think they would be any better for his son?

The forensic pathologist, Doctor Marcello Ramone, was flicking through his paper report on Millie Beaumont-Hayat, while clicking buttons that let Sarah see the pages he was reading. He was in his early thirties, still comparatively new to the profession, but he was thorough.

'It was a clean shot using a pistol. The bullet made a straight entry, tearing up the brain without damaging the skull. Death would have been instantaneous.'

'That's something at least. Any chance of tracing the weapon?'

'Ballistics are working on it. Let's see. It isn't manufactured here or widely available, the weapon I mean, and neither are the cartridges used. It suggests a professional hit; these sorts of weapons aren't available really on the street.'

Ballistics was highly developed for the Met.

'How long had Millie been dead when she was dropped off at the heath?'

'I would estimate she died around midnight, confirming my initial readings. I did some analysis on the temperature at night on the heath and how her body cooled. I think she was left there close to an hour after death, that would make sense of the data we have. But I can't confirm that exactly.'

'So she was definitely alive when she was brought into the country and must have been killed about an hour's driving distance from the heath at most. That gives us a radius to cover at least.'

'What about the state of her body? We can assume the gunshot killed her. Any indication of what was happening to her before then? She was missing for a week.'

'Yes, and there are plenty of clues of what happened to her in that week. I hope you're sitting comfortably because none of it is pleasant.'

Sarah listened in horror as Doctor Ramone described Millie's injuries, painting in the gaps of the last week of Millie's life. It made her insides curl with hatred and anger for the people who did this to her. More shocking than the fresh injuries of the last week, though, was something else: a list of injuries which Millie had sustained before she was taken. There seemed to be a pattern of violence directed at the young woman for months leading up to her being taken.

Chapter Thirteen

Moomy parked up outside the student halls in Bankside, displaying her permit clearly in case anyone complained. She got out and breathed in the air. Familiar even though that was crazy. It was years now since she had been here. Years since the worst of herself and the worst of Harry. She remembered these streets. The drunken fights. She the drunk, he the fight. No shame, no awareness that others were watching. That was the thing with London. You could always be sure that the audience was full of strangers. Unless you were really unlucky. Was she? She shut the door on her past and walked the short distance to the Globe Theatre. Reconstructed to its former glory harking back to Shakespeare, Moomy always felt it represented a pivotal image of the capital. There was so much history and depth to its existence. Simple verbal markers that could convey so much. A bit like her own thoughts. Random names and places invading her mental space. Bringing their own torments and histories.

Allow that, Moomy thought.

Declan Walsh was waiting for her outside the theatre. Emma had called him a star. And Moomy could see why. Even on first meeting him, Declan was all chiselled dark good looks and exuded the sort of confidence only actors can. He shook her hand with the right pressure, smiling into her face. His green eyes studied her, before leading her into the theatre.

They were seated on the main stage, the theatre empty. Two actors playing roles. Did he think she would be impressed? Awed by the setting, she would forget to do her job? He was pissing against the wrong tree if that was the case, she wasn't one of his predictable dates. Moomy instead was trying to unpick what he had learned and what was true. He seemed genuinely upset when he spoke about Millie's death. Then again, how would Moomy know? Millie had ended things with him and married another man very quickly. She needed to work out the balance between hate and love in him.

'Why did things end between you both?' she said.

'Things happen,' he said noncommittally. 'We just didn't think… she didn't think we would work.'

'Did she give you a reason? From what I've gathered you were both inseparable for pretty much her whole time at Oxford. Then all of a sudden she's with someone else. Things like that don't just happen.'

'It felt like it. She was my whole world. Genuinely.'

Oof. The passion with which he spoke. Moomy felt it.

'I never felt like that about anybody before,' there was a catch in his voice, his eyes looking moist. 'I don't think I will feel like this about anyone again. I still love her.'

'She didn't feel the same?'

He looked at Moomy, turning his intense eyes on her again. 'She felt the same. Whether or not she admitted it to herself, that's another story. She felt it though.'

'How can you be sure?'

'I spent nearly every day with her for two and a half years. You get to know someone. The way she looked at me, was around me. She spoke to me a week before the wedding.'

'What did she say?'

'She said she was sorry. That things might be different if circumstances were better.'

'No grand declarations of love for you?'

He shook his head.

'She wasn't having doubts about the wedding? About Oscar?'

At the mention of Oscar she saw the hostility in Declan's eyes almost immediately.

'Not a fan of his I take it? I'm not surprised. The pair of them hurt you badly.'

'Yes. I'm not going to pretend. She broke my heart, broke me in a way. I still can't hate her though. I love her. Even now.'

They were silent. The open-air theatre wasn't, as noises drifted in from the outside. Cars, voices, the river. It felt alive even when it was empty.

'Oscar though,' Declan went on, 'he was a nasty piece of work. Always will be.'

'Angry at the man that Millie chose?'

'She didn't choose him.'

'What does that mean?'

'He took her from me.'

Moomy felt herself wind up. 'Took her? She didn't belong to you, mate. She wasn't a toy.' She stared at him hard. He looked embarrassed at least.

'I didn't mean it like that. You don't know what he was like. Right from the start he was crazy about Millie. He became part of her friend circle, and he was always hanging around us. It made me uncomfortable if I'm honest. He used to make snide comments to me whenever Millie wasn't there, made it clear he thought she was wasting her time with me.'

'Snide how?'

'About my background. I'm from a single-parent household; mum worked three jobs to get me and my brother through. Oscar loved reminding me that my father fucked off and that I was on a scholarship.'

'That's why you and Millie bonded?'

He nodded.

'The two scholarship kids. It went beyond that though. We felt we were the only normal people there; everyone else seemed so accomplished, as though they didn't have any real problems. Maybe some personal ones, but actual issues like paying the bills. Stuff like that. It was all missing from their lives.'

'Did you ever raise the issue of Oscar with Millie?'

'Yes, constantly. She thought I was being oversensitive. He was clever. He never made comments in front of her. In front of her he was always so welcoming and nice. It started to cause problems between us.'

'What sort of problems?'

'She started defending him, taking his side. It irritated the hell out of me she couldn't see him for what he was. A snide little bastard. He would always get her expensive gifts and arrange amazing treats for her birthday. Like he got her a diamond bracelet for her twentieth. She returned it to him. I made her. Then he would arrange weekends in London for them, shows, Michelin starred restaurants. I was never invited, and Millie went along, saying he was just a friend doing something nice.'

'You don't think it was?'

'I could see it was him trying to buy her love. Millie could be naive sometimes. She judged too many people by her own standards, thought the best of everyone. Didn't delve too deep to question why the fuck he would be acting like this.'

'And Millie never stopped seeing him? To keep you happy?'

'Initially yes, but then she started to feel bad. How many times could she say no? I went along the first few times but it was very awkward. Plus he was an absolute asshole whenever Millie left us alone for a few minutes. If she couldn't see what it was like for me then I didn't know what to do.'

'Is that what caused you both to break up?'

Declan looked sheepish now.

'No, something else did that. I cheated on her.'

Fucking men, thought Moomy.

'It was just the once. I was drunk, she had pissed off with Oscar to some musical shite, and this girl from another college approached me. We hit it off and next thing I know she's in my room. It was meaningless sex. I felt crap as soon as I realised what we had done and as soon as I did it was over.'

'You told Millie?'

'No, there was no way I was going to risk us. I didn't tell anyone; I never saw the girl again.'

'You said it led to Millie ending things with you?'

'Yes. Even before she found out things were going wrong. You see, after I did that I felt awful. Guilty all the time and I ended up lashing out on Millie. I became even more paranoid about her and Oscar and became super obsessive, you know? It was mental the way I behaved with her. I accused her of cheating on me with him, twisted the slightest thing she said or did. Things came to a head one weekend when she had to stay with her mother in hospital. Her mother took a turn for the worse. I tried calling Millie but it went to voicemail constantly. I assumed she was with Oscar and didn't want to be disturbed. When she came home, shattered, I went into a rant. She said she'd had enough and she couldn't take it anymore. She wanted a break. Then she found out about the other girl and that was it.'

Laughter outside the theatre broke the quiet between them. Moomy didn't know what she felt about Declan. Punishing Millie for his own fuck-up? Get over that. She looked at him, his eyes blazing with shame and sadness. She had seen that look before. Weak men blaming women for their own shit.

'The way she moved on to Oscar though... literally three weeks after she ended it with me, she was with him. He loved rubbing it in my face, flaunting her. It killed me. Then he proposed and she accepted. It was mental. Absolutely mental. Who does that? Who gets married so quickly?'

Moomy didn't trust herself to speak. She knew all about that. About marriages happening in the blink of an eye. Only in her case, she knew it wasn't out of choice.

What exactly had compelled Millie to marry Oscar? And was it out of choice?

'We all make choices that don't make sense to those around us,' she said eventually.

He shrugged, turned away.

'Do you think Emma might know something? As to why?'

'If she does she's a bloody good actress, better even than me. I confronted Emma about it, said as Millie's bff she must know what happened, asked her to stop the wedding even. She said she didn't know why Millie did it, but that we should accept her decision and support her. She seemed genuinely unsure.'

'And what do you think, Declan? Why did this happen to Millie?'

He looked hard into her.

'It's obvious isn't it? The fucking Hayats. They did this to her. Or someone that hated them did this to her. Whatever. All I know is that fucking Oscar is to blame.'

Except he was missing too. Moomy looked again at Declan. The star. Was he devastated at the loss of his central role? Was he really the one that had taken Millie's light because she had moved the spotlight from him to Oscar?

Chapter Fourteen

Sarah was still thinking over the conversation with Doctor Ramone as she made her way to the tech department. Millie's life was unravelling through her dead body, the secrets and the sins done to her revealing themselves in whispers.

Romesh Kandasamy, their tech genius, was waiting for her. In his early twenties, he preferred to work for law enforcement rather than earn the big bucks for an investment bank or tech firm, although he still did consultancy work for the big players to pay for his holidays.

'Yo, detective, take a seat,' he said in his Surrey drawl. He was wearing ripped jeans and a graffiti sweatshirt. There was low-level hip-hop playing in the background. Sarah thought it would drive her insane or to daily headaches if she had to work with Romesh. 'I've been making this my priority, after the boss told me to.' He even spoke as though he was rapping rather than speaking, his words stilted.

'Millie Beaumont?'

'Yes. I got you her call history, ran some algies on it, got you a list of regulars and the oddballs. Social media is hardly there, she didn't even have Facebook. People like that still exist, believe it or not. Her laptop was picked up by tech but it's not been used since before the wedding. It did give me her e-mail addresses though, so I'm trying to get into those.'

Sarah wasn't surprised. Millie was quite academic. She didn't strike her as an Instagram selfie queen.

'What is more interesting for you, though, is this.' Romesh tapped his touchscreen and brought up a bank statement. 'Millie's account. Check the transactions.'

Sarah studied the money that came in and left. She arched her eyebrow.

'Well, that's very interesting,' she said, sending details to Moomy.

'Keep working those e-mails. I want to know if there's anything in there that might help us find out what happened to both Millie and Oscar.'

'Sure thing,' said Romesh.

—

The offices at HQ were buzzing. Everyone pretended not to watch her, but the Millie Beaumont murder was all anyone was talking about. Sarah was feeling the tiredness of the day now. It was nearly 7 p.m. and she hadn't had a break. Moomy must be frazzled, she thought. Night out getting drunk followed by a day's full-on investigation. It was more than most people could cope with. Moomy needed another talk, she knew, only Sarah wasn't her mother and she didn't know if she could abide the eye-rolling.

Sarah looked over at Moomy — flawless make-up application and fresh scent re-applied. Moomy always argued with Sarah over that. Why must she conform to the standards of masculinity to do a traditionally masculine job? Why couldn't she be a kick-ass cop and look feminine doing it? Sarah always countered her narrative with the idea that Moomy was following a patriarchal version of how she should look.

'You're the one that wears men's trousers,' Moomy had retorted.

Scott was looking at Sarah directly, avoiding Moomy. Uncomfortable by her borderline clubbing outfit.

'What do we know? I can't report back up to the powers that be that we aren't any nearer to discovering anything. How did Millie get back into the country and who killed her? I'm getting a ton of pressure on this from up above.'

Sarah knew the subtext. It had nothing to do with Millie and everything to do with Oscar. The Hayats were the power brokers in this. Millie was his girlfriend, his fiancée, his wife. As though she had no place or meaning of her own. The world was only interested in the rich and handsome Oscar Hayat. Sarah was here though. She cared about Millie, about the young woman stripped of her future so mercilessly.

Moomy updated them on her interviews with Millie's father and her childhood friend Emma. She then recounted the oddness of her relationship as told by Declan, the ex-boyfriend.

'You think something compelled Millie to marry Oscar?' Scott asked.

'I think so. You shag around if you're on the rebound. You don't marry the first guy that asks.'

'Oscar was a friend, she knew him just as long as she knew Declan. Isn't it possible they developed feelings for each other over that time?' Scott asked.

'It didn't seem that way. Millie didn't mention him to her best friend. Although her father recollected he was part of her friend circle.'

'There are some oddities which might fit this short intense romance,' Sarah said. 'For starters, Romesh found some interesting transactions in Millie's account. Oscar's mother transferred her a sum of two hundred thousand pounds.'

'When?' Scott asked.

'A month before the wedding.'

'She was probably embarrassed about her in front of her asshole friends,' said Moomy icily. 'Gave her a bung to buy a pretty dress and some jewellery so she didn't turn up to the wedding in high street fashion.'

'Possibly. Except the transaction didn't stop with Millie though. She transferred the entire sum to someone else within days.'

'Who?'

'Her father.'

'You're shitting me?'

'Do we know what he did with the funds?' asked Scott.

'Accessing his bank account is a bit more difficult. Since he's still alive.'

'You think it was a loan?' Moomy said.

'We need to speak to Bill Beaumont about why his daughter gave him that cash and what he did with it,' said Scott.

'It still doesn't explain her death,' said Sarah, 'unless you think Bill has other financial problems that might have led him to borrow money from the wrong people? You said he didn't work for years?'

'Not properly,' Moomy agreed. 'He worked from home when his wife got ill, had to give up his office work. Sold their house and everything to pay for her care. It was all in his wife's name apparently, in case anything happened to him. When she got ill it all got trapped and then used by the council to provide for her.'

'Let's catch up with Bill Beaumont,' said Scott. 'We can try and see if there's any other money connection to this. And with the mother. She's not well, so you might have to pay her a visit.'

'That's not all,' Sarah added, dreading this next part. 'I spoke to Doctor Ramone. He did the autopsy for us. It's not pleasant reading at all.'

'It never is,' Moomy muttered.

'Millie sustained a number of injuries before death. We can almost trace what happened to her from the moment she was taken through the signs left on her body. She had drag marks, scratches and bruises, consistent with being pulled from the car. Her wrists had deep tie marks, from where she was restrained for days on end. There was bruising which suggested she had been punched several times. To her abdomen, her face and her back. Lacerations on her skin in sequence. As though she was being cut as punishment for giving the wrong answer. Or to scare someone else.'

'Oscar?' said Moomy.

'Millie's fingers were also broken,' Sarah went on. 'Her left hand, the index finger, and the small finger. Ligature marks on her neck and ankles as well. She was being held captive somewhere, we can be sure of that. Her stomach was also empty practically. She had been fed water and bread for the last few days. She died in a horrendous condition.'

'Fuck,' said Moomy.

'That doesn't bode well for Oscar. Only, that suggests to me Millie was in an absolute state. How the hell did a woman in that condition get into the country without anyone questioning it?'

'I don't know. That's not all though. These were fresh wounds on Millie, sustained since her kidnapping. What Doctor Ramone also found was something much more disturbing. Millie had historical fractures and other minor injuries which had healed. Injuries she had sustained in the last few years, from his assessment. Healed fractures he said.'

'What the fuck?' said Moomy.

'It was consistent with someone in an abusive relationship,' said Sarah. She didn't have to spell it out to the two of them that the injuries being that old could only mean one thing: the abuse was carried out by Declan not Oscar.

Chapter Fifteen

Moomy was thinking. She had a few hours to plan her line of attack for the next day. How to unmask Declan the actor. What was he hiding after all? What had he been doing to Millie? Painting Oscar as the bad guy when maybe Oscar was rescuing Millie? Not buying her as Declan kept insisting, but putting balm on her wounds. How easily people turned from heroes to villains.

Most of all she was thinking about Bill though. The daughter that had been his rock, had seen him through everything, and in the end he had lost her in the most horrible way. Millie had spent her time trying to ease his pain, and he was left with the idea that she had been taken from him, terrified and abused. The loss and sadness. What must he be feeling tonight? How was he going to sleep? Moomy knew all about the love a parent had for their child. She also felt a stab of envy, as she thought of the relationship she had with her own father. And there she was crossing over. Things she had shut away. Charging back into her life. Lost in her thoughts, she didn't see them shift focus and steer her off course.

Moomy's mum loved her. She knew this, even though she had to remind herself a lot. The bitch had abandoned her after all.

They shared a life together once Moomy's five brothers had been sired. Like skittles, one after the other. It was like her dad was so ashamed at having produced a girl, he had to convince everyone about his manhood, by producing boys over and over again.

Moomy was just a blip. Girls should never be born to some men. It seriously messes them up.

But of all her children, Moomy knew that her mother doted on her the most. The only daughter, they had spent those early years in league with each other, the secret language of women, in kitchens, at the sewing machine, in the laundrette before they had a washing machine, in the market, at weddings, at *khatams* when people died.

Time and the growth of her brothers meant they had even shared a bed for a few years, and then they had slept in the same room when they had got extra beds, her youngest brother in a cot. Moomy had raised him despite being a child herself, helping her mother with night time feeds, not caring that she was tired for school the next day.

'It's good practice for you, Mumtaz,' her mother often said. Everything was good practice for Mumtaz. Everyone else had started calling her Moomy or Taz, except her parents.

'Such a beautiful name, the name of a Mughal empress, the woman the Taj Mahal is made for... why ruin it?' her father had said. He sounded almost proud.

But his bastard pride was his own, she knew that later.

But that was much later.

At the beginning, Moomy knew her mother loved her, and her father, well, maybe he loved her too in his own way.

And her brothers? She had helped to raise all of them. Especially the youngest two. She wondered if they ever recalled her, how she had changed nappies, bottle fed, baby food spooned and vomit wiped for them. Pulled faces to entertain them, sung them songs she had picked up from the radio, repeated her Qur'an she learned at the *madrassah*.

Why would they though?

Did her mother ever remember her? Yes. Moomy knew this because she never forgot her own child. The child she had lost.

Moomy's mother loved her. She had to remind herself of this every day, whenever she felt low because her natural reaction was to think her mother never did.

Haroon had been born and raised and schooled in Moomy's shadow. Her world and his were one little ghetto in inner city Manchester at the time. Their mums had met and exchanged gossip enough times. She could place him if she was pushed, but he was nothing special.

They first came into contact when she had been the sixth member substitute for her brother's five-a-side cricket team. The Khan family were renowned for their cricket prowess, and over the long, hot summer holidays they beat every local team going.

Moomy could bat a decent average, but her bowling was her masterpiece. She could multitask, which meant she spun the ball while giving the impression she was hurtling a bouncer or a fast ball. The toughest of boys crumbled under her attack.

Even then though, there was no way a girl was going to be allowed to be a permanent fixture on a team. Usually Moomy had to sit with the other sisters and make daisy chains and sing *tappe* rhymes. That was when they were allowed to accompany the boys at all.

One day her mother told Moomy she wasn't allowed to play cricket anymore, not even with her brothers.

It was shortly after Moomy had hit puberty. After that she was practising all the time.

Practising meant learning the price, look and feel of a good vegetable. Haggling and getting price reductions for the less appealing *kaddus*.

It wasn't just her, it seemed all the girls of her age were in the same boat. They used to boast about who could whip up the tastiest *aloo potato masala* quickest, whose *chapatis* were roundest and who knew the most verses from *The Qur'an*.

It was never said who she was practising for, but a teenage girl wasn't so naive as to not know. The dreaded in-laws of course. Her mother started bandying around words like *parayee*: stranger.

'I'm your daughter,' Moomy snapped one day. 'That won't change. Why do you keep saying I belong to someone else?'

'That's the way it is for us, Mumtaz,' her mother had said. 'I was someone's daughter once too.'

'You still are, Mum. You still speak to your family. Well, you send them air mails anyway.'

'Yes, but I live in your father's house, and if his parents were alive, God rest their souls, then they would be here and I would be serving them.'

'Serving? You're not Dad's slave, you're his wife.'

'Don't say such things about your dad.'

'I didn't say anything.'

'It's in your tone.'

85

'Fine. I still don't get it. No one will take me away from you. This is my house. My husband can come and live here. With us.'

Her mother laughed at her stubborn naivety.

'That would be shameful for him and us.'

'Tough. Then I'll stay single. Forever.'

'That's a sin, you silly girl.'

'We'll see,' Moomy said, deliberately burning the *roti* she was making.

In that community they all knew each other's business, all went to the same primary school and the same secondary school.

All-girls secondary school, of course.

Not many of them had worn headscarves back then. How ironic that they did now, after spending even more time in England.

Moomy used to wear *shalwars*, baggy trousers with her school uniform, though, just like everyone else. The more modern girls used to wear legging style *shalwars* or skirts with tights. Both sets used to judge each other. But in the end they knew each other.

Sometimes Moomy couldn't believe that was where she had grown up, so traditional, so formal. Maybe that's why she had rebelled.

No, that wasn't why.

Had they talked about boys? Yes. But film stars and TV stars. Not real boys. That was disgusting.

The white girls used to talk about boys; they used to shock Moomy and her friends with tales of kissing and holding hands.

Sex education lessons had been the single most embarrassing moment of all their lives. Before that they had genuinely believed in Cabbage Patch dolls and storks and miracles.

They were so… innocent… that was it… Moomy couldn't remember being so innocent… except vaguely… yes, she had been innocent.

Innocent of the cruelty of men as well.

Blocking out the past only ever worked to a certain point. Until it came knocking and threw your life off-kilter. She knew what was driving this. Bill and his daughter, that bond that she never had. What the fuck was she going to do now? She needed to solve this case as quickly as she could, it was opening up too many old wounds.

Moomy was terrified of what that meant. She was that scared girl again. The girl she had killed to become Moomy. And all she could think to do was to go to Sarah.

Chapter Sixteen

There was silence. Sarah recognised it. The silence that was her own familiar companion. The small space she occupied in the world, alone. Just her thoughts, her guilt, her failures. Her peace. Sarah put her work mobile into the safe she had built in her wardrobe, showered and then put on her loose pants and shirt, taking out the black headscarf that she had picked up the weekend before. Moomy always tried to foist colourful *hijabs* on her, with gold embroidery more suited to a wedding. Sarah wasn't interested; she needed something else from her journey. It was a nice gesture though. Moomy found it difficult dealing with Sarah's faith.

Sarah had turned a corner of her bedroom into her private space. She could have used the lounge, the space that until years earlier occupied her mother's sick bed. She didn't though. It was left empty, a gap waiting for someone who wouldn't be back. She could use Rachel's room…but that would have been too much. That would have been too much. Sarah had left it empty, like her mother's space, hoping for it to be full again. Waiting for her baby sister to come back. Rachel was sixteen, her father's daughter from another woman, but had left her father's home when his drunken rages had pushed Sarah out, followed by her mother. She had kept in touch with Rachel, even more than her brothers. Brothers that were following her father, Colin's, path.

Rachel had come to Sarah for sanctuary. Her mother, Kathy, had seen the pain in her stepdaughter's eyes and insisted she stay. She recognised the wounds that a man like Colin could inflict on the women in his life. Except, the safe place that Sarah had created for Rachel became something else.

It had been over two years now since Rachel had disappeared.

Four years since her mother first got diagnosed with breast cancer. It was a shock that diagnosis. Naively, Sarah had thought it wouldn't happen to her or anyone in her family. She blanked over the TV adverts and posters, the campaigns and information sheets. A danger, to someone else. And then it had struck. Advanced, devastating. At first she thought of hope, as her mother Kathy was brave, smiling off her diagnosis, hiding it even. Then slowly, over weeks, she had simply begun to die. They tried everything, the usual chemo, drugs, therapy. Sarah turned to alternative healers; Rachel scoured the Internet for miracles and other ways to deal with this. Nothing worked, it was too late.

Sarah and Rachel nursed her mother through those last weeks. Their lives about Kathy and her illness. And then it was over. It was gone. Kathy had left. Sarah had been devastated. She didn't get out of bed for a week; she didn't want to carry on. She felt so empty. Her mother had gone. What was left? She never understood that feeling of having your strings cut until that moment. It was as if nothing else would ever matter again. She felt a rage at the world as it kept turning. Why didn't it stop? Her mother had died!

She wanted to scream into the face of everyone around her.

The weeks became zombified months. She went back to work. Her heart wasn't in it. Her heart wasn't in anything. She became reckless, trying desperately to feel something. Her sleep patterns off, she made silly mistakes. Reprimanded by her superiors in the force, she turned to alcohol, drugs, sex. Every escape available to her. Nothing helped. The hangovers, the lows and the self-loathing after another random man left her bed. Made worse because she was with Scott. She was supposed to be with him. Together. She let him go; she couldn't take that guilt on top of everything else she was feeling.

At her lowest, months after her mother had died three years ago, was when she found her peace. She had drunk herself into a vile state, so far gone she barely understood who she was and what was happening around her. She was arrested by a colleague, PC Zak Mirza. He recognised her from a training course they had gone to and rather than read her the riot act he had taken her home, got her sober, him and his wife looking after her for the night. She stayed with them for two days. It was the height of Ramadan. And in those days the first glimpse of something hit Sarah. She saw the way they came together; she saw a solace in the way they believed.

Her conversion to Islam wasn't immediate. She took months to make the decision. She was scared it was a knee-jerk reaction to something, to her mother's death; she would regret it later. Use it as a bandage and then pull it off when the wounds were healed. Except, she found it was the only thing that helped her, then, when she had nothing else. Praying alone to a newfound God.

Slowly she came to. She gave up the drugs and the men. The alcohol took longer. Her guide, an American called David Trevelyan, who was a convert himself, explained to her she didn't have to be perfect. Hell, there were Muslims born to the faith who did everything they weren't supposed to. He guided her to find her spirituality, guided her to Sufi mystics, Rumi poetry. And slowly she found her way back to being able to function.

By that time it was too late for Rachel. She had found her own path, the wrong path. And she was lost to Sarah.

Sarah laid the mat down, the direction towards Mecca already clear in her head. She raised her hands, folding them over her chest and started to repeat the words in Arabic she had learned by rote. Feeling the release, the centring. The drug of choice.

The end was the bit she was aiming for, when the motions that had to be done were finished: the one-on-one prayer. Prayer for her mother, her peace of mind, her father, her brothers and most of all for Rachel. She prayed Rachel was alive, that she had survived the wars.

When she was done, her phone buzzed. It was Moomy. Said it was an emergency. She needed to come round.

–

'Don't you have any liquor?'

Moomy was sprawled on Sarah's sofa, her jacket thrown casually. She was wearing a midi dress and boots. Her trademark. Her hair loose, the blonde highlights clashing against her dusky skin.

'No,' Sarah said, putting down a cup of tea and plate of biscuits. Moomy sniffed at them and gulped her hot tea, wincing as it burned her mouth.

'Careful,' Sarah admonished.

'Yes, Mum. Can't believe you don't keep any liquor. Nothing at all? Not an old bottle of wine or stray can of beer anywhere? Come on. What happens when you wake up and realise being a Muslim just isn't good for you?'

'I hope that day doesn't come. Why, is that what happened to you?'

'You know what happened to me.'

'Men happened to you, Moomy, not God.'

'Whatever. These were bastards thinking they were acting for religion.'

'You know there's a difference.'

'Look, I didn't come here to get judged, okay? What I choose to believe or not is my business. I'll follow the rules that fit me. You go on and become a jihadi bride; I'm following normal stuff.'

Sarah flinched, as though Moomy had punched her. Jihadi bride. That's what did it.

'I'm just saying. Don't question me finding God when you lost Him.'

'Fuck off. I need to talk about my family.'

'What happened?'

'I hate all of them. My stupid fucked-up family. Especially my mother.'

'From what you told me, your mother did the least to harm you.'

'She should have done more to protect me.'

'Your mother was a victim of circumstance just as much as you ever were.'

'I don't give a fuck. Why won't they just let me be?'

Sarah didn't have the answers. What she had was tea and a sofa bed. She never let Moomy use Rachel's room. Moomy never asked why. It worked.

Chapter Seventeen

They were gathered in one of the conference rooms, a juxtaposition of old and new, as thick red carpet and velveteen curtains, wooden tables and chairs, were patched with giant touch screens and the latest tools for communication and policework. Space was a major issue, especially with the Mayor and Prime Minister in a pissing contest to try and increase police numbers. Specialist units like Sarah's were being shipped out. She had an hour before everyone else turned up. The constables, the admins, the tech support, the liaisons. The room would be full of people who would be working at this case, behind the scenes, doing all the things that she needed done but didn't have time to. It was unfortunate but in cases like this Scott would get the credit, possibly some sent her way and at a stretch Moomy and her tech genius Romesh. The silent, key people that made everything link and fall into place; the people who did the less glamourized aspect of the job, from securing a crime scene to running traces. They were hardly ever given the kudos they should.

Still she wasn't about to think over the dynamics of the force, she had some time to Facetime Istanbul. Inspector Orhan Avkan loomed large on one of the full screens on the wall in front of her. How things had changed, the world so inter-connected, information able to flow in such an open and easy manner. He had an accent but his English was clear. She didn't expect anything else, and assumed John Hayat would have put pressure on the highest parts of Turkish power she knew. They would make sure he had a foreign trained investigator. That unconscious bias and racism that existed in everyone, John more confident of Orhan's abilities if he had trained with New Scotland Yard or the FBI.

'The case gained much notoriety here as you can imagine,' Orhan said, dressed in uniform, his face handsome, hair dark, eyes blue. There was earnestness there. 'The press were on this story, it had so many elements of a soap opera. After the killing of the journalist, you know the Kashoggi case?'

'Yes, of course, in so far as I followed it on the news.' He was the Saudi journalist who entered the Saudi embassy in Istanbul, never to be seen alive again.

'That really affected how we treated this case also. We didn't want Turkey to be seen as some location that was dangerous, where people get kidnapped and killed.'

Sarah wondered at this, an initial thought – did the Turkish government smuggle Millie out, to prevent backlash against her being discovered there? Sarah dismissed it, the timing would not have worked, Millie was found too close to the time in which she was killed.

'It was not good for our reputation, on top of which John Hayat has a lot of business interests in Turkey. We needed to ensure he felt that he was being looked after.'

'And I'm guessing you were key to this?'

'Yes. I trained for a year with the New York Police Department and also did an internship with Interpol.' Sarah nodded, her assumptions verified in a roundabout way. 'My family are also very well placed in Istanbul society, so he trusted me to help find his son.'

'Was it necessary to pacify him?'

'I am sure, inspector, you also understand what it can do to an investigation if family are causing a problem?'

Sarah agreed, she already had a sense from this case, that was exactly what the Hayats were likely to do. She had come across their type before. The rich and powerful, they didn't believe in rules or being questioned by anyone.

'Can you talk me through your investigation? Any suspicions especially you may have had, your theories,' she asked.

'We immediately put resource into this, as soon as it was identified who the kidnapped couple were. There may be this impression that we are a large country, prone to corruption. We leak your teenagers into Syria and act as the meeting place for spies and smugglers. Some of this may be true, but we are also a modern European nation with the best policing. These men that took the Hayats did not come from nowhere. We have our watch lists, people that we can pinpoint in a situation like this.'

'The likely suspects,' she added helpfully.

'The usual suspects,' he said grinning at her. 'So we went through who was in the area, who may have been paid to run this hit. And we knew from the driver it was a hit. The bullets recovered are standard use in much of our gang related activity, so we pushed our contacts and informers. These big gangs always have weak points and they tell us what we need to know. Sometimes it's the truth, sometimes the fear of the gangs is worse.'

'And what did your sources reveal?'

'Nothing.'

Sarah didn't hide the surprise and frustration from her face. Was Orhan stalling or was he being genuine?

'You see, we could not even trace a hint of this back to any of those usual suspects. We normally get an inclination as to who might be responsible, which family, which gang, even the nationality of the person. Whether this is Daesh related or not, or political. Foreign or domestic agents. There is always something, no matter how small. With this, we didn't sense a change in the rhythms anywhere.'

'There must be something?'

'There really is nothing. We have searched for where they were taken to, that entire area was covered with teams looking for clues. Tyre tracks, sightings, reports, rumours. I will save you the bother of searching through all of the paperwork. There is nothing there I'm afraid. Whoever did this, they were well prepared, they knew the intensity of the investigation and they covered themselves.'

Sarah appreciated his summary, but she would check the documentation and evidence herself, just to be sure.

'Millie didn't just transport herself into this country. What about smuggling routes or air traffic?'

'Everything is being looked at again, but we understood this was a possibility from the start of our investigation. We put an alert on our borders. Turkey has extremely complicated borders, just from our land mass and which nation states we are next to. Still, the search is ongoing in that aspect.'

Sarah nodded. She understood how this might be the case, but it did nothing to quell her anxiety. She asked Orhan to keep her updated, but she knew there was not going to be anything helpful coming. It was Millie and her death here in London that would be the key to solving this.

Chapter Eighteen

Victor watched his mother sob in Spencer's arms, kissing his face and giving him a litany of her plight. Stupid bitch. He felt like smacking him. And her. Useless idiot. Victor was the one holding the reins, running the business, the rock his father was relying on. Spencer? He had shown what he was. Being out of action for so long. Forget the fact that it was Victor who had got him into that state. Spencer should know better.

The envy turned into anger, and he snapped at his mother, not meaning to. Spencer looked at him with hostility. Victor didn't care. Spencer was no one to fear, neither was their mother. Victor was the one they needed to be scared of.

Victor coldly called one of the maids, asked them to get his mother breakfast. In the breakfast room.

'I don't think I'm well enough,' his mother said. 'I can barely function, Victor.'

'It's fine, Mother, some change of scene and fresh air will help you. Plus you can breakfast with Spenny. What say you, Spencer?' Spencer had spent hours throwing up, after sleeping for close to eighteen hours. A day when Victor had called an emergency board meeting and stood in for his father. Assuring them that the Hayats were not crumbling under Oscar's disappearance.

They would find Oscar's body in the same state as Millie's. Then he would just have to deal with Spencer. John Hayat had gone to Istanbul, to meet his secret service guy and find out more details about what happened there to Oscar. They would then make a return trip to London, trying to work out how Millie had ended up there. John thought she might be a decoy, to throw them off the scent from Turkey.

Victor was done with the domestic reunion high drama. He needed to get back to Hayat HQ. Dig in even further. And prepare for Spencer's downfall.

'Get dressed,' he said to his mother, as though she was a child. He knew Spencer wouldn't say anything today. Afraid that his antics from the night before would be sent to his parents. Including a rant about how he hated Oscar and Millie. How he was glad that common gold-digging whore was dead. It was pitch perfect, as though Victor had written it himself.

Victor's phone buzzed as he was on his way out of the townhouse to the office. It was his father. The police wanted to speak to his mother. He wanted Victor there, make sure she didn't say anything stupid. Anything incriminating.

That was all he needed, to be her fucking babysitter.

–

Bill had slept badly again. Images of Millie had killed his sleep. His beautiful, sweet Millie. Eaten up by the choices she had made. The house, even though small, felt frightening. He saw ghosts in the corners, heard whispers calling his name. Unsettled, he would wake through the night, his own fear stopping his sleep. It was when the sun was up that his body seemed to relax enough to sleep. By then it was too late.

Tired when he woke up, he didn't feel like facing the day. There were accounts he needed to work up, money trails and transactions he needed to sort out. People relied on him. Trusted him. The irony. They trusted him with money.

After doing his accounts he would have to visit his wife. She might not know he was there, he could probably not go. Only, he would feel the guilt. He would feel he had failed her if he didn't show. He had failed Millie. What sort of father was he? What he asked her to do? At the end. How could he live with himself?

He was making himself a coffee when he got a message from the cop from the day before. DS Moomy Khan. Said she needed to speak to him. He had wondered how long it would take for them to find out. A lot quicker than he thought. He debated if he should make a run for it. Get away, now, from everything. But he wouldn't do that to Angie. He would stay until she wasn't here anymore. He felt sick at the thought he might go before her. Without Millie there was no one left to look after her.

–

John met Ari Newman at Ataturk Airport, but he didn't have the answers that John needed. Charting one of the Hayat private jets, John had made the journey through diplomatic channels. It was a speedy process; he was hoping to be back in London at night. The police were already questioning his wife. Who knew what they might discover next.

Ari was ex-Mossad turned private security operative. John had used him for a number of years now and Ari had always delivered. They were in the back of a blacked-out Mercedes, heading to the villa where Oscar and Millie had planned to spend their time.

He sometimes wondered if it had been the right thing to relocate from America. That's where his businesses were, but Lara had hated it. She couldn't navigate the rules that society functioned by at their level. In London, her name and bearing and experience put her at the top. After a few years in America, Lara had insisted they return to London. Just before Spencer and Victor were born. She wanted her children raised in the world she knew. The people, the places It was John who felt out of place here. In America they had loved John. He was rich. He had made his money there. He was the American dream. And they loved that, the poster child. In London he was just another foreign billionaire who was trying to break in. Always treated as an outsider. Still, it was America and his work for the embassy that meant he could pull strings when he needed to. Only, he hoped that the secrets he held would not be exposed.

'How can you have nothing?' John said, raising his voice. 'The police are inept. They will never find who did this. You are my only hope, Ari. Only you know the truth.'

Ari was wearing shades; John hated people who hid their eyes. He couldn't read them properly.

'I hired my own forensic team, flew them out from California. They scoured the site of the crash, but nothing. I accessed the Turkish police database, re-questioned all the witnesses they had. Every car that might have been on these roads leading to the villa has been checked. This is a city of ten million though. It is a place where people can disappear. There is no CCTV culture like London.'

'Ten million people, one of them must know something.'

'Let me follow my protocols, I will have some answers for you.'

'If I wanted to follow protocol I wouldn't have hired you. I want you to look at the things police can't or won't.'

'Again I did all of this. The last week I spent looking at kidnapping gangs, organisations that trade with ISIS, groups that form people trafficking and smuggling networks. I used every contact I had here. And nothing. There was no hint even of one of them being used to pick up Oscar and Millie.'

'Ari, my son is missing. His wife has turned up dead. You know the truth. You know where to look. Find him. Please.'

John was no longer a billionaire calling the shots. He was a desperate father begging for the life of his son.

A son Ari was more and more convinced was already dead.

Chapter Nineteen

Moomy decided to tackle Bill first. He was the furthest away, and she was in the mood to drive, try and clear her head. A head full of thoughts and memories. Thoughts of Haroon, memories of her past.

Bill looked exhausted, washed out. Worse than he had the first time Moomy had met him. There would be no recovery from this. He would learn to live with the pain. Like people did with chronic bone ailments or lingering diseases.

'Can I get you a coffee?' he said, his voice hoarse but also slurred. Obviously, he'd just woken up, hadn't spoken to anyone for hours before he slept.

'I'm fine, thanks,' Moomy said. She felt like a bitch for being here and asking him what she had to. He'd just lost his daughter; his wife was seriously ill. Fuck. But it had to be done. 'Why don't you make yourself one?'

He looked at her intensely, trying to read her. She kept friendly on the surface. He made himself a drink and sat nursing it as Moomy did what she had to do.

'Bill, we found some transactions in Millie's bank accounts. Money transfers that don't make any sense. Can you help explain them?'

Bill looked away, swallowing his drink.

'Two hundred thousand pounds,' Moomy said, just to be clear. 'It came into Millie's account from Oscar's mother. Do you know why Lara Hayat gave your daughter that money?'

Bill didn't reply.

'And can you tell me why Millie then gave you that money?'

Bill put his cup down, wiping his face as though some invisible mask had been holding it together.

'Lara Hayat? Are you sure?'

Moomy nodded.

'I thought it was Oscar.'

'Is that what Millie told you?'

'I assumed. I asked her repeatedly where it came from. She wouldn't tell me. So I assumed it was him.'

'You have no idea why Lara Hayat gave your daughter two hundred thousand pounds weeks before she died? Weeks before she married your son?'

'Honestly, no. I thought it was Oscar.'

Moomy didn't dwell on the thoughts in her head. Bill had taken the money, despite his misgivings and suspicions about where it had come from. Not deliberately, but had he also ended up being one of the reasons – perhaps *the* reason – Millie had entered that world?

'What did you use it for, Bill?'

He looked up at her, flinching, as though he just realised she was there. His mind obviously on why Lara had given the money to Millie.

'Things haven't been easy. You know the financial problems we were having since Angie got ill. Everything I built up was in her name. I was struggling. We had to take the council to court. They froze Angie's assets, in

105

case we abused the fact she was ill. By doing that they stopped us giving her the care we needed to. They released money for things like care workers and items she directly needed. But the mortgage, the bills, the things that kept the house going – they didn't care about all of that. And her care home bills, they charged full whack and the assets dwindled away. They wanted to sell this house, pay for her care. I was desperate.'

'What did you do?'

'I took out a loan. Lots of loans. I maxed out my credit cards, took every legal loan I could. And then when they weren't enough, I took out a loan from someone I had met through work. I did his books once. I knew what I was getting into, and still I did it.'

'A loan shark?'

'Yes. Funny thing is he was trying to get me to sell this house to pay him back. I needed the cash. Millie came through.'

'Lucky, really, she had a rich boyfriend?'

'It wasn't like that,' Bill said angrily. 'I didn't whore out my daughter. I sat her down and told her that we would lose the house. Told her she was to go and live her life. That I would find somewhere. Millie, though, wouldn't hear of it. She first sold the jewellery Oscar had given her, then raided her own savings. When that was done, she said she had raised the rest of the money to pay off the loans and save the house. I begged her to tell me where she got it from. She wouldn't say, just told me to do what I had to do for me and her mother.'

'Millie asked her future mother-in-law for that much money to save you?'

Bill nodded.

'And this loan shark, he was happy with the return? He didn't try and ask you for more?'

'No. I helped him out with his accounts. He went easy on me. Accepted the money I gave him.'

'Are you sure? He didn't have a grudge against you that he took out on Millie?'

'Very sure. I'm aware he might bend the law but kidnapping and murder aren't really his style. Breaking windows and kneecaps is.'

'Did he threaten you?'

'Yes.'

'So you were scared and desperate? Millie would know that. She would be prepared to do anything to help you, I'm guessing?'

'Yes.'

'Even ask her fiancé's mother for money.'

'If that's what you've found out.'

'The question is, why would Oscar's mother part with that much money for Millie?'

It didn't make any sense. If the Hayats were worried about people targeting their wealth, as John had told Sarah, Millie asking for the money would have played into their fears that their son had been targeted by a gold-digger. So why exactly did Lara Hayat give Millie that money?

Moomy thought of something else then. A throwaway remark to Sarah, about them paying so Millie could bling herself up. Maybe the money was meant for that. Channel it to Bill for the house and care fees so they didn't look as poor as they were. And more money to whitewash Millie herself, get her the latest in designer treatments and clothes?

But what price did the Hayats exact in return?

Moomy knew all about families and the price they expected their children to pay.

—

Things changed for Moomy irrevocably at Haroon's brother's wedding. It was his eldest brother, she knew that, the doctor. How Haroon's parents had lorded that over everyone. Oh look at our son the doctor, look what we've done.

They didn't mention the fact that the woman he was marrying was a girl who had been on his course. It had been hushed-up gossip at that wedding, but everyone knew they were girlfriend and boyfriend. Such big words back then.

Moomy had grown into her own, turning sixteen, her figure naturally curvaceous and toned. She did plait her hair down her back and wear glasses, sort of like a semi-glamorous nerd; like Wonder Woman at her day job, Haroon would say one day.

She was wearing ferozi blue with silver embroidery and fake silver jewellery. Haroon was one of the *sarwalah*'s best men, sitting on the stage in a white *sherwani*, and as Moomy had accompanied her family to congratulate the newly married couple, and given them a cash donation, Moomy had overheard Haroon asking his brother J:

'What's the capital of Venezuela?'

'Caracas.' She said it without thinking.

Haroon looked at her, and in that moment something had clicked. He was supposed to be a local genius, not only with a doctor as a brother, but at the local grammar school as well.

On paper Moomy and her friends had written off the skinny wimp, with his preppy haircut and assumed he was probably arrogant.

At that moment though, Moomy caught his reflection in the corners of her spectacles, and she thought he had a very honest smile, and her heart started skipping to something else.

They spent the rest of the wedding exchanging shy glances: Haroon coming to talk to some of his real blood cousins who were sitting near her at one point, Moomy making sure she walked past the stage when she was refilling plastic cups with soft drinks, her back straight, her plait over her right or left shoulder, depending which side the stage was on.

A week later Moomy's parents were asked if they wouldn't mind their daughter helping Haroon – a great hope for the local community – with his Geography GCSE.

Her parents agreed, as long as the kids were chaperoned, of course.

Haroon's older brother, Jahangir, J for short, was roped in for the job. His parents thought maybe the studious environment would rub off on him too. He hadn't quite matched his doctor brother and the Oxbridge potential of Haroon.

The oldest of Moomy's brothers, Liaqat, was her chaperone.

Both J and Liaqat ended up playing Carrom Board in the other room, or watching TV or playing cricket or football in the garden. There was no way they would be chaperoning anyone.

So it had been Moomy's mother who would watch them. She sat at her sewing machine, making the jeans and trousers and jackets that her husband and sons sold at markets, while the two kids would discuss concepts such as interglacial terra firma, screes and other geography terms. They were seated on opposite sides of the coffee table, Moomy's head covered with a *dupatta* at all times.

In truth, Moomy and Haroon were writing each other love letters, playing noughts and crosses, hangman, writing poetry.

They had bonded over those lessons so tightly that they had lost all reason.

Moomy cut her finger and wrote his name in her blood. He did the same.

'See that? My name and yours, in blood, together. That's beautiful.'

'What you on about? It looks disgusting,' she had said.

'I think it's romantic.'

'Is that what they teach you at your posh school? How to be a soppy twat?'

He pinched the back of her hand, electricity shooting through her; she swore her heart stopped, that she missed important lung functions every time he did that to her.

They were supposedly at the library and at an after-school cross country running club, respectively.

They were actually sprawled out in Birchfields Park. It was far enough away for no one to recognise them. Always the risk though. How exciting.

The blood looked coppery, tasted tinny as he took her finger in his mouth, as she sucked his finger in return.

'Isn't ingesting blood *haraam*?' he asked.

'Isn't being alone with me *haraam*?' she said.

'We're in a public place, interruptible at any time, our clothes are on, heck you even have a *dupatta* on your head. The devil makes up the third when two people are alone in a room somewhere. Not like this, not in public. I have procrastinated over this many times. Our love is *pakeezah*: pure.'

'Isn't the film *Pakeezah* about whores and brothels?' Moomy said.

'Shut up. Let me be in love.'

'Love? You really love me?'

'More than life itself,' Haroon said.

Her heart lost another moment somewhere. Did those missed heartbeats go somewhere? How easily he had said those words.

Life itself. Life itself. How foolish she was to have believed him.

But there, as the pink blossom swept around them, like a scene from a movie, there was no need to disbelieve.

Mingled blood. Their blood would mingle again. Many times. Each time tragic.

'Here, listen to this,' he said.

'What is it?' she asked, as she took his headphones and portable CD player.

'Un Amor. Gypsy Kings. It's gorgeous, so sumptuous, takes you to a different place.'

'Baby, you're being a pretentious posh boy again.'

They lay with one headphone each, not touching, but being caressed by the sounds of the Spanish guitar, the fluffy pink petals in their hair, on their faces, and they were in a different place.

–

'What university are you going to?'

'Dunno. Haven't thought about it much,' she said.

'Haven't your parents asked you?'

'My intelligence is a shock to them,' Moomy said. 'I don't think they ever gave it a thought. Girls don't go to uni in my family. Apparently. I'll be the first. I think they're disappointed. They probably wanted me married at eighteen.'

'Right, this is the United Kingdom, not some barbaric village. Even in Pakistan literacy amongst city girls is on the up. I really don't think you give your parents enough credit; you are far too sanctimonious sometimes.'

'Sanctimonious. That's a nice word.'

'Patronising. That's a really nice word,' Haroon said.

They were in the library, at the back, where the Black and Asian literature was kept. Where no one came. Where the librarian couldn't hear them.

'So where are you applying? You have to do your UCAS forms next year.'

'Probably Manchester.'

'Manchester? No way. We have to get away, escape the doldrums, discover our potential. The Universe is a big place,' he said.

'Yeah but it's a bit far to commute to anywhere else.'

'You mean you'll live at home? What about student life? You have to immerse yourself into the whole experience. That's a huge part of the learning curve.'

'Don't be stupid. You're a boy. I'm a girl...'

'Thank God...'

'I can't go away. Probably. So if it's not Manchester then it's probably marriage.'

'Don't apply to Manchester. Tell your parents you didn't get it. Let's go to London.'

'I thought you were Oxbridge? Your parents keep telling everyone.'

'I want to be with you so...'

'Oh yeah? You think I'm too thick to go to Oxford or Cambridge? You arrogant...'

They sat in silence, for an hour, then he gave her a headphone and they listened to *Kuch Kuch Hota Hai*. The love story they both liked from their childhood.

How ironic she thought later. Except real life never matched reel life.

Eventually they left the library and he walked her to the end of her street. He said sorry. Moomy never did. Even back then.

–

'Haven't you got anything that doesn't make me look like a nun?' Moomy stared at herself in the shapeless loose clothes that Sarah had given her. Her dress cast aside.

'You're going to go home, get a change of clothes and meet me in the office.'

'Whatever.'

Sarah was tired. She had stayed up late with Moomy then woken up to read the dawn prayer. Now it was another full day at work. A day when she was determined to make some headway with the Millie Beaumont case. Time was running away she felt, time when someone was probably torturing Oscar the way they had tortured Millie.

Chapter Twenty

He remembered that night clearly, how could you forget? The road had been dark and dead, no lights and no traffic. He took it frequently, it was just another part of the route, mapped out so there would be minimal risk. He sometimes wondered how he had ended up here, doing this for a living when there was so much other stuff he could have been doing. Still, when you had bills to pay, kids to feed, a wife demanding something better, it was easy to do. He didn't know how he had been selected for this, maybe word had got round that he was broke, that money would be useful right about now, that he might be willing to do anything for it. Anything. Desperation made fools of the most resolute men.

It was always a task that involved keeping his heart in his mouth. Every stop a risk, a place he might be discovered. He knew now what they were looking for and how to avoid raising suspicion. He knew also how people meant to be securing the borders didn't always do that. That everyone had a weakness and that these men and women, too, had been bought off by the same people who were paying him.

Pretend you don't see anything.

Those were the easy days, when someone he knew was on duty. When it was a stranger his heart battered against his chest and he sweated buckets. He looked guilty as hell. Still, they let him through, no questions asked. Thousands of miles with cargo that was invaluable. Who it was for, he didn't know. Who sent it, he didn't know either. All he knew was where to pick up and where to drop off. If he got caught, he really was a dead end. It was a safe way to do business by those running this. All the risk was his.

Still, he had made it; he was driving through these deserted country roads, unobserved and nearly at his drop-off point. He checked the instructions on his phone: his satnav said ten minutes until rendezvous point. He felt the urge to have a slash. The nearest rest stop was probably miles away and so was home. Fuck it, a few more minutes wouldn't make a difference.

He parked up by a line of thick trees. This whole area was trees and farms, just empty nothingness. Who knew that wilderness this thick and off the radar existed?

He unzipped and pissed against a tree, fear creeping over him as he looked into the darkness and the shadows. Was that a face, a figure? Was something staring back at him in the trees? He shivered despite himself, laughed at how freaked out he was. Grown man getting the jitters.

A twig snapped. He jumped out of his skin; urine splashed on his shoes and jeans. He swore into the night, looking around him. What was going on? Who was there? Must be some squirrel or something. He should get out of here, but he looked around him, transfixed by the fear.

He almost screamed as a car sounded and headlights blinded him. Screeching to a stop next to him, two men got out, tall and well built. This wasn't good he knew. What the fuck?

The one speaking to him had a thick accent.

'Where are they?'

'Who?' This was not good. He was in the middle of nowhere and these idiots could be anyone.

The man didn't wait for an answer. He nodded to his colleague, who started to force open the back of his van.

'What the hell are you guys doing? Stop.'

The man nearest him pulled out something dark from his pocket. Even though the car headlights were in his eyes, he recognised the outline of a gun when he saw one. He gulped hard, frozen, terrified. He only wanted some extra cash – nothing was worth this. He made a judgement. Fuck whoever was running this, these guys were here, with guns.

'Hang on,' he said, and opened up the back of the van.

It looked harmless enough. There was his cargo of material for soft furnishings. Rolls and packets of materials neatly packed. There was no room for anything else. But these guys knew there was. While the man with the gun kept it trained on him, his colleague started to pull out the material. He knew. He was looking for the false bottom of the van.

Enough stock discarded and the smooth flat metal surface of the van was exposed. The man knocked on it hard, spoke to his colleague in a foreign language that sounded Eastern European or Russian to him. The man then used a wrench he produced from inside his jacket pocket, and forced open the false bottom. The small space that customs never found or deliberately didn't find.

He felt his heart go mental, his shirt wet from sweating despite the cold. The man inside the van finished what he was doing and lifted up the trapdoor-like covering of the hidden space. He never really knew what was there: he didn't look or ask. Just knew that if people were paying him that much and going to so much effort to get him to move things, then it must be important.

The man inside the van started taking out small packets in soft pouches. He imagined they contained precious stones of some sort. So that's what he was part of then. And then the small bags stopped and instead the man pulled something else out of the trapdoor. Something that should not be in such a small space, something that would struggle to survive in a place this constricted.

It was a woman. And he had a feeling she was dead.

–

He was having nightmares. The body. The gun. That's not how this shit went down. When he did his deliveries they normally went another way. He handed over the package, which was tiny usually, he got the cash in return. End of. This though, how the fuck had they done that? And when she moved. He nearly jumped out of himself. How had she survived those conditions? You would struggle to fit a child in the back of that van. How did they get a full-grown woman in there?

He had tried not to look, but he couldn't help it. She did not look good. He could see the damage even in the distorted car light. The way she walked, the noises she made. In pain, yet she was walking drunk. They had drugged her. If she was a stowaway then surely they would have just put her in conscious. The driver didn't do that. The people he worked for knew that much, at least, he was very clear about it. No people. He didn't think it was right and he didn't want to take the risk. You heard all sorts of stories with people just dying while caged up in the back of your lorry or truck. Nothing was worth that. He liked what he did. No one got hurt. Until now. What the fuck had happened?

The man with the gun had kept it pointed between him and the girl. A threat for sure. Don't do anything stupid. One of you will get shot. His colleague pushed her to their waiting car. She really was out of it, not making any sound as she was manhandled. As though she was scum.

The man with the gun came close to him, and put the barrel against his forehead. He felt his heart explode, closed his eyes. Shit, shit, shit. This was not meant to happen. He waited frozen, terrified. No. This couldn't happen, not now. He had kids, he had a wife.

'I didn't see anything,' he exclaimed.

'Yes and you make sure it stays that way.'

When he opened his eyes the man with the gun was smirking at him as he thrust a plastic wallet into his hands. His payment. It felt bulkier than any in the past. Extra money for the stuff he had seen. That he would never remember seeing.

He had watched as the car drove off into the wilderness and collapsed against the side of his van.

–

Oscar felt the searing pain. Not him. Not physically. It was what they did to Millie. Whatever happened between them, whatever this was. He didn't want to see her suffer like that. How did it all go so wrong?

They hadn't hurt him at all. That was the agreement, they said. Millie was fair game. He watched as they tortured her. That wasn't the plan at all. What had happened?

And now? He was scared. They said they would let him go. When?

And then it went wrong. Horribly wrong.

His mouth was gagged, his hands in plastic ties. He struggled, but nothing. Millie screamed, her voice burning itself into his head. Then they gagged her and carried her out of the room.

Things got worse. Someone smacked him over the head, everything going black. Was that the plan? He didn't even get time to answer himself.

Chapter Twenty-One

Sarah wasn't expecting a Hayat family committee when she came to meet Lara. The townhouse in Knightsbridge was like a dolls' house. The four storeys, the identikit square windows, the red brick. Inside a maid opened the door revealing a surprising staircase, before showing Sarah into a receiving room. It was tastefully decorated, but over-decorated. Heavy furniture, a pale green with cream and coral undertones carried through the entire room. Someone had made it their life's work to ensure everything from the lamps to the cushions to the rugs were perfect. Someone who made a living from the laziness of the super-rich to decorate their own homes.

Lara Hayat herself was just as carefully placed as her furniture. She was blonde-haired blue-eyed, her face ageless in a rich way. Money could really buy you everything, thought Sarah, even the illusion of youth. Lara was dressed in a smart dress, her arms covered. Just diamonds at her throat and ears, huge diamond ring on her finger. Tasteful but expensive pieces. Her son Victor was with her. He had her eyes, but his father's dark hair and features. He was dressed in a designer suit and impatience.

'What is it you want to talk to my mother about?'

'There are just some issues I need to clarify.'

'She has nothing to do with Millie's death. You should be out there finding Oscar, not wasting your time hassling her.'

Sarah tried to keep her gaze cool. She had barely sat down; why was Victor accusing her of harassing his mother? He seemed agitated, uncomfortable even, with having the police in their home.

'Hopefully we can clear this up quickly. It might even help with finding Oscar.'

Lara put a hand on Victor's arm, a gesture that didn't seem to affect him. Victor ignored it and went on.

'What do you want to know?'

'You have to forgive my brother, he's not known for his charm.' Sarah turned to look at the man who had just walked in. He had his mother's colouring, offset with a deep tan. 'Spencer Hayat.'

Spencer sat next to his mother so she was now boxed in between her sons. Sarah saw her lean towards Spencer, and he in turn put his arm around her.

'I got this,' Victor said, who seemed irritated further by his brother's arrival.

'How can we help?' Spencer asked, ignoring Victor. Sarah could see the easy confidence that emanated from Spencer in comparison to his brother. Victor had shades of gruffness that his father displayed. Spencer looked like the advert for a Knightsbridge son, his blond hair thick, a New England pressed shirt and creases in his jeans.

'I need to speak to your mother. Although, while you're both here, maybe I can ask you some questions about your brother?'

'What would you like to know?' Spencer looked enthusiastic, open, keen. Not worried or sad. Victor gave him a disgusted look.

'I spoke to your father earlier. He couldn't think of anything specific that might have made Oscar a target for what happened. I'm guessing that Oscar only showed your parents one side of his life. I know it's difficult to betray a confidence, only if it can help us, then I would ask you now. You would know your brother better than your parents probably. He wouldn't hide himself from you both. Is there anything that might explain what happened? Why someone would want to target him and Millie like this?'

Spencer furrowed his brows, shook his head. 'I can't think of anything. What about you, Victor?'

'I barely spoke to him, no idea what he got up to,' Victor said.

'You barely speak to anyone, unless it's about money or the business,' Spencer said jokingly.

'Someone has to take an interest, it's not all about spending the cash.'

'Where would we be without the great saviour?'

'You weren't close to your brother?'

'Define close,' Victor said.

'How often did you see him?'

'He was at university for the last three years. Hardly ever. Birthdays, Christmas, weddings.'

'He went to university late? He was helping your father in his business, I believe?' asked Sarah.

'Not sure how much help he was,' said Victor.

'So, you weren't close even before he went?'

'Not particularly.'

'Victor and Oscar both worked for my father though,' Spencer said.

'And what about you?' asked Sarah.

'I set up my own business. A chain of gastro pubs.'

Victor scoffed.

'I like being independent,' replied Spencer.

'Independent? It was still Father's money that started up your venture.'

'And Oscar?' interrupted Sarah. 'Did he do anything apart from work for your father?'

'No,' said Victor.

'What about in his private life? How was he?'

'He was a bit shy if I'm honest,' Spencer said thoughtfully. 'Not really the partying sort. I mean he went, hung out with us. Not really his scene though. Preferred his cultural pursuits. Art galleries and museums.'

'You don't know of any altercations or incidents that might have put him in danger?'

'Nothing,' Spencer said.

'Can I ask how the business is run? Do you all have an equal say?'

'It's a complicated multinational,' said Spencer. 'We have a board.'

'The family doesn't retain controlling interest anymore?'

'Of course we do. We are majority shareholders, we make the important decisions. My father has final say over every major decision.'

'How are the shares split?'

'Father and Mother control the company.'

'And where is the company heading? Was Oscar going to head up the company eventually?'

'You mean if our parents died?' Victor said coldly.

'The truth is, we both benefit with Oscar gone,' Spencer said honestly.

Victor glared at him.

Their mother looked at the floor. Yet it was her that Sarah really needed to talk to. Alone. To find out what kind of secrets she was hiding.

Chapter Twenty-Two

Declan Act Two. That's how Moomy saw it. Same place, The Globe. Same time of day. But Declan was now in a different role.

'What are you rehearsing for? I never did ask.'

'*Othello*.'

'How apt. What role are you playing?'

'The main lead. It's a special adaptation. The entire cast is made up of Afro-Caribbean actors, apart from the one role that originally was.'

Moomy didn't trust herself to speak. She was all about empowerment. Changing the narrative. But the casting she'd seen of late was a bit off the chart. Why must *Richard III* be played by a black woman? Why not write a strong role for a black woman instead?

'How is that working out for you? Playing the hero?'

'It's a great role and the first time I've had the chance to portray it.'

'Who's playing Iago?'

'A fellow actor.'

'That's the really exciting role to play in *Othello* though, isn't it? The jealous best friend.'

'Yes, he's definitely the most layered. We all love to hate a villain, don't we?' He laughed. Clear laugh. Fake laugh.

'Tell me, how was your relationship with Millie? Before Oscar took her away from you?'

Declan's anger was immediate, his voice loud. 'He didn't…' Then he quieted himself, lowered his voice. 'He didn't take her from me. We broke up before they got together.'

'Are you sure of that?'

'Yes.'

'You said you weren't happy about her seeing him as a friend. About the lavish gifts and weekend outings. How your jealousy got the better of you. How you had it out with her. So tell me, Declan, did those confrontations stop at arguments? Or did you show her how you felt too?'

'What do you mean?'

'And what did you do to Millie to make her aware of just how upset and jealous you were?'

Declan flared up again.

'What is this? What exactly are you trying to establish?'

Moomy regarded him coolly. She had no time for dickhead men who used their physical strength to threaten and subvert women. She'd had enough of that in her life.

'We found some interesting things in Millie's autopsy. We found healed fractures. Recent. Before she was taken. Within the last few years the pathologist is thinking. The time she was with you.'

Declan's eyes were on fire, the colour in his face sunburnt red.

'How fucking dare you,' he said.

Moomy kept her voice low and even. Menace in every syllable.

'Do not raise your voice at me, or use that sort of language. I'm a police officer. So unless you want me to arrest you and question you at the station, I suggest we sit here on centre stage all very calm and civilised.'

'I'm sorry,' Declan said, genuine contrition on his features.

'Is that what you said to Millie? After you hit her? That you were sorry?'

'I didn't…' he began loudly before softening his tone again. 'I didn't lay a finger on her.'

'Someone did. More than once.'

'I loved her.'

'I'm not questioning your love, Declan. Maybe you loved her too much. To the point of possessiveness?'

'That's not how it was.'

'Something happened to give her those injuries. Something cruel and vicious.' Moomy held herself in. Declan was a monster if he hurt Millie the way the forensics were suggesting. Yet she couldn't blame him for her personal crap. Couldn't take it out on him.

Declan seemed to hit a wall, his resolve and his anger disappearing.

'I promised,' he said, his voice a whisper. He coughed it away. 'I promised Millie I wouldn't say anything, it feels wrong. She loves her parents. I can't…'

'Her parents?' Moomy didn't hide the surprise on her face.

Declan seemed to be in turmoil, his breath laboured, his hands wiping his face. Then with the choice made, he breathed out, breathed in. His leg started tapping nervously as he spoke. Moomy listened to him, her heart breaking with every word he said.

Chapter Twenty-Three

The two boys had gone, leaving Lara Hayat alone with Sarah. There was a tension and silence between them. Sarah saw a change in the woman without her children. That helpless act seemed to drop instantly. Now she looked like a woman observing her prey.

A clock marked time somewhere and Sarah caught sight of a Victorian clock tower, mother-of-pearl inlay and crystals sparkling on the wooden structure. Gold filigree on the hands.

'A gift from the Turkish Ambassador. It was given to one of the last Ottoman sultans by Queen Victoria.'

'That's quite something. What was the occasion?'

'No occasion. John invested in helping their gas supplies or something. Maybe steel. I don't pay attention to my husband's business ventures, barely keep up with my own.'

'Your family own half of London from what I can tell.'

'Yes, I suppose we do. I never feel as though it's real if that makes sense? They just become addresses and buildings and income. As though they are someone else's. I inherited them, my children will inherit them from me. An almost invisible inheritance. Property is the most boring and yet the most lucrative way to make money, don't you think?'

Sarah had bought her mother's council flat on an estate in Elephant and Castle; most people she knew even in their forties like her didn't have their own home in London. Boring but crippling for people who were at the beck and call of their landlords. Still, she wasn't there to judge the wealth of the Hayats.

'And what happens to that wealth? Your sons seem to think it will be an equal split?'

'Does that matter?' Lara's tone seemed to shift a gear. She went from softly spoken to sharp in an instant.

'Mrs Hayat, this conversation stays between us. You don't have to tell me anything. What I will say, though, is that anything that I need to know will eventually come to light. I don't have a vested interest here. My only interest is finding Oscar and preventing what happened to Millie happening to him.'

'Please, God, I don't think I could bear it. My heart is already destroyed with him missing. I need my son back.'

'Then help me find him. By being as honest as you can and as open as you can.' She nodded imperceptibly. 'Is the money going to all your children equally?'

Again the hesitation, the battle inside. Sarah knew people though. She knew that the love Lara had for Oscar was real and that love would win out.

'No,' Lara said, softly, as though if she said it too loud it might be heard by someone other than Sarah. 'Oscar is due to inherit everything.'

There it was. The secrets of the Hayat family. The one thing that John hadn't said, when he had been the heart-broken father, looking for his son. He hadn't mentioned the fact Oscar was sole heir to his billions. And by default so was Millie.

'It wasn't my choice. John insisted. He said the eldest child had rights. He thinks so differently sometimes. We have made vast sums of provision for Victor and Spencer. They will never be poor. They just won't ever be as rich as Oscar. John doesn't want the family business to break up by in-fighting. He wants control to rest in the hands of one son: his eldest child.'

So Millie was going to breed the next generation. Lara probably thought Millie beneath her son. Was it just about the money or was it more? Was it about the colour of Millie's skin? Angie had been born to immigrant parents from St Lucia. Sure the Hayats had Arab blood, but was marrying someone black just too much for them? Too much for Lara in particular, this woman whose family traced her lineage back to who knows when. Marrying John she could pass her children off as white, especially Spencer, but Millie? Oscar's children would not look anything like Lara. And that money, that ancestral money? Going to the children of that woman? Sure. But what about Oscar?

'Oscar is worth a lot of money then?'

'Billions.'

'Yet his kidnappers haven't asked you for anything?'

Lara looked away, the terror in her face clear.

'Can I ask, Mrs Hayat, about money? In particular about two hundred thousand pounds. Money you trans-ferred to Millie. Weeks before she was to marry your son. A match which I believe you weren't entirely happy with. What was the reason for the money?'

Lara was back to fighting mode.

'I don't have to answer that.'

'No. Not yet, but eventually I will need to know.'

The threat was there. Tell me now or under different circumstances. Maybe at the police station. What would that feel like?

'Was it a payoff? Did you attempt to bribe her into abandoning the wedding?'

'Don't you think I could stretch to more than that?'

'Not without raising suspicion. From everything you've told me I'm guessing your husband keeps a tight control over the finances of the business. Two hundred thousand, so much for most people, might be something you spend regularly though. Anything more and he may have started to suspect? Was it an agreement of some sort? A regular payment to Millie to stay away from your son? You knew she was in need of money maybe?'

'It wasn't like that at all. She asked me for some cash and I didn't say no.'

'You didn't ask her what she needed it for?'

'No.'

'Come on, Mrs Hayat, the girl your very wealthy son is about to marry asks you for money and you agree? A girl clearly after your heir for his fortune? You just gave her the money?'

'Yes.'

'Mrs Hayat... do you want Oscar to turn up dead like his wife?'

'No, please... I...' She played with the diamonds on her wrist, her real god, the real strength of her confidence and her life. 'You have to understand Oscar was worth so much. Not just financially, but he was my first child. Always the one who loved me the most. We always get told, don't we, not to have favourite children? Yet Oscar has always been the one who I felt the most for. You see when he was born my father was still alive. I didn't have much to do with the business. Oscar was my focus. In the years after, my father passed away and by the time Victor and Spencer were growing up I was so busy, I barely had time to raise them. They were given over to the help and the nannies. Especially Victor. He's the youngest, and I hate saying this, but the coldest. His first memories must have been of me going away. By then Oscar and Spencer were old enough to travel with me, so I would sometimes take them when Victor couldn't go.'

'And then your pride and joy brings home the most unsuitable girl?'

'You make me sound like such a snob. I'm not. Look at who I married. John was not born into my world. He was so rough when I met him and yet I loved him beyond anything. The vain peacocks positioning themselves in the Knightsbridge set all failed to impress me with their Eton and Oxbridge education and their galivanting around the world spending their parents' millions. John was so shy in a way, not posturing, so real. I knew that when he looked at me he saw me for who I was. He didn't need my money. Maybe he wanted the family connections that marriage to me would give him, but even that was attractive to me. I felt as though it was an equal marriage. We completed each other, complemented each other. So I'm not this cold-hearted, snobbish cow.'

'Then what was the issue with Millie? Her skin colour?'

'Please, I am not racist. Look at my husband.'

'He looks pretty fair to me.'

'You are being facetious.'

'I'm asking the questions people don't like. Millie was a total outsider, wasn't she? Poor and black.'

She pffd and waved her hands as though Sarah had offended her.

'There was no issue. Millie was beautiful and clever and sweet. She just wasn't what I wanted for my son. She didn't bring him anything. I wanted Oscar to marry someone who could match him, who he could trust. Who I could trust. Why shouldn't I worry about Millie only being interested in my son for his wealth?'

'So what was it? A bribe? A test? You gave her the money to prove your suspicions. And how did that work out?

'She took the money, didn't she?'

'Money you gave her to not marry your son?'

Lara didn't disagree.

'And then still married your son.'

'Doesn't that tell you everything you need to know about her?' Lara said quietly.

'Are you happy she's dead?'

Lara Hayat didn't reply. Which was answer enough.

Chapter Twenty-Four

Moomy felt a chill as she spoke to Bill Beaumont, her earlier meeting with Declan crashing around her head, his words painful even now. She didn't know how to broach the subject. She should have done it face-to-face. But she was a coward. She wasn't always so scared. There was a time when she had taken the biggest risk of her life. Back then. Back when. Now she needed the distance. Bill was being asked by her to carry out an act of betrayal in a way.

Bill was at the care home when she called him. Moomy was immediately more on edge thinking this was the worst place for him to be. She had to know, though, what the truth was.

'Bill, I have to ask you some more questions. I have to tell you things about Millie that I don't want to. And yet I must.'

Moomy recounted to him the injuries. The fractures on her arms, hands, ribs. Healed, but real. Fractures that Moomy had assumed were the result of Declan.

Bill had started to sob even before she had finished. And she knew then it was true. Moomy gave him time to compose himself, offered to call him back.

'It wasn't her fault,' he said. 'She didn't know what she was doing. It was the illness. She was frustrated, she was confused and scared. She didn't know who we were, thought we were there to hurt her.'

'Is that why you had to move her to a care home?'

'I couldn't deal with it alone. Millie was going to give up her place at Oxford for me. I couldn't let her. I had to make the choice, the most painful choice. Just before Millie went away, I made that decision. I had to save my daughter, even if I can never save my wife.'

'The injuries to Millie, they were done by your wife?'

Bill had lost himself, openly sobbing, making it difficult to hear.

'Yes… it's a symptom of the illness, something they don't tell you about. Some people get so bad they react like this. Imagine being in your home and not recognising the people there, and then those people are trying to touch you and change your clothes and force food into you… how would you feel? How would you react?' Moomy couldn't say. If anyone tried to force her to do something now she would kick the fuck off. Not like before, when she didn't have a choice and had to go along with what others in her life had decided for her.

'I understand,' she said. She didn't. She sympathised and she accepted the difficult place Bill and Millie and Angie were all in. One day everyone is okay. The next no one is.

'Bill, I just need you to outline the incidents you remember for me. I will then match them to Millie's injuries. Just so I can be sure.'

He agreed. And Moomy knew then that Declan hadn't been behind those injuries. But still, he was definitely not in the clear as far as she was concerned. Spurned by Millie, just how far would he have gone to exact revenge against her and the man he felt took her from him?

–

Moomy broke down in her car after her conversation with Bill. In her head were thoughts of fathers, daughters and first loves. Millie had ended up dead, in a way Mumtaz had too. To create Moomy.

Why was her head so lost in her own thoughts? Why now? Why couldn't she escape? Yeah fine, life had kicked her. She got over it. She moved on. So why did it keep trying to remind her? London was massive. And yet Harry had turned up again, she had bumped into that prick in this city of millions. She thought she had lost herself from her past. How the hell had Harry come back into her life?

City of millions. Disappear. Reinvent. Relive. Escape.

It didn't work. They found you. The things that strangled you. The conversation she and Harry had had as teenagers, still etched in her mind. Moomy angry because she had so much potential. And in the end being a girl had meant she had paid in ways that Haroon was never expected to.

'Are you going to marry someone from back home?' Haroon had sounded apprehensive, unsure, younger than the teenager he was.

'Don't know. Haven't thought about it. Aren't you going to marry me?'

'Me…' He coughed and spluttered, spilling his Coke can in the grass.

'I guess not. What about loving me more than life itself?'

'Of course I will,' he said regaining some composure. 'Once we gain academic plaudits, carve out careers for ourselves, become independent. I meant it. My love is not seasonal.'

'How long will all that take? I'll be married off with two kids by then,' she said.

'Seriously?'

'Seriously. Maximum, I'll get to the end of my degree if I'm lucky. My dad wants me out of the house. I'm too much of a burden for a misogynist.'

'That's fine. We can get married as soon as we graduate. Work can wait. I will move heaven and earth, slay any dragon, climb any tower... but you will be no other man's wife but mine.'

'Words are cheap. You look a bit too skinny to be a hero anyway.'

He put a sulky mask on. She threw dandelions and grass at him until he relented and threw them back.

They clasped hands, lying in the debris, her face covered by her *dupatta*. He sat up on one elbow and blew gently, then moved it back with his finger; her hand moved to her stomach, she bit her lower lip, her eyes closed, aware of his scrutiny.

Haroon brought his face forward, and breathed gently on her lips, careful not to touch them, before tracing their shape with a plucked yellow flower.

It was the single most erotic moment of Moomy's life, a moment she had failed to recapture in the arms of any man. Even Haroon's.

They were careful. They knew it wasn't okay to be going steady. Boyfriends and girlfriends were not acceptable. Moomy had no-one to speak to except Haroon. And her diary.

She gave him a codename: she called him Ranjha after the erstwhile doomed lover from the tragic Punjabi love story *Heer Ranjha*, often called the Asian Romeo and Juliet, and wrote essays of inner turmoil about him.

They were careful. They never got caught.

Her diary was not so careful. It got caught all too easily.

Moomy was confronted by her mother. Luckily, her mother could barely read English, but she did see a giant heart with the names Moomy and Ranjha written in red felt tip pen.

Moomy had been threatened, tell all or face the same questions from her father. So she had poured out how she had met someone, how he was a decent guy, how they were in love, how they were going to get married, how, how, how…

Her mother's face had turned ashen and Moomy felt the earth shift under her.

'You silly girl. Have some shame. End this now.'

'But, Mum…'

'If your father finds out he will break both our legs. For my sake…'

'Yes, Mum…'

Betrayal. That seems too harsh a word. Circumstance, compromise, the way things are. Just are. That would be fairer.

But of Moomy's empty heart that cried betrayal?

Hush that heart, because no one is listening.

–

'We can't meet ever again,' Moomy had said.

'How Victorian. Why not?'

'My mum knows. If my dad or brothers find out they'll kill you. And me.'

The blossom was bruised, clumped in puddles, looking like junk and decaying now. The grass was wet from a summer rain. It felt chilled.

'I won't let them. This is just the first test of our love, there will be so many more as we progress. Let's not fall at the first hurdle, we have so much more to give.' Haroon the earnest.

'It's too dangerous. What if someone else finds out?' Moomy the realist.

'No one will. Trust me.' Haroon the optimist.

Trust him? So she did.

Get found out? Oh, how she did.

Her mother confessed what she knew, and Moomy was lectured and locked away. No more library visits ('It's the summer holidays why are you going to the library anyway?') no more unsupervised trips out of the house ('You don't need to see your friends on your own, take your mother with you').

Her mother asked her point-blank if she was still a virgin.

'Of course I am! What do you think you've raised?'

'I don't know any more.'

There was only one way to avoid any scandal. There was only one solution to this problem. They would go on holiday as a family to Pakistan and let Mumtaz clear her head, and when she came back her head would not be turned by such notions as *pyar mohabbat beghayrat*: love and shame.

'They're marrying me off to my cousin,' she said.

'Don't be absurd. This is the nineties. You're over sixteen. They wouldn't be so bold, it's illegal. It's just a family holiday.'

'My middle brother let it slip by accident. They found me a boy, he's twenty-two. Rehan. That's his name. He's a graduate apparently, my dad's nephew, he'll come over here and work as an engineer or something.'

'Moomy… no… this isn't happening, I won't let it. I'll send my parents to your house and ask for your hand in marriage. This is ridiculous. We have to fight this. Have some faith in the love that we share.'

He was beginning to annoy her with his self-absorbed romanticism.

They were whispering into the phone, her family praying, playing cricket, cooking. Moomy had sent a message via a mutual friend and had picked up the receiver with measured precision, before it even rang.

'It's happening. What else can I do?'

'We need to be prepared, start hoarding away money and essentials. London. It's big enough to hide in,' Haroon said.

'Run away? We can't,' she said.

'Do you know what is happening to you? Some strange man is going to marry you, and get his filthy bastard hands all over you. I'll die before I let that happen. No one will touch you while I'm alive.'

'Haroon…'

'We are doing this. We're running away.'

They packed and decided a night when she would creep out of the house. She had no money, so stole some of her mother's jewellery. She was sure it would be okay and they would repay her mother one day.

Except Haroon got caught. He confessed all to his parents. His brother J got beaten to a pulp by their father. Why wasn't he chaperoning his younger brother? The blame was placed on J, as Haroon stood shamefaced, his mother protecting him.

And then Haroon's father had his first heart attack.

Moomy put the jewellery back and they both knew there would be no running away.

'Mumtaz is their daughter. I cannot interfere. And neither will you,' Haroon's father had said from his recovery bed.

'Let's call the police, there has to be legal recourse.'

'Have my parents arrested?'

'If that's the only way, then yes.'

'Let this go, Haroon. We have no option.'

'Do you know what your life will be like? Are you aware of the death sentence you're assigning yourself? And me. Do you think I can exist, seeing you as another man's wife, day in, day out…'

'You'll be at uni soon enough. Loads of girls get married back home, it's not so bad. I might even be happy…'

Her words sounded so devoid of the fear she was feeling inside. The unfairness of how her life would unfold, in comparison to his.

'That hurts, Moomy. How you can foresee a life with a stranger, with another man. It cuts deep, and you twist the knife with those words. I can't let you marry anyone. You're mine.'

'Then you marry me.'

'My parents...'

'Forget them. This is happening, Haroon. We aren't strong enough; we don't have the ability to go up against our families, our traditions, our culture.'

'This is not tradition or culture, don't repudiate Islam in this way. It's a barbaric custom of forced marriage...'

'I am going into this with at least some knowledge. I'm lucky they didn't just ship me off and get me married off and hold me prisoner.'

'That was their intention,' he spat.

'I know but... marry me. We know the *nikah* ceremony. *Tu mujhe kabool, main tujhe kabool*: you accept me and I accept you. Simple.'

Moomy was attempting to take control of a destiny that seemed to be galloping away from her. She could leave him, knowing she was tied to him. That whatever else her parents did to her, she had chosen who to marry first.

'We need witnesses, an Imam, a contract...'

'God and the Angels can be our witnesses. The whole Universe that God created can be our witness.'

Witness to the naivety of children. Star-crossed and doomed. But Moomy couldn't see that back then, only now when she looked back on it.

Chapter Twenty-Five

They were sipping at the tea that Lara had brought to them. The silent maids bringing a trolley service of cakes, sandwiches and tea. When they were gone Sarah wondered just how much the staff saw, their silent presence invisible probably to the Hayats. She had to pick carefully who she spoke to, if she was allowed. Neither woman touched the food. They were too wrapped up in their discussions. Sarah didn't know if any of the food was halal either. She was still struggling to work out what she could and couldn't eat.

She got that pig was a no-no. Which was a killer since bacon sandwiches were her go-to comfort food. They were a bitch to give up, worse than the alcohol. And she got every other meat had to be halal. Moomy didn't help much, stuffing her face with whatever she wanted to. She was so lapsed it wasn't even worth asking her anything. Her answer to every question was, 'Have some vodka and a sausage roll and fuck the rules'. But then people loved telling her about gelatine and E numbers and the debate about cheese and lobsters. She couldn't cope so she stayed vegetarian and only ate meat when she was sure.

The tea tasted different. It was a stupid thing to think, just because it was served in some off-the-wall priced china and on a trolley by maids. Only, someone had really thought about it. It tasted amazing. She put the cup down, focusing back on Lara Hayat, the doyenne of the property empire that her missing son was going to inherit. And the woman who was trying to take her place.

'What was the deal you offered Millie?' Sarah asked, breaking the sounds of china and metal spoons. They were in the heart of Knightsbridge yet there were no sounds from the outside world. Money could even buy you peace in London it seemed.

'Two hundred thousand every quarter, for the duration of her mother's life. Her care would be done at home by private nursing staff. Her father could give up work.'

'How did you know what her Achilles heel was?'

'I did my research.'

Sarah looked at the composure on Lara's fake face and felt loathing. She had found the stress that the Beaumonts were under, the one thing that might break Millie. Millie wasn't some cold-hearted gold-digger. Lara had dangled the one thing in front of her that Millie didn't know she wanted but realised her parents needed. Like the serpent in the Garden of Eden. Actually did she believe in the serpent story now? She knew the Garden of Eden was in *The Qur'an* and the fall of Adam and Eve, but was it the same? She made a mental note to find out. Another thing. It seemed as though she was starting from scratch.

And these people. Sarah had dealt with people from different backgrounds over the years, brushing up against those in power early on in her career. Working in London you got the bottom of the heap, the knife crime and the drug dealing, right to the top. She was part of the team that had brought down an MP in the past. It was why she was trusted to deal with the likes of the Hayats. At one time it was such an alien world. Her own background not preparing her for what people like this did with their lives and their money. Now though, it was different. She had become accustomed to it. The rich and their messed-up ways. Nothing surprised her any more.

Moomy, on the other hand, was new to this world. It was why Sarah kept her away from interviewing Lara. She would have been dazed by the money and the polish. Not for long but still initially. It took a lot to bypass that level of wealth and arrogance.

'How did Millie react when you approached her?'

'Oh, she put up a good show at first,' Lara said, her hands as if dismissing Millie's protests. 'That she wasn't after Oscar's money; she claimed she didn't know about him inheriting everything. Liar. Of course she did.'

'How would she know?'

'Oscar knew. He probably told her in a moment of drunken weakness. He could be indiscreet about such matters, didn't realise what a big deal it was.'

'And your other sons? They were okay with this financial split?'

Lara stared hard at her, there was no way the mother serpent was going to betray her children. She didn't react at all.

'What happened to change Millie's mind?'

'I urged the girl, encouraged her. Sent her brochures of the life her mother could have. The new home they could buy, in Central London near the best hospitals in the country. The brilliant care she would receive. I made her see.'

'Made her? How? Did you threaten her?'

'Threat is such a loaded word. I persuaded her, explained to her.'

'Harassed her through messages no doubt?' Sarah would check out what the communication had been between Millie and her future mother-in-law.

'Whatever it took to make her understand.'

'And when did she?'

'A few weeks before the wedding, she agreed. She was in tears, again all for show. Couldn't wait for the money to come through fast enough, I'm guessing. Greed is a disease. In all of us.'

'Even yourself?'

'Yes. I don't hunger for wealth and riches, yet I hunger for happiness for my children. My Oscar...' The cold brittle voice wavered: at least she genuinely cared for her sons. Millie was just an inconvenience.

'What were the terms of these payments?'

'Millie would break off the engagement and all ties with Oscar.'

'Not stating the obvious, but they got married? Did you have an agreement in writing?'

'Of course. I don't give away so much money without it. In case John ever asks. He loves his audit. Something about everything needing to be above board and legal all the time. While he's busy playing with men who have flouted the law throughout their business lives. You don't become rich by being legal. Fact.'

'And if Millie broke that agreement?'

'Then I would show Oscar and the money would stop.'

'So didn't you try to stop things when you all headed off to Bali for the wedding?'

'I called her in, screamed at her, told her I would expose her to Oscar.' There was fury on Lara's face, and Sarah could picture just how she would spit fire, how Millie must have felt being on the receiving end of it. 'She was a clever one though. She told me that she was going to do it in Bali. When we were all gathered there, she was going to elope before she got to the altar. She said Oscar would never give her up, he was so madly in love with her. The only way was to humiliate him and his family, that way he would never want to see her again. And I fell for it. I fell for her little scheme. I even had a backup in waiting to catch my broken son, heal him, a woman worthy of him. As I said, however, Millie was just too clever for all of us.'

Sarah's mind was a mess of ideas and confusion. Millie took Lara for a ride? Or did she mean to call off the wedding? Did something happen in Bali to make her change her mind? What exactly? 'I sat there on the front row, mother of the groom, resplendent in my Chanel even if I say so myself. And I beamed, the biggest smile, my son thinking I was happy for him. I waited and I waited, my heart soaring, knowing she wasn't going to show. And then the music started. Every guest had their face turned towards that bitch, none saw the utter devastation and betrayal on my face. There she was in a Vera Wang, a dress that Oscar probably paid for, diamonds all over her. I had to stop myself from throttling her in front of everyone.'

'You didn't stop the wedding?'

'I wasn't prepared, I didn't have any proof on me. I was determined to break it all as soon as the vows were done. Get it annulled. Oh, Millie thought she was so clever, but she had no idea who she was dealing with.'

'What did you do?'

'I pulled Oscar aside during the reception, and I showed him the agreement. I told him everything.'

'How did he react?'

'He was horrified, shocked, confused. Why did she marry him then? I told him he needed to end it with her, he needed to let Millie go and he needed to annul the marriage.'

'I bet he loved that, his mother interfering in his life that way? He was a grown man. What did he say to you?'

'He said he would deal with it.' She didn't answer Sarah about just what her son might have said.

'Did you confront Millie at all?'

'Yes, when I got her alone. It was the morning after, before they departed for their honeymoon. I told her Oscar knew and it was all over. She told me I was deluded and that she wasn't going anywhere. Oscar loved her and if I wasn't careful I would be the one who left his life.'

So there it is, Sarah thought. The complications of the marriage. Lara desperate to get rid of Millie, scared she would lose her son, feeling betrayed. Oscar himself feeling as though he had just married a woman after his family money. A woman he had pursued relentlessly for years in Oxford, and she had turned out to be the one thing he hated. Yet they went on honeymoon together; he didn't abandon her as soon as he found out. In Sarah's mind ideas were forming, shapes she didn't like the feel of. Just how desperate were the Hayats to get rid of Millie? Were mother and son in league with each other?

She dismissed this idea. Lara was genuinely afraid for her son, even Sarah could see it every time she spoke about him. And there was no way Lara would put her son at risk. Getting Millie killed, she was seemed very capable of. Harming Oscar? No.

There was no ransom though. What did that mean? Was there more to Oscar's disappearance in that case? Was he behind this? His revenge for Millie, in his eyes, betraying him, or did he accept her reasons for why she did it? She took the money to help her parents and married him for love anyway?

Sarah felt closed in and oppressed by the room, Lara's cloying perfume, the incense being released into the air to fragrance the home. Enough, she thought, she had to get away from here. So she could think and piece together just what the Hayats had done to Millie Beaumont.

Chapter Twenty-Six

Victor watched his mother crying in Spencer's arms. The stupid bitch. Why couldn't she keep her mouth shut? He was panicked now. Knew what the police would be thinking. Oscar was to get it all, the businesses, the fortune. He and Spencer bequeathed little trinkets to keep them going. Neither of them getting the family business. Victor deserved it. He had worked harder for it than either of his brothers; he had been the one to help his father through some tricky situations of late. While Oscar swanned off to play preppy student at Oxford, Victor had helped deal with the financial crisis that the company faced. They had lost a fortune on the steel and gas side, his father getting into bed with some dodgy Russian gangsters. Literally getting into bed with the hookers they supplied, shitfaced and signing away all sorts of rights to their pipelines across Russia. It was Victor who had made sure the deal was reversed, with Ari's help of course. They had staged a mini military-style operation to deal with the gangsters, and save his father. Save the business that Oscar was going to inherit.

With him gone, Victor had angled himself to take over. Sure Spencer was older, but he was incompetent. Victor had made sure of that. Spencer's vices were all pay-rolled by Victor. From the drugs to the women. Stupid Spenny too dumb to even realise. The blond Greek hero too pretty for his own good.

Victor didn't hate his brothers, they were his flesh and blood. They had grown up together, playing childhood games, supervised by various nannies and au pairs. They had been home-schooled for most of their early childhood, only heading off when it came time for Eton and then university. Victor didn't think much of anything, until he turned eighteen. Then he was considered old enough to know the truth. The callous truth of his parents, and how he and Spencer would get nothing. Millions compared to the billions that would be his. And the seeds had been planted, the hatred growing in him ever since.

He watched again with loathing at his mother and brother. How could she tell the police? They would work out soon enough that the people with most to gain with Oscar gone were himself and Spencer. She had ruined everything.

Victor stared hard and cold at them both. Enjoy it, he thought. Where Oscar went, it won't be long until Spencer follows. He would make sure of it.

–

Ari watched as John dribbled in his sleep, grunting in his boar-like snoring, wiping his thick face in his dreams. He didn't feel anything. He had stopped feeling a long time back, his whole life about not having empathy or caring. His father was a general in the Israeli Defense Force whose dream it had been to train Ari to become the best. The best spy, the best assassin. He had taken Ari under his own regimen, and he had broken Ari. Or tried to.

Ari looked out at the clouds underneath the jet, no idea where they were. He could have checked, he had enough equipment to always pinpoint exactly where he was, had even embedded himself with a tracker under the skin. For now, he wanted to feel that sense of nowhere and nothing. The freedom.

Despite his father's best efforts, Ari had followed his mother into medicine. He had trained as a doctor, but only after years of working with the army and Mossad. Caught between the dichotomy of saving and taking lives, Ari couldn't cope and had ended up having a breakdown. The pressure his father put him under, the stress his work put him under, Ari had crumbled. He had literally lost his mind.

Recovery was slow, painful, long. He lost both his parents in that time, in that decade. And when he came to, all he wanted to do was to be nowhere, away from every memory of his past.

So he had become what he was. Someone in the shadows, the man people like John Hayat relied on. Working between the edges of light and dark, where the things ordinary people didn't want to think about happened. He was fluent in Hebrew, Arabic, German, Russian and even had rudimentary Urdu, Hindi and Chinese. He could operate in practically any corner of the conflicted globe, because the language he spoke most was that of violence. And everyone understood that.

John snorted in his sleep, twisting his big frame in his chair opposite Ari. He reminded Ari of his father, the same Middle Eastern tough patriarchal nature, the belief in himself and something greater. Ari didn't like to think how John's approval was a poor substitute for the approval he had once sought from his father.

Maybe it was why, for John, he had crossed lines that he might not for others.

The Russian affair had been particularly brutal. Ari had regressed years of healing when faced with that situation. He had practically been behind the destruction of a criminal bloodline. Sure the people killed deserved it and more, still killing is never without payment. He still tasted it all. The blood and death, as he orchestrated the death of more men than he cared to recall. In his nightmares he still saw it all.

Victor. Ari wasn't afraid of anyone. Not even of Victor. But he didn't trust Victor. The man was dangerous. He had seen in him the sort of determination and destructive coldness he had only ever seen in terrorists. A steely commitment to his cause. He had seen it in the operation against the Russian gang they had taken down, his motives clear to Ari.

He knew John would never say it openly, but John felt it, too. He felt the threat that Victor posed to his other children. When John constantly told Ari to check there was no link to the Russian operation, that this wasn't about retribution, the subtext was clear to Ari. Make sure Victor isn't behind Oscar and Millie's disappearance.

Ari wasn't sure and in all honesty he knew Victor was capable of anything. Even this.

Chapter Twenty-Seven

Romesh had been eating a greasy Chinese meal, the smell invading Sarah's senses. She realised she had only drunk tea today. Why was she forgetting to eat again? She also wondered where Romesh put it all; she could eat air and still never be as thin as him. Maybe it was all the typing.

He was clicking between screens, pulling up documents and images for Sarah to look at, evidence of the things he was telling her. She was always slightly in awe of the speed at which he worked, her own one finger touch-typing a testament to the times she had grown up in.

'I was going to flag these to you, regular calls to Millie Beaumont from Oscar's mother. And I mean almost daily calls and messages.'

'Do we have the messages?'

'We don't have Millie's phone, so just waiting for her phone company to release them to us.' He sounded sanctimonious and it grated on Sarah. It was a game they played. He had tricks up his sleeves but wanted someone to acknowledge them.

'Romesh…' Sarah said, a note of warning in her voice. She wasn't in the mood for games.

'Lucky for us though, I can crack her WhatsApp and, lucky for us, that's how Lara Hayat messaged her.'

Romesh showed the messages that flowed between Millie and Lara, outlining what had been agreed. The messages were on a daily basis, reminding Millie of the conditions and how much money had been agreed. But the messages towards the wedding were more threatening.

Lara: Don't play me, Millie. You will regret it if you go ahead with this wedding.

Millie: I don't take kindly to threats. You need to trust me. I agreed to this. My mother is more important to me than your son and your family.

Lara: You don't deserve my son. We both know that. Do what's best for us all.

Millie: Best for you more like. Maybe I will marry your son after all? I'm sure Oscar will be more than happy to pay for the things you promised.

Lara: You are so naive Millie. Every pound in this household is controlled by John and me. Oscar can't give you anything. How can anyone be so selfish? Think of your parents. Stop playing games. Or you will lose.

Millie: It's funny because from where I'm standing, I hold all the cards in this game. So losing doesn't really seem like an option.

Then after the marriage.

Lara: Don't think this is over. You will regret what you did today. I won't let you get away with it.

Millie: Do your worst.

Do your worst. Sarah looked at the words, the threats so clear. Had Millie pushed Lara too far? It seemed that way. Millie playing a game that would see her dead.

But she couldn't compute how Lara would put her son at risk. Unless the idea was to kidnap them both, kill Millie and then release Oscar at a later date. Millie was dead. So was it just a waiting game for Oscar to turn up?

Except, who would Lara hire to do this? Was Oscar involved or did she do this alone?

Sarah thought then of John's right-hand man. Would he be available to the whole family? What sort of services would he provide? He was a mystery and Sarah needed to know more about him. Was he just about investigating or was he doing something much more sinister?

Then again, was Lara such a good actress that she could fake the concern for her son?

'Any messages between Oscar and Millie?' she asked Romesh.

'That's the odd thing. Nothing.'

'What do you mean?'

'I can't find anything.'

'That's strange, isn't it?'

'Yes... unless she deleted them all. And I mean deleted them all as soon as she got them. You see her messages are backed up every night at 2 a.m. Most people are defaulted to this setting. That's how I got access to them, I recreated them from her cloud backup.'

'I didn't hear any of that,' Sarah said, knowing it wasn't legal, helpful but not legal.

'She must have deleted the messages from him, I presume.'

'Why wouldn't she keep them?' mused Sarah. 'It's a normal thing to do, keep old messages, go back and reread them?'

'Unless they stuck to text messages or Snapchat. Although we did check and Millie didn't seem to have an account for that, and there isn't a lot of traffic between the two of them over text either.'

She didn't understand why Millie deleted her messages.

'

'Thanks, Romesh. Any advance on how Millie got into the country?'

Romesh cracked his fingers and knuckles and started swiping his screens and typing away.

'We know, I guess, more than others how porous our borders are,' Romesh said solemnly. Sarah understood what he was saying. There was this idea that the flow of immigrants was monitored, that travellers came through official ports, or even hidden under lorries, all having to cross borders. But there were thousands of miles of coast and so many different ways to get into the country that she didn't like thinking about. It was naive to think a terrorist would simply get on a plane with a liquid weapon and fly into the UK. Or disguise themselves as a refugee in a little dinghy and try and cross the English Channel. Sarah was all too aware that there were too many possibilities and thinking about them would give her nightmares if she let them.

Just as many routes out of the country, she thought. A route her sister was taken on. Invisible, disappearing, disappeared.

'I think we should focus on flights,' Sarah said. 'Doctor Ramone didn't mention anything particularly about the forensics indicating a recent sea voyage. There would have been trace elements. And I don't even want to think about her being stuck in the back of a lorry. She was alive, so it would have been too risky to do.'

'Yes and from Turkey to London. Long journey. So flights.' Romesh swiped his screen. 'It's unlikely Millie came through a normal commercial flight. I doubt a struggling passenger like Millie would have been easy to get through security. Conscious or unconscious.'

'I agree. So routes into London that aren't monitored?' suggested Sarah.

'I don't think she was brought into London at all. I'm thinking private jet, with some sort of diplomatic or billionaire status, to a smaller airfield. Relaxed security, easy to bring over a passenger. Or even cargo.'

Sarah caught the glint in his eyes. It was something she had thought herself. If Oscar was with Millie, the easiest way to get them here was in cargo, unconscious. And private jet made sense. The pilot wouldn't have checked luggage or cargo if it was someone trusted. Or protected.

'Check the Hayats' fleet. They have a couple of private jets I think.'

'Five actually. All across the world. There's one stationed in London. I've checked the itinerary, it's taken two flights in the last week. The first this morning taking John Hayat to Istanbul. It's on its way back now I believe.'

'And the first flight?'

'Was taken the day Oscar and Millie went missing. The interesting thing is John flew out with a passenger named Ari Newman.' Sarah kept her face neutral, but twigged just who Ari was. The 'help', the man John was using to assist him. 'He came back alone, though, no other passengers were recorded and there was no mention of cargo.'

'Would it be mentioned?'

'Yes. Anything like that which isn't hand luggage would usually be recorded as potential commercial enterprise.'

'And the pilots? All in the employ of Hayat?'

'Yes.'

'I think this is still the right vein to search under. Check all private jet journeys this week, there can't be that many. I want passenger details and check for any cargo shipments. Especially anything with diplomatic links. And let's check anything odd at border crossing involving lorries and any other vehicles. There is no reason why Millie and Oscar weren't brought in the usual way.'

Sarah wasn't convinced though. There were too many risks using those routes. Too many unknowns and potential stop and search checkpoints. It would take either Millie or Oscar to wake up and cause a fuss. No, the journey into the UK had to be quick, and private jet was the way Sarah would have chosen.

'Can you get me details on Ari Newman? His last known address and contact details.'

'Already have. One step ahead of you, dude. He's flying back today with John Hayat. No known address in the UK. But if you get your skates on you can probably meet his plane.'

'I'm not a dude, but thank you.'

'Sure.' Romesh was already lost in his screens, swiping to find her more facts and solutions.

Chapter Twenty-Eight

They were crowded around a long table in one of the conference rooms. Scott was visibly shaking with impatience as they filed in. Moomy, especially, rattled him; she was laughing with one of the admin supports, Ayan, a young Somalian girl who was on a fast track. Moomy stood at the doorway gossiping until Sarah coughed, and she rolled her eyes, dragging herself in. The door closed on the four of them.

'Update,' Scott barked.

'Millie Beaumont aged twenty-two, found shot in Hampstead Heath. So far we don't know where she was shot or how she was brought into the country. Given the high-profile nature of the family it seems logical that there has to be some ulterior motive to this. This isn't a random killing.'

'Have you spoken to the family?'

'I spoke to Millie's dad,' said Moomy. 'Also her best friend and ex-boyfriend. Sad story with Millie's mother's illness, really rocked that family. Angie's condition got to the stage where she was physically assaulting Millie and her father. Her ex was a piece but mainly he was jealous, I think, over Oscar. Although the picture he portrayed is of a jealous and possessive Oscar more than anything else.'

'There's also the money trail,' said Sarah. 'Lara Hayat had been funding Millie. She claims it was for her mother's care, but we found transactions and bookings made in Lara's name for dress fittings and haute couture. Jewellery even. Millie was being scrubbed up for the pictures. And worse than that. Lara has admitted paying Millie off to stay away from her son.'

'What do you mean?' said Scott. He looked scared more than excited by this revelation.

'We found messages between the two of them. Angry and threatening. Millie was being pushed to her limits from what I could see. Everything we know about this young woman is that she was an intelligent, likeable and genuine person. Yet the messages she sent to Lara – they spoke of real frustration against her mother-in-law. As though she had snapped. A very different Millie to the one her friends and family have shown us.'

'Possibly the real Millie?' Scott asked.

'I don't think so,' Sarah countered. 'Nobody can hide those character traits that well for that long.'

'I agree,' said Moomy. 'Declan was very much about Oscar being a controlling psycho. Millie was an innocent girl being played in his eyes.'

'So we have motive for Lara Hayat?' Again, the hesitancy in Scott's voice. *He really didn't want it to be the Hayats*, Sarah thought.

'It's a difficult one. She was paying Millie not to marry her son. Millie went against that deal, Lara admits to confronting Millie, telling Oscar. So she must have been angry. Angry enough to orchestrate a murder? People have killed for less. She certainly had the money. But would she have put her son in harm's way? That's the bit that doesn't work for me.'

Scott stayed silent, the room oppressive as he did.

'I don't want any noise from this, but I need Lara to be checked. Romesh, do it digitally and quietly for now.'

'I'm still struggling to place her as being behind this,' Sarah said. 'No mother would risk their child in this way. Also, the Hayat family have enough suspects. Lara told me Oscar was going to inherit everything. John Hayat had some weird notion of firstborn inheritance. Spencer and Victor will get comparatively tiny settlements. We need to look more closely at that dynamic. Either of them could have been desperate enough to arrange this too.'

'These rich freaks, man, who does that?' said Moomy. 'First child gets it all.'

'Try the royal family?' quipped Romesh.

'What do we know about the wealth?' Scott said.

Sarah repeated what was public knowledge. The marriage between Lara Wickham and John Hayat, the fortune combined. Property and natural resources.

'There doesn't seem much to say about it,' said Sarah.

'Sorry I think there might be,' Romesh added. He swiped across his computer screen and read some notes before talking to them. Scott was looking less impressed as the time went on. Moomy looked eager to get on with it rather than rehashing everything to Scott.

'What are you looking at?' Sarah asked.

'It's old newspaper articles. They've all been digitised now and we have subscriptions to most of them. I've been running searches in the background all day today, and I think the algorithms have finally come up with something.'

He plugged his tablet into a loose cable which connected to the overhead screen. The room was flooded with snippets from newspapers, connected by bubbles and arrows and Romesh's notes.

'Summary?' Scott asked.

'Okay, so there was an announcement, of course, when Lara and John got engaged. This is going back to 1989. It was quite a thing, the English rose marrying the brash American billionaire.'

'I think we've done that to death,' Moomy said.

'Yes, of course, but what I've managed to pick up through my research is something else. The love story might not be as much of a love story as thought previously.'

'What do you mean?' Scott moved forward interested.

'I went back a few months and looked at the finances of both companies. Both have closed books, private companies mainly. But I found this in an old copy of the *Financial Times*. It was about Wickham Estates, the property business that Lara was heir to.'

Romesh opened up documents on the screen, Sarah skim reading what it said.

'It claims there were serious worries it was about to go under?' she said, something dropping in her head.

'Yes. They were in some serious trouble. Bad property investments mainly.'

Sarah felt adrenaline running through her. The resolute Lara Hayat and her love for her husband. All of it rubbish.

'And after the marriage?' she asked.

Romesh tapped his screen and pulled up more articles.

'Two years later back in profit.'

'So basically Lara married John to save the family business?' Sarah said. 'She said her father was still alive while the children were young. I think Lara was married off to John in some sort of arranged marriage.'

Scott stared at her intently.

'Why does this matter?' he said carefully.

'For one, it explains her reaction to Millie. Lara married for money; she may have seen in Millie a reflection of that. She understood the motives of someone who in her eyes was a gold-digger, because she was desperate for money herself once. And she might do anything to protect a fortune she feels she was sacrificed to save?'

'I still don't think the evidence is strong enough,' Scott said. 'You've given me a plot for *Dynasty*. A young woman was murdered and dumped in a public park in London. The press are only holding off on this because the Hayats have put a stop to them printing anything. This is not good enough. We don't know where she was killed or who did this. Do you understand the pressure I am under?'

Sarah was surprised. Scott rarely lost his cool. No doubt he was getting grief from the Foreign Secretary pushing for a resolution. A resolution that did not point fingers at the Hayat family.

Chapter Twenty-Nine

Moomy got the hot guy to interview. He was all ego and Savile Row, sitting behind chrome and glass. She was still smarting after the brush down with Scott, the asshole. He was right though, they were struggling to find anything concrete. She was here to find out if any of the brothers might have anything to add or help. The Mayfair head office of Hayat and Wickham was Georgian stucco mansion on the outside, marble and oak on the inside. Receptionist with a stick up his ass. Moomy said no tea and coffee, crossing her legs, leaving her jacket off. She could wrap men like Spencer Hayat round her finger. All blond hair and blue eyes, which kept staring at her cleavage.

'How did you feel when you found out about Oscar? About him inheriting everything?'

'Not quite everything.' Colour rushed to his face. This he was embarrassed about, ogling her he wasn't. 'But yes he was going to get most of it. I don't know, some outdated notion of inheritance Pa has. I don't understand it but I accepted it.'

'Straight away? You didn't argue or question your parents?' Moomy saw the dark circle tell-tale signs around Spencer's eyes. Partying or working hard. One of the two. The brothers had agreed to speak to her at the office. They didn't want their mother disturbed further. Such loyalty. They also kicked up dust because apparently Sarah had already spoken to them.

'Of course, it was natural to ask why,' he said. 'I mean these are huge sums. There was more than enough to go around, you know? Why did Oscar merit it all? The accident of birth. I mean, you know, that's just weird.'

'What did they say?'

'No arguments. It's what my father wanted and that's what would happen. We were given a choice. Put up with it or lose everything. And you know the stuff we get, it's not small. I'm talking like a hundred million each.'

'Yes, but it's not the billions that Oscar would inherit. Oscar and Millie.'

'No, she wouldn't get it. You see, if they had kids then the eldest would get it. Pa's tied in the money to about five generations or something.'

'Can he do that?'

Spencer shrugged.

'He's done it. So yeah, their kids would get it. Not Millie.'

'And if Oscar died? Before him and Millie had children?'

Spencer looked uncomfortable, his eyes unable to meet hers. Although still able to meet her breasts. Moomy realised he wasn't lecherous, he was nervous. He kept dropping his eyes because he was nervous to meet hers. Except, they unfortunately kept falling where she didn't want them.

'I'm guessing you, being next in line, would inherit everything?'

Spencer nodded.

'Pa's always going on about being salt of the earth, immigrant who did well. But you know what? He's the biggest snob of us all. Don't know how he ever agreed to let Oscar marry Millie.'

Moomy hid her surprise. This wasn't the image of John Hayat that Sarah had conveyed. Or that John himself had put over. Was he happy at Oscar's choice? Or was he so cheesed off that he would gladly shift his inheritance plans? Moomy understood how parents could visualise their children as commodities. That coldness. She didn't believe in the all-powerful love of parent for child. It was difficult to convince others. Someone as successful and stable as John Hayat, why would he lack a normal paternal instinct? Normal didn't count for jack in her experience.

'How did you get on with Oscar?'

'Fine. We were fine. Brothers. Like all siblings, I guess. We had our rows but generally we got on well.'

'You didn't resent him for the money?'

'How could I? It wasn't his choice, was it?'

'No. You were never tempted to change things? I mean with Oscar and Millie...'

'No way, not at all.' Spencer was very emphatic. 'Wrong brother.' He clamped his mouth shut. 'I loved him, I would never wish anything like this on him or Millie. I'm not some cold-hearted mercenary. He's my brother.'

'So tell me, who do you think might be behind this?'

He didn't have to say it though. He already had. Wrong brother. Which only left one alternative.

Same set-up, same money, only totally different energy. Victor Hayat was like a cornered leopard in the Canary Wharf HQ offices. Why they needed different offices she didn't understand. His eyes were blue, dark, sharp, fixed. Shark's eyes. Staring into Moomy, staring through Moomy.

'What are you insinuating?'

'Nothing. It's a question.'

'I loved Oscar. He was my brother.' Moomy noticed the difference. Spencer spoke about Oscar as though he was alive. Victor as though he was already in the past. 'I wouldn't have wished him any harm. And it's a bit far-fetched, isn't it? What are you trying to say? I would kill both my brothers to inherit a fortune?'

'There's only one brother left?'

'That's sick. I wouldn't kill Oscar or Spencer.'

'Rumour has it you weren't happy when you found out about the clauses in your parents' wills.'

Victor didn't hide his anger. Moomy had already interviewed the staff in the office. The secretaries loved to gossip. None of them said anything about Spencer. Clearly they were in love with his model looks and his charming personality. Victor was an asshole to them, acted like their boss. Which, to be fair, he was. They claimed he always acted as though he, not John, owned the company. Companies. It was odd how Lara Wickham had simply given up control of the day to day running of the business and stood aside. Let her husband do her bidding. What was that all about? Reminded Moomy of her own mother. Silent as Moomy's life fell apart.

Victor with his olive skin, his dark hair, his foreign features. His harshness. He was set up from birth to play the other son. Moomy felt something bordering on understanding. The darker fallen angel standing next to the bright sun that was Spencer, and the spinning planet that was Oscar. The staff were understandably very worried about Oscar and had little to say about him.

Victor though. They all spoke about his naked ambition. Don't shit on people when you're on top. Because they will stab you first chance they get.

'You're basing everything on rumour? Is that what the police are reduced to now? I mean I know resources are scarce, but still.' He smirked at her. 'And yes it's no secret. I was livid. I had given up my life for this company. Even as a teenager I was the one interning here in my school holidays. I stayed in London for university, went to LSE, just so I could stay a part of it. I worked weekends with my father, every emergency I was there. And while Oscar swanned off to Oxford, I was here. I proved myself again and again. And still it made no difference. And you know what? I accepted that. I accepted that I would only ever be a cog in the Hayat-Wickham empire. And that was fine. It was my legacy to be one of the support acts. When Oscar took over he would find me just as dedicated as my father did.'

'But now Oscar won't take over.'

'Yes.'

'Unless he comes back.'

'Yes.'

'Do you think your brother is still alive?'

'I hope he is.'

'And if he isn't?'

'Then my family need me more than ever.'

'Did you know Oscar's itinerary for his honeymoon?'

'Vaguely.'

'Meaning?'

'I mean I wasn't that interested. Only that he was going to be away for a month. Whisking Millie around the world.'

'And did you know the destinations he was going to?'

Victor shook his head. Moomy opened her phone. The good thing about a society wedding was the amount of video footage available. Although there were only meant to be official photo and video images, Emma had filmed parts of it for Millie. She had sent through what she had to the office. One particular video was of great interest, the main reason Moomy was now keener than ever to question Victor Hayat.

Moomy let the video clip play. It was Oscar thanking everyone for their contribution to the wedding.

'And Victor. Thank you for planning and paying for the honeymoon. I don't know where we are going but I'm sure it will be fantastic.'

Moomy stopped the video.

'So, let me ask you again. Did you know where Oscar and Millie were going on their honeymoon?'

Victor looked at her as though he was going to tear her throat out.

Chapter Thirty

The sun was melting into purple grey dusk when Moomy got home. Her meeting with the Hayats had left her feeling dirty and drowned in the past. She needed to speak to Sarah, let her know about the barefaced lies Victor had told her. The denial and then the admission. He knew what time Millie and Oscar would arrive in Istanbul, what time the car would pick them up and what route it would take. He had planned it all to the last detail. A kind brotherly gesture. Or something more sinister? They would have warrants to do searches on his financial history in the morning, although given the Hayats' standing it might be wishful thinking. She checked her phone again. Maybe Sarah was off praying somewhere. She had the annoying habit of wanting to visit every one of the million mosques in London to try them out. Freak. And she kept trying to rekindle something in Moomy. *Leave it*, she had told her. Moomy was too fucked up to think about those things. Had been on her own journey to get to where she was.

Moomy went to have a soak. Mistake. Alone, closed eyes, thoughts of Harry so close. Her past so close. The oppression so close. She was back there. Back with Harry. Back in that place. The place she had died.

Haroon and Moomy married each other in secret. Just the two of them, alone.

His family were at the hospital. Her family were all busy by some serendipitous occurrence.

She wore a red and gold *shalwar kameez* she'd had made for Eid. He wore his *sherwani* from his brother's wedding.

They exchanged the simple vows.

'That's it. I am your wife now. That marriage in Pakistan won't mean anything.'

'You need to tell them, stop their circus in its tracks. No Imam will marry you if you are already someone's wife. That's adultery. And bigamy. Women can't have more than one husband.'

'Haroon... you live in a parallel world to most of us. I will be married off, we both know that. I won't protest. The time for protesting won't present itself.'

'What do you mean? Are you implying suicide? No Moomy. I couldn't stand the idea of you damned for eternity... please...'

'No, you silly boy. Surrounded by a whole load of freshies in some dodgy village, you think I'll get a choice to protest? But...'

She couldn't look at him as she said it.

'I can't stand the thought that that man will be my first... my body, my soul, everything is yours... wow, I sound as soppy as you do now...'

'Moomy we can't, it's forbidden...'

'You just married me with the Universe as witness. There's nothing purer than our union. I'm your wife. Do this, Haroon.'

'We can't... let's wait, plan it properly...'

'This is the last time we'll be alone, Haroon... please... I can take a thousand nights of that man crawling all over me, as long as I can hold onto this, know that it doesn't matter because in reality, my marriage and my wedding night was with you...'

He tilted her tear-stained face to his, and kissed her moist eyelids, tasting the salt water. He kissed her cheeks, and then her mouth.

They put on *Kabhi Kabhie* and *DDLJ* as background music. She had dreamed of sharing his bed. Finally she was in his room. Not the way she had envisioned it. Still. It was real.

Haroon kissed her neck, her collar bone, her neck again. Moomy kept her eyes closed throughout, imagining, feeling, like a star in the heavens, she was luminous, alive, burning with passion.

He took his clothes off, and slowly removed hers. She opened her eyes to see his face poised above hers, his hair falling on to his face, his upper lip and brow beaded with sweat, seeing the tiny, normally invisible hairs. She felt herself naked and felt him against her.

She covered her body with her *dupatta*, turned her face as he stroked her body through the thin material, the golden embroidery scratching her skin. He kissed her throat again, and she closed her eyes, grabbing the constellations with her hungry, raw fingers again, travelling through an explosive galaxy.

He kept her body covered, moving the *dupatta* only enough to be able to rest his bony thighs inside hers, his heart crashing against his ribs, crashing against hers. There was darkness behind her closed lids, and Moomy became a being of dark matter, harnessing herself as Haroon manoeuvred himself, entered her.

She opened her eyes, gasping with the pain, her nails digging into his back, her eyes wet with tears, his fixed on her, worried he had hurt her, but she nodded, and he carried on. The pain soon gave way, and she longed for the dawn in her self-created twilight, shadows falling over them.

They clasped hands, Moomy turned her face to her fingers intertwined with his, and a tear slid from her eye onto the pillow. She saw the stars and arched her body, Haroon exploding at the same time.

The stars and moon disappeared, as though someone had blown them out, as she reeled, her body speaking in tongues that only a woman could know.

Slowly, they followed the map back to reality, crawling in the darkness together, their hearts beating, their bodies locked.

They made love again, this time more sure, not so terrified of the consequences, dancing in ecstasy with the celestial beings.

They got dressed and Moomy went home. It was the last time they saw each other before she went to Pakistan.

Haroon never got to see his child that had been conceived that day.

Allow... allowed... forbid... forbidden... how did someone else have the right to change your life like this? How could someone you love hurt you so much...?

–

Everyone in the village seemed to know Moomy was there to get married. Her grandmother, a toothless old crone who said Moomy was as pretty as the moon, her uncles and aunts, exchanging sly glances and inappropriate giggles, her cousins, who started to call her *dulhan* bride as soon as she landed.

The water made her ill, the food had flies on it and there were ants crawling everywhere. The village didn't even have a name. Just a number. Chak 69: Village 69. The toilets were a communal trip to the fields in the mornings, and electricity lasted two hours a day. There were two TV sets in the entire village.

Lost in this labyrinth of familial nightmare, Moomy spent her days screaming inside, while sitting immobile on the outside, a marble statue, like the Hindu deities from Bollywood films.

She was going to be fed and trussed and decorated and venerated in her bridal regalia, before becoming a sacrifice.

The poverty irritated her. She knew a quirk of fate had separated her from being one of these girls who collected buffalo dung to dry and use as fuel, who spent their entire days dusting courtyards and cooking, before administering their husband's every desire.

What was she saying? A second quirk of fate had brought her crashing back to this world. She was about to join their legions.

Except she was special. She was a golden calf. She had a British Passport. And Rehan would get one too once he married her.

She thought of suicide but lacked the courage to damn herself to an eternity in hell. She dreamed that Haroon would turn up and rescue her, but her secret, internal daily vigils for him appearing on the horizon à la Shah Rukh Khan in *DDLJ* just didn't happen.

Her parents barely spoke to her, in case she started something, said something.

In the midst of this Pakistani village, surrounded 24/7 by strangers who were supposedly family, Moomy never thought she could feel so much loneliness.

—

'No,' Moomy said.

She had been dressed in a bright red and gold *lehengha* and tons of jewellery. Her hands were covered in intricate *mehndi* henna patterns. She looked at these as the woman within her decided to assert itself.

Her father quickly cleared the room. Moomy was alone with him, her mother and the Imam.

'No,' she said again.

'In accordance with Islamic law I have to ask you a final and third time... do you Mumtaz Khan accept Rehan Khan as your husband, in accordance with Shariah and the agreed dowry that he has paid you?'

Words like *kabool*: accept, and *haq mehr*: dowry whirled in her head; her heart crashed against her ribcage. She looked up in defiance, staring at the old man with the beard down to his waist, daring him to marry her off.

'I'm already married,' she whispered in Punjabi. Where had this come from? She could have spoken up so many times before, stopped this charade. Now here it was though, her reality and her fate sealed forever. This felt like the last breath that Mumtaz would take. So she had spoken up.

The Imam looked shocked.

'*La hawla wala quwwata*,' he said, a prayer to ward off the devil, then turned to Moomy's father.

'What *baqwaas* nonsense is this? I am fed up of you, you shameless girl.'

'It's true. I married Haroon. I'm his wife. This marriage is illegal.'

'Illegal? I'll give you illegal…' Her father bunched his fists ready to strike her.

Her mother held his hands back.

'What are you doing? Don't beat her, we will have *bezti* shame in front of everyone.'

Bezti? Shame? What about their *beti*? Their daughter?

'Make her agree, or I will kill her.'

'Mumtaz, please…'

'I'm married to Haroon. So you can force this, but it will be a lie. And Allah is witness to your evil. Go on, I dare you.'

'Why are you saying this? What marriage?'

'We did our own *nikah* marriage ceremony. Just me and him.'

'And who was witness to this sham?' her father said.

The Imam followed their conversation, but didn't understand a word. He spoke Punjabi, Urdu and Arabic but no English.

'The entire Universe,' Moomy said.

The words had sounded beautiful, strong, true when Haroon had said them. In this room with the mud walls, the pigeons on the roof, the darkness from no electric, they were as hollow as they were untrue.

'You need two witnesses and a contract and a dowry. Did you have all these?'

'No, but…' She faltered.

'Now listen to me, you foolish girl. You will marry Rehan, even if I have to force you. And if you don't... I will divorce your mother!'

Moomy saw her mother's eyes, like a deer before a hunter's shotgun, absolute cold white terror.

Fuck, fuck, fuck. They may have screwed her over, but she didn't have it in her to do this to her mother. Moomy could see the puppet strings, see how divorce would mean death.

So to save her mother, Moomy agreed.

As the word *kabool* left her mouth three times, and as she signed the contract and as she accepted everyone's congratulations, Moomy wondered if a living death always came with such fanfare.

–

The wedding night was a joke. Rehan had to prove his manhood, so there was no doubt of what he expected. Or what was expected of her.

He gave her a gold chain, bright Pakistani gold, and in return he took her body.

She lay back as he pumped himself inside her. Neither of them were naked; he didn't even kiss her, just went straight for her, and within a couple of minutes it was over.

He fell asleep afterwards. And Moomy let herself cry.

–

There were tears in her eyes now as she remembered the unfairness of it all. She hadn't asked for this, for her life to

be so messed up. Who was there to help her back then?
Who was there to help her now?

Chapter Thirty-One

Higham Airbase was located halfway between Higham and Rochester, just over an hour's drive away from Central London. Sarah had hit the M25 and luckily missed the notorious tailbacks and traffic, easing her Toyota down the motorway and through the Kent countryside until she reached the small tucked away airbase. It had a very sparse look to it, as though it was merely a collection of outhouses on some large farm. Hangars holding small private jets. She looked out for any signs of military presence but there were none. She guessed it was an emergency backup, probably not properly used for those purposes since World War II.

The sun was melting and dripping down the sky as she parked up, like broken egg yolk, giving off the last of its heat. The weather was unsettled in itself, didn't know if it was summer or autumn. This time of year was always a little unsure, as though venturing into puberty.

The first signs of life she saw were what passed as flight control, a middle-aged man in a small office attached to one of the outbuildings. Rob Thorp was genial, bored probably with the lack of traffic in and out of the airbase. He had books on military history and the Trojan wars piled up on his desk. Against the basic set-up the actual flight control computer systems seemed like another world.

'Sit, detective, can I get you something to drink?' he said, offering her one of the odd mismatched chairs dotted around the room.

'No, that's okay. I need to head back after this. When are they expected?'

'They should be landing in the next half hour. Mr Hayat's car is already waiting for him on the landing strip.'

Sarah looked out to see the shape of a Mercedes parked up some distance away.

'He'll go straight from the airplane? What about customs and security?'

Rob gave a husky laugh, the sort that ex-smokers have.

'People like Mr Hayat can afford to bypass security.' He grinned at her, but the questions on her face soon changed his expression. 'They would have had ID checks at Istanbul by the local aviation team, and the pilot is obliged to check as well. All cargo is, of course, subject to usual custom inspections.'

Sarah didn't hold much trust in these protocols if they were all manned by people like Rob. It was all too relaxed, as though money could buy you ease of air travel as well as everything else. No queues and thorough security checks here.

'Personal baggage is legally subject to inspection; we have X-ray machines,' he added. 'Only, for people like the Hayat family they are rarely used. The problem is the jet is theirs, the pilot is theirs. It's like asking someone to go through security before getting into their own car.'

Sarah nodded her understanding, Rob sounding more and more defensive under her cool gaze.

She could picture it now, how someone with the right connections and money could easily use this method for their own personal tricks.

'What about the passenger manifesto?'

'That is tight. We know everyone who is on the flight leaving the start country and everyone who gets off here.'

'If they're going to get straight into the car?'

'The pilot again will have to send through a disembarkation report to us, but we rely on the stringent checks done on take-off. I checked the passengers correlated with the flight itinerary when Mr Hayat left for Istanbul.'

'And at the Istanbul end? Are they using one of the main airports?'

'No, it's the private airbase of one of Mr Hayat's friends I believe. High up in the Turkish government.'

Sarah again thought just how easy it was to manipulate all of this. It was unlikely petty criminals would manage to manipulate and twist the security protocols of two countries, but someone like John Hayat, trusted billionaire, why not? So if the Hayat family were behind Millie's death – any one of them – could they have used this way to bring her into the country?

'Who else in the Hayat family has control of the private jet?'

'They all have access. Only, Mr Hayat needs to sign off on any travel. They don't make regular journeys, are quite careful compared to some other travellers. You'd be shocked at how some families use their jets. Like we use cars for popping off to the supermarkets.'

'No odd flights by the Hayats?'

'Not really. They have the usual birthday sort of stuff. Spencer Hayat chartered the jet to take his mates to New

York for his twenty-first. That was something, twelve already drunk lads. They all had to be processed properly, security vetted and checked. Only the family get relaxed security. That was a busy day.'

'Spencer's the only one that had that sort of birthday flight?'

'Yes. The other two are much more sober. Victor only flies for business. Oscar the same, usually with their father. The only times Oscar used it personally was when he took his girl to Paris and Madrid.'

'Millie, you mean?'

'Yes. Shocking what I've read in the press about them disappearing.'

Sarah didn't say anything. How they had managed to avoid a press leak so far was beyond her. She checked the sky again, wondering if there was anywhere for her to pray the late afternoon prayer before the sun set. She was still in a state of ablution and had her handy compass to show her which way to pray.

'He used it a couple of times for a friend of his in the past too. Nothing wild, all very subdued.'

'Which friend?' Sarah asked absently, wondering when she could broach the subject of prayer.

'I can't remember the name, some Indian chap. His best friend.' Sarah didn't know who Rob was referring to, but if anyone beyond the family knew about Oscar's life and anything that might help them understand what had happened to Millie and him, possibly this friend would know.

'Can you check and let me know, please?' Sarah asked.

Rob seemed reluctant, but he had an in-built respect for authority so agreed.

'Do you mind if I pray?'

Rob's face went from confusion to bemusement.

'Yes, sure, if you want to. I'll check on this. Are you okay to pray where you're sitting?'

'I'll need a corner somewhere.'

Sarah got her compass out and worked out the way to Mecca. She found the corner that gave her enough room. She didn't want to see the look on Rob's face as she took out her travel prayer mat from her coat pocket, and her headscarf. She put it on, and tried to shut off his presence as she prayed.

When she was done Rob couldn't meet her eyes, was busy typing away at his computer, and shuffling paper. He coughed a couple of times.

'Did you find out the name?'

'Yes, erm, yeah. It's a Paul Chandan. I have an address and contact number.'

'Thank you,' Sarah said, taking the details down.

She had taken off her headscarf, once again looking every bit English. There was thick silence between them, Rob giving her furtive looks.

'I wasn't expecting that,' he said. 'I mean I'm used to some of our Arab sheikhs doing that. One of them even prayed on the tarmac before they flew once. I just didn't expect… I didn't realise you were…'

Sarah knew what he was thinking. She probably had mixed parentage, Bosnian or Arab, English mother or father. She didn't wear her religion overtly, people just assumed. They found it difficult to make sense of someone they had thought of as Sarah Heaton, English to the core, being Muslim. Especially because she didn't act and look like the crazy converts they had seen on TV. Where was her face cover, her hook and her fiery rhetoric?

'I became Muslim a few years ago,' she said.

'I see. From what?'

'From nothing really. My parents and me were C of E, none of us particularly with it. We weren't big church-goers in my family.'

That was one of the reasons she had felt so empty. She didn't have the faith gap filled in when her mother was going through what she did, when Sarah went off the rails afterwards.

'How did your parents react?'

'My mother wasn't around to see it. My father, well, he's from a different place. He's having to adjust.'

She didn't go into detail about how her father was all about England for the English, and that meant white and Christian and straight. Muslims were about the worst thing in the world for him. He usually asked her when she was going to blow herself up and had even made reports to the security services and the police about her, claiming she had been brainwashed and was a threat to the country.

'Yes, I can imagine,' he said. 'It is so… different?'

'I guess.'

'I mean, I'm surprised… I… sorry I'm being rude, intrusive.'

'It's fine, honestly.'

'I just mean, well, how they treat women, I'm just surprised when women decide to do it. Or is there a boyfriend involved?'

He winked at her, checking the lack of a ring on her finger. It was an attempt to lighten the mood between them.

'You shouldn't believe everything you read,' Sarah said.

Truth was she was still coming to terms with the details. Moomy seemed to think the religion was about keeping women in their place, under men, which was why she had given up on it. And it was true Sarah was aware of the misogyny that was practised by some cultures, using the faith to back them up. Then again she had met women who were fierce, independent thinkers, who embraced the faith. Sarah had found her peace in the mysticism and serenity of worship, and so far no one had tried to oppress or control her. 'And no, I didn't convert for a man.'

'Well whatever works for you, detective,' said Rob.

–

Sarah had been waiting on the runway by John Hayat's private Mercedes. The chauffeur looked apprehensive about her presence, avoided eye contact. This wasn't usual protocol, she knew.

John got off the plane first, took a few moments to register she was there, but then relaxed his expression. He shook her hand, but looked apprehensively over his shoulder. No one else was coming off the flight.

'Detective? You have news?' he said.

'Not yet, Mr Hayat. We are still doing all we can to find Oscar and find whoever did this to Millie. Did you get any further in your investigation?'

'Nothing. I tried everything, contacted everyone I could. I have many powerful friends in Turkey, they are all assisting but so far nothing.'

He looked dejected when he spoke, genuinely frustrated and worried. The longer Oscar was missing the darker the places his mind must be taking him.

'Is Mr Newman still on board?' Sarah asked. John looked affronted, as though he was being accused of something. He didn't reply. 'Do you mind if I speak to him?'

John looked back at the plane, unsure what to do, then shrugged. Sarah walked up the steps to the jet and found Ari Newman in one of the plush seats looking at her.

'Hello, Ari,' she said. 'Hiding from me?'

He kept his face impassive and hard.

'Small world,' he said. 'You're looking good.'

Sarah took the seat opposite him, tense, and looked into the black eyes she knew so well.

Chapter Thirty-Two

Romesh had lost track of time again. It happened often while he was concentrating, trying to work out patterns, break down and into networks and histories, make links and find answers. He had always been wired differently, blamed his mathematician parents from Bangalore and San Francisco. From his early years he had been subjected to puzzles, equations and instead of watching TV had been keen on working out math questions. It had helped though; he had studied mathematics at Cambridge and ended up working for the government in various IT roles, after a stint with a couple of investment banks and hedge funds, where he had earned the cash that paid for his swanky flat in Shoreditch.

Romesh thought this was his time to give back for a few years, do something worthwhile. Before hitting the big league again. His girlfriend, a genuine computer whizz, was already in Silicon Valley working for a tech giant. It was only a matter of time, he guessed, before regular visits became a demand to be in the same place at the same time.

He stared at his screens, scrolling through code and data, trying to let his mind do the linking for him. He had the uncanny ability to see things before other people, to go down alleyways that other people wouldn't twig. A throwaway online placeholder, like a throwaway comment, that would come back to him and hold everything together.

As he scanned the information he had available online for Millie Hayat, he became more keen on looking for her friends and husband and what they might tell him. He had saturated what Millie had to say to him: the money was the biggest red flag she had. His attention focused on her friends: did they have something to hide, had they done something together that might have made Millie a target? He then turned his attention to Oscar.

Oscar was a strange one. On the one hand he was all out there, obsessed with his Instagram feed especially, pictures of every one of his activities. Looking good in every shot, filtered and posed. He had splashed images of everything. Two images in particular came up. There were tasteful shots of the engagement ring, and then one picture of the married couple. Taken against a sunset, Millie looking up at him, Oscar gazing down at her in love, their hands clasped against his heart.

I have found the woman who completes me, my soul mate, my all.

These lone shots of the ring and the wedding were his most popular posts. Searching for Oscar online the wedding picture was the first one that came up.

Oscar seemed clean from what Romesh could see. The Hayats had released details of his finances, in so much as they had copies of bank statements clarifying that Oscar hadn't made any transactions since he had been taken. Romesh checked for any other credit that might be associated with Oscar, in case he had cards or loans that his family weren't aware of. What Romesh wanted to see was a financial transaction that might cast some doubt on Oscar, but until he had full access to Oscar's bank account that was unlikely. Unless he turned up dead or they issued warrants against the Hayats, their entire finances were opaque. And he knew there would have to be one hell of a reason to get that warrant issued.

His breakthrough came when DI Heaton sent him details of Oscar's friend, Paul Chandran. Paul was not the son of a billionaire and his history and personal details were not as hard to break into. Romesh did a credit search, online search and within an hour he had unravelled everything.

Sarah wasn't answering so he called Moomy.

'You better get here ASAP,' he said. 'This is going to blow your mind.'

Chapter Thirty-Three

The captain and flight attendant had also disembarked, the private jet silent. Sarah looked around at the leather seating, the LED TVs, the sofa, the bar. It looked more like a lounge than an airplane. It was also a lot bigger on the inside than she had thought.

'So this is what you do now?' she said, finally looking at Ari. 'Thug for hire?'

He looked good, she hated to admit it, but he did. Dark hair and eyes, his face was all angles, stubble only enhancing everything. He was wearing jeans, tight black T and a midi black jacket. Functional but smart. She was being harsh she knew. Ari had turned into a private security expert who helped wealthy clients, like John Hayat, who needed state level security. They weren't afforded it by the governments of the world.

'Man has to make a living,' he said, his accent faint but there. 'And you? Still trying to save the world. Pointless job.'

She ignored him. She knew why she was doing her job.

'You think this is fate? Our meeting under such precarious circumstances?' he said.

'Hardly. My job is to turn up rocks. You're usually lurking under one of them. It's only ever a matter of time.'

He laughed at her.

'Nicely put.'

They had met a couple of times during her career with the Met. The first time had been innocuous enough: Ari was one of the hundreds of diplomatic staff who didn't pay their congestion charges or parking fees. Sarah had just started in her post and was tasked with chasing down fines, a placement with the Diplomatic Protection Unit. Ari had surprised her by taking her for dinner and they had dated for the six months that he had been in London.

A couple of years later, as her career had been on the up, she was called in by the American Embassy to investigate a possible homicide. One of their workers had been found dead in her home. Ari was her liaison, on secondment to the US from Tel Aviv. The homicide had turned out to be suicide, but she and Ari had again picked up where they had left off. Until he had left the country, this time without telling her. She felt cheap and used.

It was only after meeting him again, when he was providing security for an international aid organisation, that he had explained his rush. His father had died, and the death was sudden and hard on him. It had taken him months to process and understand. Months in which he hadn't reached out to her or anyone.

Sarah understood that when her own mother passed away. And now? They were in such different places in their lives. Ari had become some sort of shadowy operative and Sarah had been through her own conversion. Still, she felt the electricity that was there.

'I hear you've joined the other side now,' he said.

'Meaning?'

'You became Muslim?'

'Why is that the other side?'

'Don't you hate Israelis by law?'

'Don't patronise me. And you're not exactly flying the flag for Israel any more. More like the dollar sign straight to your private bank account in Switzerland no doubt.'

'I knew I told you too much when we were together.'

A flash of them together. Raw and passionate. She shut it away.

'I don't hate anyone,' she said. 'Except people that break the law.'

'Give it time. I'm sure I'll see you on a pro-Hamas demo soon enough.'

'You're impossible,' she said, her irritation rising.

'Isn't that what you liked about me? Oh sorry, or have you left me behind now that you are born again? Fresh and clean. Free of the memories. Right?'

Sarah wished that was true. You could change everything, only the memories never did go. What she could change was how she reacted to them. Apart from her sister. That memory always winded her.

'Stop dicking around, Ari. How are you going to play this?'

'John pays my bills, I have immense loyalty to the Hayat family. So I will play this the way they would want me to.'

'Even if that means you waste time and get Oscar killed? Unless you know where he is already?'

'What are you implying?'

'I'm implying that the Hayat family were pissed off with Oscar bringing some common into their ranks. Millie was not supposed to be part of their world. So was this how they safeguarded their billions from being diluted? Saving their bloodline?'

'This isn't *The Da Vinci Code*, and they aren't some sort of sacred royal bloodline. If they were that bothered they would have disinherited Oscar or paid off Millie.'

'They tried and failed to do the latter that though.'

'Yes. She was clever, took the money and the boy.'

'You knew about it?'

'Of course. Lara Hayat asked me to sort out the details. Secure transactions her husband would not know about. You see, John really doesn't have the time to check Lara's spending, unless it's something significant. We were going to transfer small sums, ten or fifteen thousand a time, charge it to different ghost companies, all of them linking to a central account under Lara's name. From there, Millie would be paid.'

'Without John knowing. And yet he wasn't too thrilled at the match either?'

Ari looked impressed when she said this.

'You really have done your research then,' he said. 'John worked hard to make his money. Not always legally, but extremely hard. That, he tells me sometimes, was the easy part. Getting to where he is in terms of the social world, that is something else.'

'He seems to be okay. He has the ear of governments all around the world.'

'Yes, because of money, steel and gas. You think the British establishment welcomed him though? You think someone like him would be allowed to marry Lara Wickham? You see, in America it is different. His wealth buys him respect. In London? No-one cares unless his granddaddy was some relation of the royals or some other aristocrat. It's like the Arab sheikhs or the Russian oligarchs. They will be allowed to spend their money, but they can never buy into the status circle.'

'Yet he has done?' Lara Wickham had become Mrs John Hayat. He had managed it somehow.

'Yes, he has. He got lucky. Lara fell in love with him. Her family were dead against it; they see men like John as crooks. In the end, she was an only child, they had to give in. John had one giant advantage. He was richer than the Wickhams.'

Sarah looked out of the window. She saw John's car still parked, waiting for Ari. The airfield was deserted. Rob had told her nothing else was due to arrive that evening. She felt tired. This world she had stepped into was giving her a headache. She got the secrecy of the diplomatic world, understood spies and politics. This was something else though. The value of money above everything else. Had Millie strayed into something even she didn't quite grasp?

'But it wasn't like that, was it? The Wickhams were broke when they met John Hayat. An immigrant billionaire on the outside. They sold their daughter and her breeding to a man who pumped money into their failing businesses. I don't think the Wickhams were against the marriage, I think they actively arranged it.'

Ari made no comment.

'Millie, though, what was she bringing to the family? Except the wrong colour? John might be an outsider but Millie was really an outsider.'

'John has spent decades being the joke, the foreigner. He loved it when the Russians turned up. They gave him the respect the grand families Lara knew never did. And what he wanted was for his children never to suffer that.'

Sarah understood that.

'He wanted to make sure his children were part of that world,' Ari added. 'Millie would take his family backwards in his eyes.'

'So he had her killed?'

Ari stared at her. He didn't deny it.

Chapter Thirty-Four

Moomy was not in a good place. She didn't know why she was spiralling so much. It was Millie, she thought. Or rather Bill. He loved his daughter; he didn't feed her to the wolves. It was unfair. No, she was being pathetic. Millie had died horribly. Moomy needed to get a grip. She needed a drink. She needed for it not to be happening.

She focused, instead, on what Romesh was showing her. She tried Sarah again. Phone off. That meant she was with someone. Probably work. Definitely work. Sarah was too straight-laced now to do anything fun. Moomy wished she'd known her before she'd become such a bore.

Then again maybe Sarah hated the past as much as Moomy hated hers. She rarely talked about it anyway.

'So, Oscar pretty much is invisible online on the face of it. And by invisible I mean he's a personality, a thing. Oscar H. Plenty of photoshopped pics of him skiing, snowboarding, kayaking, skydiving. He's a maniac for stuff like that. Wearing designer clothes. He's very clever though. He never gives away where he's doing these things. There are no actual details about his life.'

'It's like a PR campaign you mean,' Moomy said, looking at the images.

It's what the super-rich did these days. Flaunt their wealth by stealth, showing off doing all the stuff ordinary people with jobs and mortgages couldn't do.

'Yes. It's all like that. I checked out linked accounts, but his Facebook is private, and he has thousands of followers on Instagram. It's hard to tell who matters. Even with the Oxford set he was in with Millie, not much went on.'

Maybe they were too clever to do so much where the world could watch. Moomy didn't have any social media accounts. She had no interest in seeing what her fucked-up extended family were all up to. Unless it involved rotting in hell. She wanted front row seats for that.

'Paul Chandran is a different matter though,' Romesh added. 'His settings are so basic it's not even funny. His Facebook is public for the most part, he's very candid about his life on Instagram and I even managed to follow him on Snapchat. He loves himself totally.'

Moomy saw the images Romesh had found. Paul posing in various garbs. He was an off-the-wall dresser.

'Is he auditioning for *Joseph*? And is he wearing lipstick?'

It was true. He had shiny lips in most of his pictures. There was no hiding here. Paul was camping it up online and didn't give a damn who saw. Moomy wanted to befriend him already.

'Quite the character,' said Romesh. 'This is Oscar Hayat's best mate. They met at Eton and have been inseparable ever since. So on Paul's social media I finally found Oscar. Not a lot. But enough.'

'Show me.'

Romesh pulled images up, highlighting and expanding captions. He zoomed in on a couple.

'I don't know how these snuck through, but this one especially. It's on Facebook. Going back a few years now.' The image showed Oscar with his head on Paul's chest. Paul's hands were clasping Oscar's head, his eyes closed. The caption underneath:

More than life.

Romesh pulled up another picture. It showed a woman in a fur coat, legs out there, knee-high boots. After a hard night, make-up smearing, looking tired. She had Oscar and Paul with her, under each arm. They looked just as wasted.

'This one, Paul is tagged in the picture. Oscar has stopped anyone tagging him. Paul hasn't. The woman is a mutual friend, Dippy Clarence. She's an It-girl, socialite, usual rich trash. But look at the caption.'

Playing gooseberry to my bffs.

'That's quite suggestive. And they left this on Facebook?'

'She only tagged Paul. The night was Dippy's prom, and both of them turned up as her date. Paul was tagged in dozens of pictures that night; too many he probably didn't bother looking at them all.'

'What are you thinking? They're a secret item?'

Romesh smiled at her, revealing very white teeth. He had them fixed during a few months working in the New York office of a hedge fund, apparently. They were so perfect they scared Moomy.

'There is a lot more. So, I decided to let my train of thought follow, and I used Paul as my target. The guy is leaky, he's an art historian or something, clueless when it comes to technology it seems. I have his e-mail, his mobile, a list of his favourite things. All from his online profile. So I checked something out. I reset his Grindr password.'

'How?'

'By resetting his e-mail password.'

Moomy looked shocked, but then realised Romesh was working within the law for the right people.

'So he has a Grindr account?'

'Yes. Only the app doesn't store messages really. He's saved a few, but live messages are on the app itself on his phone. What is clear, though, is that Paul is gay; he's okay with it. And he has this little diamond symbol on his profile.'

'Which means?'

'Which means he's selling sex.'

'Why would he have to do that if you're thinking he's in a relationship with Oscar?'

'Exactly. So when I looked a bit more closely I realised the diamond has a little word in front of it. It says "want". He's basically looking for escorts.'

'Okay, so Paul is into all of that, what does that have to do with Oscar?'

'This.'

Romesh pulled up bright yellow and blue messages against a black background. Moomy's eyes followed them, her mouth opening in shock at what she read.

Chapter Thirty-Five

The air in the confined space of the plane was stale. Sarah wondered what was happening on the outside. Her thoughts loud in her head, as Ari went to the private on-board bar to get himself a drink.

Sarah wasn't buying it for now. Whatever else was going on, she didn't believe John was a cold-hearted, callous murderer. And it didn't explain Oscar's involvement in the plot. Why put his own son at risk? Was John biding his time until it was appropriate for Oscar to be released? There would be questions asked of all of them.

'What were you looking for in Istanbul?' she asked.

Ari had poured himself a drink, gin and tonic. He was never a big drinker even when they were together. *Is that what they were?* Was it really a relationship or just something they did while they were in each other's worlds? No, if it had been, her feelings wouldn't linger like this. She thought of him too often, and his reaction to her proved that what they had shared was something. A cliché, but if timing and opportunity had been different, maybe they would have had a future?

'Oscar,' he said, cheering her from the bar. He took his jacket off. His arms were visible now, the tanned skin, the veins, the muscles. He stretched them over his head, revealing an inch of flat six-pack, before returning to his chair with his drink. Sarah declined his offer, even of water. She wanted to avoid peeing until after sunset, so she didn't have to redo her ablutions for prayer.

'In particular, what were you looking for?' she asked.

Ari shrugged. Sarah felt her words were hollow as she spoke to Ari.

'I'll say the same thing to you I said to Lara Hayat: the more you help me the better prepared I will be to find Oscar. And to find Millie's killers. That's if you want them found.'

He looked unmoved.

'Come on, Ari. Don't hide things from me. Be honest. What did you do in Istanbul?'

Ari threw back his drink, slamming the glass on the table between them.

'Sorry that was harder than I intended,' he said, looking amused. 'Before Istanbul, I went looking for something else. I was in Ukraine.'

'Isn't there a civil war going on there?'

'Of sorts. It's reached a stalemate. Neither side particularly wants to escalate given the nuclear powers involved. I wasn't there to help with that though. I was looking for someone.'

'Oscar?'

'No. Not directly anyway. A few years ago, John got into some trouble. He needed a gas pipeline to flow from Iran to Europe. It was the biggest pipeline in the world, most of it underground. All pretty normal. Except the pipeline came to the attention of the Popov family in Georgia.' Sarah looked blank. 'Notorious gangster family, Russian origin but settled in Georgia now. They do it all from people trafficking to drug runs to weapons markets. All illegal trade is their domain. Nasty people. Now they see an opportunity with John and his pipeline to go legitimate. The new head of the clan, Dimitri Popov, is Harvard educated, good-looking, smart. He doesn't want to spend his life in fear or in the shadow of violence. He has an American WASP wife, probably the main reason he wanted to change.'

'Women will do that to you. Damn them and their morals,' said Sarah.

'You should meet some of the women I have.'

'I think I can guess more than most what they're like.'

'Dimitri wants out. But he wants to do it by investing in the pipeline. Laundering his illegal cash basically. And John? Well, he's a businessman. But also he's scared, genuinely, of what the Popovs might do to him and his family if he refuses.'

'Come on, he can afford the best security. Don't let it get to your head, but you don't come cheap and he has you.' She said it matter-of-factly, it wasn't an ego boost. Ari, though, couldn't help smiling at the compliment. 'So he went along with it?'

'Yes. Remember this was also when the world's markets were crashing. The effects of the recession were still being felt, especially by steel and gas. John had lost a fortune, and so he agreed to help Dimitri. He let him have a stake for the cash. All good.'

'I'm guessing not for long though?'

'No. Things turned nasty very quickly. You see, Dimitri tried to close down the darker side of the business. The trafficking, the drugs. All of it. Fine for him and his wife, but the rest? He had a whole operation that he was trying to shut down. And most of them weren't on board. What did they get if Dimitri became legitimate?'

Sarah had a sense she didn't want to hear the rest.

'They set up a meeting with Dimitri. They wanted to tell him what they thought about his plans. All the smaller men involved, the ones waiting to take over from Dimitri. They told him straight he could do whatever he wanted, but the bad stuff keeps going on. So that leaves John with a problem. How can he work with Dimitri knowing that he is still into trafficking and drugs? And how does he back out of that deal?'

'I guess politely telling a man like Dimitri Popov wouldn't work?'

'He wouldn't have got the words out before they popped a bullet in him.'

'So he sent you instead?'

'No. John was having a breakdown. He didn't know what to do. It was Victor who got me involved. It was Victor who asked me to deal with it.'

'And you did?'

Ari didn't say anything. He looked away. She would be told some things, but not everything. Not even by him.

'When Oscar and Millie disappeared, John thought it might be retribution. He said that to me. They've come for revenge. Blood for blood. That's how the world works out there. So we assumed that someone had decided to pay John back for Dimitri.'

'The pipeline?'

'The whole thing fell through, there were too many risks. Victor found another way through Azerbaijan instead. None of Popov's associates were needed. Smaller scale but it did the job. Victor traded in larger volumes for less profit but safer guaranteed profit. He's very sharp that boy.'

'Well, we all know about sharp boys. Why were you in Ukraine though?' Sarah asked.

'The only men loyal to Dimitri ended up there. Running some online fraud scam. Big change from what they used to do. Fuck you up but not with a bloody nose. I was there to make sure they weren't involved in Oscar and Millie's disappearance.'

'And they weren't?'

'No. But how can you trust what they say? So I located every member of Dimitri's operation who might have had a hand in this, traced them and checked them all. I couldn't find their fingerprints in any of this. But you know that part of the world, it's nearly as bad as this part of the world. Power and money. Corrupted to the core, the world over.'

Ari looked tired then, went to fix himself another drink. 'You sure you don't want one?'

'Very sure. Okay, so you checked out the Russian angle. What else? What else were you doing in Istanbul?'

Ari sat down, staring out of the window. The car was still parked there. She knew that John would want to know word for word what they had discussed. She also knew Ari would make up a story to cover himself. To protect her. Might even give John the sordid details of their past.

Sarah knew it wouldn't come voluntarily, so she prompted him instead.

'Victor Hayat. The man who planned the honeymoon. You know he lied to my colleague about doing that?'

'Victor lied? I didn't expect that from him.' Ari laughed at her, taking a swig of his drink.

'I think John hired you, not just to make sure that the ghost of Dimitri Popov wasn't haunting him, but also that this wasn't a case of fratricide.'

'You make it sound so sophisticated. It's brutal murder for money. Greed and ambition. Bastards have been doing it for centuries.'

'Is that what this is? Victor killed his brother for control of the family fortune?'

'Oscar isn't dead.'

'Millie is. I'm guessing we will find Oscar's body soon enough.'

'No. I don't think this is what this is.'

'Would you tell me if Victor was involved?'

'Of course not. You're not paying my bills.'

'How can I believe you then?'

'You can't.'

'Ari…'

'I don't want to discuss this further. Arrest me or let me get off this plane.'

Sarah knew she couldn't do anything officially yet. Not only was John Hayat covered by his work for the US Embassy, but there was no evidence, nothing concrete to make any of this stick.

'How are you?' he asked quietly, tracing the rim of his glass, staring at her reflection in it. Distorted. Her but not her. That's what she must be to him now. 'I'm sorry about your mother.'

'It's been a while. You couldn't reached out and told me that in the last three years?'

'I wanted to. Many times.'

'Who told you anyway?'

'I kept an eye. You were always the one that got away. The only one in some respects.'

Sarah felt herself react to his words. She didn't want to, willed herself not to. But Ari had something about him.

'Why did you convert?'

The question surprised her, making her catch her breath, before answering him.

'Why does anyone do anything? I needed answers. And the pain of losing her, knowing she was gone…Ari you know what it's like. You told me about your father. You understand. Even the drink and the nights out and the rest of it, none of it helped. I was a mess. And I found my answers. Things just started to make sense.'

'How?'

'I guess I was feeling lost and alone. And then I wasn't.'

'So, are you on the fast track?'

'For what?'

'Becoming a Jihadi Jane?' He laughed at her as he said it, but stopped seeing her reaction.

'It's not funny, and you of all people should know not to be intolerant or ignorant.'

'Sorry,' he said holding up his hands in defence. 'Why aren't you wearing the headscarf?'

'My choice. If it feels right I will. I wear it to pray and that's enough. For now.'

'Your choice. You might regret your choices one day.'

'Then I will live knowing that they were my choices and my mistakes.'

She got up, but he grabbed her hand.

'Have dinner with me. Please.'

She pulled her hand from his grip and left him without replying. There was no going back, and no matter how helpful he had been over the case, she still wasn't convinced by his opinion on Victor. There was also a lack of reference to Millie. Did she not matter, or was Victor involved in her death? There was something that Ari and John were hiding about him and she would find out.

Chapter Thirty-Six

The MI6 building stood over Vauxhall like an alien spaceship ready to depart with the chosen ones at any given moment. Moomy was convinced that was its purpose. There was no other explanation for the design. As the evening burst over London, though, she wasn't there to meet anyone from MI6; she was, instead, headed to a chic little flat in an upscale residential complex on the Albert Embankment. The concierge tried his posh twat act. She gave him a verbal finger and one flash of her ID and she was up. Glass and chrome vomit lift and corridors. Hotel more than home.

She had called and made an appointment. Apparently he wasn't fussy. Made it clear he didn't fuck women. Moomy said she wasn't a woman. Fully. He asked for a face pic. He said she didn't look bad for a tranny. Although he could still tell she was one. Cheeky fuck.

He opened the door in a police uniform. He had asked her what she wanted. She thought it would be a laugh. The look on his face when she showed him her badge. Priceless.

They were in the lounge. Probably cost more than her entire life. How much was this guy earning? He had asked for £250 an hour when she had called. Sex was extra.

Overnights were two grand. Who the fuck had two grand spare to pay for a night with this freak?

He was shaking, lighting up his vape. Brazilian. Here illegally, she thought. Now his life was about to fall to shit. They both knew it.

'Listen I'm not VICE, I'm not here to bust your ass over the sex stuff. And I'm not Home Office either, so won't be checking your immigration papers.'

He relaxed a little.

She didn't add that they would all be round tomorrow to do him over.

'I need to know about this man.' She showed him a picture of Paul Chandran. 'And this one.' Oscar Hayat.

Luciano studied the two pictures, nervous. He didn't even hesitate or talk about client confidentiality. When his own dick was on the line he was happy to let it hang out.

'This one I recognise,' he said, pointing at Paul's image on her phone.

'What did he call himself?'

'Paul. That's what he calls himself.'

Very original.

'He did all the booking.' He studied the picture of Oscar more closely. 'This guy he could be his boyfriend. I'm not sure.'

'Why?'

'He always wore a mask. Over his eyes and nose. Like those Venetian types, you know from Venice?' Luciano's voice was very sing-song, high and annoying. She was mainly annoyed because she thought he sounded fake.

'I know. So you never saw his face? And Paul?'

'He was fine, very open about it all. I got the feeling the other one was married. I wasn't allowed to speak to him before or after.'

'How many times did you meet them?'

'Only twice. They didn't book me again.'

'Twice? And you remembered?'

'Oh yes, darling, I remembered. It was such an odd set-up you see.'

'How?'

'Paul messaged me, first through Grindr then through WhatsApp. He arranged it all. Said that he wanted a threesome with me and his boyfriend. That's all fine and good yes, I do that no problem. I am versatile and they said that is fine and good too, they will both fuck me. Eventually. First they wanted some of the other things I offer.'

Moomy tried to picture Luciano delivering the sort of things he promised on his profiles. Domination, rough sex, verbal. He seemed too effeminate to do any of that. Maybe that's why they didn't rebook? He was a disappointment?

'They said they wanted me to be, well, how can I say...?'

'I'm sure you can find a way. Listen all of this goes no further, okay? I don't want to do this officially. So you tell me now what you can and that's it. Your name will never come up.'

He nodded. Big believing brown eyes. Naive fucker.

'They want me to say things first. Like swear and shout, and then they want me to say quite horrible things. I'm not a racist, I don't have problem with anyone.' He said it so quickly Moomy knew why. To make it clear to her that what he was about to say wasn't him, that he didn't hold her race against her. 'They asked me to call them names. Tell them to go back to where they came from. Shout abuse at them. Paul gave me some phrases.'

'Did you keep them?'

'No, he made me delete my messages when he met me. I was scared by how aggressive he got about it when I met them, I wanted to react, but they were two and in my home.'

'Then what?'

'Again all of this is normal. I give it to mens all the time. No problem. The weirdest thing was the other side.'

'Weirder than this?'

'Maybe not to you,' Luciano said defensively. 'To me, though, yes. Paul said he didn't want his boyfriend to know that I was an escort. He wanted me to act like I had met him on Grindr and had wanted a threesome after seeing his pictures. It was very strange. He said his boyfriend must never know that I was being paid. I had to act like I was enjoying it. Natural.'

Moomy didn't think this was weirder than wanting someone to shout racist abuse at you. Still, Luciano might remember this part more.

'That's it. So you met them twice and this happened both times?'

'Yes,' he said.

He looked like he was quite tough with his facial hair and muscular build. The voice, though, it was just a no-no if toxic masculinity was what they were after. She couldn't take Luciano's word for it, that the other man was Oscar. Still, it was enough to go on. Luciano was one of the escorts whose messages Paul had saved on his profile.

When Romesh loaded it up and downloaded Paul's saved messages, Luciano was there. A bit of further research had got them his phone number from another escort site.

'Anything else about them?' she asked.

'No... well, maybe. I got the feeling that Paul, he was really in love with the other guy. Everything was about giving the other guy pleasure, making him happy. As though his own needs were not so important? I think this Paul was truly in love with him.'

'And the other guy?'

'He barely touched Paul when we were having the sex. He kissed me and made love to me, only now and then being with Paul. I felt bad for him, since he had gone to so much effort for him. I think he felt jealous too. When this other guy was with me. I saw it in his eyes. Like jealous anger. It scared me a little.'

Moomy asked to check security videos for the nights that Paul had met with Luciano. Paul was visible on both occasions, but his guest was not. He had a cloth cap pulled low, and a scarf wrapped around his mouth, shades finishing off the disguise. Moomy tried to work out from the build if it was Oscar, but couldn't. She asked for the footage to be sent to Romesh, see if he could get her a match. In the meantime, she was off to see Paul Chandran and find out more about his relationship with Oscar.

Chapter Thirty-Seven

Paul lived in a detached house in Hampstead, owned by his parents, according to the land registry. It was a good hour's walk from the Heath. Yet only a fifteen-minute drive. From where Millie had been found. The house, and the Eton story, screamed rich to Moomy. She drove her Mazda through the streets, which were eerily quiet. Hampstead wasn't spacious, it wasn't countryside. It was peaceful though.

She had only called Paul when she was already close to his home. She didn't want to give him a heads-up or time to plan or escape. Romesh had got her location details; Paul was home. Or his phone was.

After the courtesy call it took Moomy five minutes to get to his door. No time to escape. He didn't look ready to anyway. He was barefoot and wearing shorts and a T-shirt. More ready for bed than running away.

He showed Moomy into his kitchen, where a maid was making drinks for them. She was dressed in a tight sari, her silver hair tied back in a harsh bun. They exchanged some words in Hindi, which Moomy understood, before he dismissed the maid. He handed Moomy tea in a mug, staying seated at the kitchen island rather than moving into the lounge. This was clearly going to be a quick conversation in his mind. Moomy had other plans.

'You've known Oscar a long time?' she said, looking around the clean kitchen, which was bigger than her entire flat. She had a bad habit of always comparing how little space she had to other people. She had bought into location. At the sacrifice of room.

'Yeah, since we started at Eton, around eleven. First day and we became best friends really. It was a help having someone in your corner. It's a cruel place to be friendless, so I was glad to have him.'

'How were you at Eton? What sort of things did you get up to?'

'Nothing special really. We studied hard, played hard. Eton has its own rules and traditions. It was a great experience.'

'You didn't get into any trouble?'

'Well, we got caught smoking a few times. That was it really. Truancy, going on a few wild nights with some girlfriends. Usual stuff.'

'Girl friends or girlfriends?'

'Both. Girls we had grown up with, we were all dating each other at the time. It was very incestuous that whole circle.'

'Anyone special? For you or Oscar?'

'Not really, just messing around. Nothing serious.'

'What about Dippy Clarence?' Moomy saw a moment of recognition pass over his face. 'You all seemed very close?'

'Yeah, she was cool. Oscar dated her for a while. Only a couple of months. Stupid teenage stuff. After that we all became good friends. We're like the Musketeers. She's devastated about Oscar. Sent her right back.'

'Right back to where?'

'She's in rehab. Dippy's just a dead cliché. Proper drink and drug habit, we're talking Amy Winehouse levels. In and out.'

'Why did they break up? Oscar and Dippy?'

'They weren't really together, it was just dumb stuff. Sorry, why is this relevant? You said you needed some information to help with the search?'

'Yes, we're just exploring all angles, the search has focused on Turkey so far. We're just thinking outside the box a little. Speaking to everyone who knew him, trying to build a picture that might help.'

Paul looked genuinely sad when she spoke, genuinely heartbroken. Moomy drank her tea which was cooling fast. Paul hadn't touched his own. His fingers were tapping the island top.

'You know Oscar better than his own family probably, more *intimately*.' Moomy enunciated every syllable of the word. 'If there's anything that might help us understand what might have led to this, any clue that might lead us to find him. In confidence, now is the time to tell us.'

Paul shook his head as he spoke.

'I wish there was. I wish I knew something that would help. Oscar was everything for me, my best friend. I would do anything for him.'

'Anything?'

'Yes.'

'Would that include harming Millie?'

Paul froze. She could see the fear and anger spreading on his features.

'Tell me, Paul, does the name Luciano mean anything to you? Brazilian, hot, escort?'

'No, it doesn't. What the hell is this?'

Moomy let him rant, swearing, livid, agitated. She then pinned him with her eyes.

'Sit down. Shut the fuck up. And listen.'

Moomy told him what she knew. About the threesomes. The arrangements. She didn't divulge they had cracked his e-mail and Grindr. That was pre-emptive and illegal. She told him everything Luciano had.

Paul listened, his hard eyes dropping into piteous begging. Don't tell his family, don't tell anyone. He looked furtively at the door, closing it, in case his maid heard. Moomy confronted him with the video evidence from Luciano's property.

'The other man with you. Was it Oscar?'

'No, absolutely not,' he said, clear about that. Lying through his dazzling teeth? 'It was someone else.'

'Who?'

Blank expression, mind turning. You wouldn't have to think about something like that. Not unless you were making up a lie.

'So, how close were you and Oscar *really*?'

'We were best friends yes, but that's it. Nothing else.'

Moomy showed him the picture from Dippy's Facebook. And the picture from his own Instagram. The captions underneath.

'Why would she claim she was a gooseberry? Getting in the middle of you both?'

'It must be a joke, that's all. I can't remember, it was so long ago.'

'And yet here is this woman that Oscar dated, who must have known you both better than most people. It's a very blunt term. And this picture, your hand is sitting on his chest in a very intimate manner. No? Paul, I think it's best you are honest with me. Because I have enough to take you in for questioning.'

'For what exactly?'

'Oh, I don't know. If Oscar had something to hide – his double life with you, for a start – then it gives him plenty of motive to set up his wife's death. In fact, you, as the jealous lover would have more motive. Don't you think?'

'It wasn't like that.'

'Then tell me what it was like.'

Silence.

'It's not him. It's not Oscar,' Paul repeated.

'Then who is the man you took to see Luciano? Who is the man you paid these escorts for? The man you claimed was your boyfriend? Because you know when I take you into custody it's all going to be laid out. Every sordid detail. Your family, your online history, any gay apps you use, the financial transactions. There will be more like Luciano. There will be scandal and press. Is that what you want?'

Paul was breaking now, his eyes beginning to leak. His whole life, his identity, the secrets and the lies. All of it about to unravel. He was probably picturing his future, the future that Moomy was condemning him to. Torn between love and loyalty. Honesty and martyrdom.

'Please, don't do that. It will destroy them. My parents. Please.'

'Come on, love, don't play the victim with me. Your parents are loaded, people of the world. I don't think they will give a shit. So, let's not use that whole I'm an oppressed gaysian card.'

'Maybe, the gay thing, they know anyway. I mean it's never said, but they know. The escorts though, that bit. The things you told me about Luciano. That would destroy them.'

'Your choice. If you're honest now, I won't take it further.'

Paul wiped his hands over his face, making keening sounds. Theatrics. Moomy held her line.

'What do you want to know?'

'Everything,' she said.

Chapter Thirty-Eight

The night was oppressive, warm. Sarah couldn't breathe as she lay on her bed. Moomy hadn't returned her calls. Romesh was trying to get hold of her. Ari had messaged Sarah. Voicemail of hate from her father. She wanted to shut it all out. What had she done? Why had it turned out like this?

She thought of her mother. Thought of the nights she had been busy working, the days when she had been fighting for justice. Time she could have been with her mother, holding her, comforting her. If she had known her mother was going to leave her, not get better, she would have gladly sacrificed the time. Put her life on hold for those years. But she didn't. And now she never could. Never again would she be able to touch her mother's skin, feel her delicate bones in the body that had given up, heard her voice. It was just a whisper in the last days. But it was something. Just seeing her mum look at Sarah. She was too busy working, trying to build a life, a career. Trying to make her mother proud, desperate to be something while her mum was still alive. Failing on all counts. Now, feeling ravaged and destroyed by the guilt Sarah felt.

Just five more minutes to say goodbye and tell her mother she loved her. A sign from somewhere that when Sarah had said goodbye that it would be the last time. If she had been with her mother on that last day, she could have told her she loved her, that she was sorry. Instead, her mother slipped away, silently, alone. What must she have felt?

Sarah didn't even bother wiping away her tears. She screamed into the empty flat, gut-wrenching, animalistic and raw. Pain and guilt and grief. There were only ever her screams. Nothing coming back. Nothing to say it was all okay. That she was forgiven.

She jumped out of her skin when she heard the voice. She thought it was her sister at first. Then realised it was Moomy. She had her spare key, had let herself in. Moomy didn't switch on the lights, she just came in and held Sarah. Let her rock in her grief against her, let her tears soak into her clothes. No judgement, no reassurances, just let her be.

After an age, Moomy got up and got her some water. Sarah drank it silently as Moomy wiped the tears from her face, the snot from her nose. She got her another glass of water, stroking her hair as she drank it back.

In a gesture she knew was probably painful, she watched as Moomy laid out the prayer mat, and got Sarah's headscarf out.

'I'll be in the lounge, drinking vodka I brought with me. Like those Indian restaurants. Bring your own beer.'

Weak smiles, but Sarah watched her go. She got up, washed her hands, face, arms and feet. Then she did the only thing that plugged her grief. Didn't get rid of it, just dammed it up. She prayed.

Moomy hadn't touched the vodka bottle yet. Sarah knew she wouldn't. It was a rule in her house for Moomy. No drinking. Moomy brought bottles with her whenever she visited, always leaving with them unopened.

'I'm sleeping here again,' said Moomy.

'You know where everything is.'

'Hell yeah, I do. What about you? You going to be okay?'

'InshAllah.'

'Don't start that with me, please.'

'Hey, you bring the vodka I'll bring the Allah. Fair trade.'

Moomy glared at her before massaging a kink from her neck.

'What did Paul Chandran have to say?' asked Sarah.

'Do we have to?'

'Yes.'

'Poor sod. He let it all spill out. I gave him my usual bullshit about confidentiality and not using any of what he said blah, blah, blah. He told me a story. About how he and Oscar had developed together into young men, had started experimenting with each other at Eton. It carried on after that.'

'They were in a relationship?'

'No, not at all. He was very clear about that. He said Oscar just liked to have fun. He said he dated girls, had girlfriends. They just got their freak on together. And that became more intense over the years.'

'Intense how?'

'They were getting drunk, high, chemsex. That sort of level. Went from normal vanilla sex to kinky to then proper *50 Shades* stuff. Extreme domination type crap until they ended up trying stuff like the verbal shit Luciano did.'

Sarah got herself some cold water from her fridge. Moomy opted for a Coke Zero. For the vodka, she joked.

'So, what was it? Friends with benefits?' Sarah said, feeling the icy water in her throat.

'In a way, yes. Oscar had a dark side he liked to explore with men; Paul was his way to do it. They usually just tried it with each other when Oscar was in the mood. Paul said he had met other men apart from Oscar and without Oscar. Then when Oscar wanted to try the weirder things, he arranged it so that he used an escort. He thought that if they picked a random guy he might spill. So they were buying men and their silence.'

'That clearly worked.'

'Hey, it nearly did. None of them knew Oscar, he always wore that mask. No-one came forward in all the time Oscar was missing either.'

'True. So what was this?'

'Paul basically said that a few times a year he and Oscar would have sex either with each other, or with a third party. That it wasn't about being gay or having a boyfriend. They were just screwing around, so there was no issue with him marrying Millie.'

'He was just going to carry on afterwards?'

'No, Paul said that wasn't the case. Oscar had stopped all of this when he got serious about Millie. Claimed he was giving it all up. To be honest, I think Paul was devastated; he loves him clearly. The look in his eyes when he talks about him. The things he did for him.'

Sarah considered what Moomy was saying.

'Payment for the escorts were always done by Paul?'

'Yes.'

'So you think that if Oscar really wanted to be with him or live a different life, Paul might be the one to pay for a hit on Millie?'

'Possibly. Only, I don't think so. I don't think Oscar would have married Millie if he wanted to live with a guy.'

'You think? John Hayat would be okay with his chosen heir being married to a man?'

'Maybe not. If that was the case, he could just give it all to one of his other sons. There was no need for Oscar to get married, kill his wife and then what? He still can't live with a guy.'

'No, but he can live as a heartbroken widower, while he carries on sleeping with men.'

Moomy paused and considered this. She shrugged.

'You want to bring Paul in?'

'No. Not yet. Oscar is still missing. There would be no point.'

Moomy yawned. 'I'm going to hit the shower then go to sleep.'

Sarah watched her go, this woman who had entered her life and provided her with comfort when she had lost everyone. Filling gaps that her own mother and sister had left, that her hate-filled father and brothers had created.

She checked her phone. Romesh said he was going home but they needed to speak urgently in the morning. Ari had called several times. He then messaged her while she had the phone in her hand.

I know about your sister. I think I can help.

Sarah's heart burst against her ribcage. Did he really know, or was he playing her?

Chapter Thirty-Nine

This was bullshit. That was all. Bull. Shit. She was a grown woman hiding away at her friend's flat, her boss's flat, and why? Because of her past. Because that bastard past had found her.

Moomy was craving the vodka. She needed it badly. No, she didn't. Yes, she did. She didn't go for the drink, Sarah would never admit it, but she would be hurt. Without the alcohol to numb her though, her thoughts were left unchecked. And as she closed her eyes, Moomy was back there. Drowning again.

–

Her breasts felt swollen, and the sickness they had put down to the water and heat was morning sickness. Two months after her parents had left her and gone back to the UK.

She had missed a period before she had got married to Rehan, but had thought maybe it was stress. When the second one went AWOL she knew she was with child. And she knew it was Haroon's.

She wrote to him, told him about it. He didn't reply. She was devastated.

In some existence that was made up of eighty per cent madness and twenty per cent sanity, she could plug into happiness whenever she touched her belly. There was hope growing in her.

She didn't even pass it off as Rehan's. The village just assumed and her parents were called long distance and told. They sent cash.

In fact they seemed to send a lot of cash.

Moomy didn't quite know what Rehan did. They said he was educated, had a degree, so he wasn't allowed to work in the fields like his brothers and cousins.

He seemed to disappear all day, come home, demand to be fed and then spent the evening and night singing Pakistani film songs into Moomy's ears, as he proved his manhood.

Moomy couldn't have care less. When she started to show she told Rehan he couldn't have sex with her any more. Studies had showed it could harm the baby.

He continued singing songs in her ears as he wanked off against her back.

He wasn't so bad. He was quite good-looking in his own way. He just repulsed her. She felt like a captive, kidnapped in an ancient battle, some other man's wife, taken in servitude and bondage to her conqueror.

In the third trimester the pregnancy became unbearable. Moomy was feverish, tired, swollen, barely lucid, crying for Haroon and her mother. There were days she couldn't leave the bed, soiled herself, was moved around like a doll.

The baby kicked at her, gnawed at her insides, the delight she felt at its existence turning into dread and terror. Still, she had clung on.

Rehan took to sleeping in the courtyard, unable to stand her weakness. Moomy wondered if he took other women. But then who would he take?

There was a *kotha*, a brothel in a nearby town. But where would Rehan get the money? The answer was obvious. The money her parents sent.

Why did she even care? Another woman's misfortune meant she would be spared.

Through thirty hours of the most agonising labour, when Moomy was convinced she was dead, would die, spewing blood and human plasma, Moomy eventually had her child ripped from her insides.

She was too shattered to realise anything, slept for ten hours straight. When she woke up and demanded to see her baby, they couldn't meet her eyes, told her to rest.

She screamed like a banshee until they relented. They brought the child in, clean, wrapped in a white sheet. Still.

He had cried for ten minutes, they told her, before being silent forever.

Finally Moomy cried, rocking back and forth, holding her child, her only reason for living.

She called him Haroon. Her mother-in-law said Moomy had been saying that name a lot in her delirium. They understood now, it was the name she wanted for her baby.

Her parents were told. Rehan asked them if they wanted to speak to their daughter. They said no. She had been through enough. Moomy was numb to their rejection already.

'You have to go to the UK and invite me from there,' Rehan said.

'Why can't we just do it from here?'

'They want to see you working in the UK, see you can support me before they will let me in.'

'Let's just stay here.'

She was broken. She didn't want to go back, to see the lives being lived by the girls and boys not forced down the road she had been. She didn't want to see Haroon. His love gone, proved to be as fake as his promises. She wanted to live out her life in this nothing place. Pretend she was never anything else except Rehan's abused wife. Only Rehan wouldn't let her.

'Are you crazy? I only married you so I could get to the UK and get away from here. I don't want my children growing up here, barely able to feed themselves, growing up ignorant and uneducated.'

'You seem fine,' Moomy said. 'You're not starving or uneducated.'

'Here,' he said, throwing her an envelope. 'Your parents sent you a ticket.'

'I don't want to go. I like it here. My son is here.'

'Don't be absurd. We have to go on and live. This is why my family treat you like a queen. Haven't you noticed how you don't have to cook and clean and do all the things my sisters and sisters-in-law do? Because you're our golden ticket.'

'Sorry, Rehan, you picked the wrong lottery ticket. I'm not going anywhere.'

He grabbed her plait, twisted it in his hands, his face close to hers, spittle hitting her skin. She refused to acknowledge the pain.

'Listen to me, you stupid bitch, this is too important for me and my family. You mess this up and I will beat you every day until you die. Do you want that?'

She didn't, but she couldn't leave her dead son. Not a single person in this place would care about him, look after his grave. She would not leave her child. Whatever she had to suffer. Then the woman inside her spoke up again. The woman that she was meant to be, if things had gone the way she had planned. Take the ticket and get out of here, you silly girl.

So Moomy packed her bags. Her mother-in-law had confiscated her wedding jewellery the day after the wedding, so she had nothing of value.

She made them stop the borrowed car at the graveyard and prayed over her son's tiny grave. She took a handful of the yellow dirt that covered it, and put it in a glass jar.

'I'm sorry, my baby, I won't be back. But I'm taking you with me. And know this, I loved you for every second you breathed, and I will love you for every second that I breathe.'

-

As a married woman, her parents assumed the ghost of Haroon would have evaporated.

It had been two years, and he had left for university. He didn't make the grades for Oxbridge, went to UCL instead.

Moomy saw Haroon's father, aged because of his heart attack. Haroon's mother barely acknowledged Moomy when they met by accident at a *khatam*.

She asked how Haroon was. His mother looked daggers at Moomy, asked her how her husband was.

She had been back a month when she decided she would never go back to Pakistan, or stay in Manchester, where she would eventually be forced to call Rehan over.

Her movements were less curtailed. She packed a rucksack, held the jar of dirt from her baby's grave, took the money her father had given her to open a bank account and make a visa application for Rehan, and left for London.

Before she went she took hold of her plait that had grown long down her back – a thing cherished and loved by her mother, oiled regularly – and cut through it using heavy-duty scissors. She left it on her mother's bed.

Her parents didn't dare call the police, told people Moomy had gone back to Pakistan. Rehan had married another cousin, had managed to immigrate to Canada. Where he worked in a chicken shop. Eventually her parents told people she had died in childbirth. Haroon told her this much later.

Dead to her parents. Dead like her own child.

–

Moomy ended up in Southwark, at a women's refuge. She got a job in retail, attended evening classes, did her A levels and got into the London School of Economics to study law.

She had lost all semblance of innocence by then. Fuck had become her favourite word. She didn't track Haroon down or get in touch with her family.

London was lonely, with only the battered women of the refuge for company. Moomy kept to herself, opening up to the counsellor she was offered sometimes, usually trying to forget.

Her GP said she was probably suffering from postnatal depression. So what if there was no baby to show for it. It still happened.

Moomy just had one determination: get revenge for the murder of her child. She wasn't thinking straight and didn't know who was responsible.

Everyone? The entire world? Maybe she could start at home and with Haroon? Or that entire village?

She'd know when it was done.

–

Moomy was lost, dreaming, suffocating when Sarah rushed into the lounge, switching on the lights. She was shouting, fully dressed.

'We have to go.'

'What's happened?' Moomy said, her eyes blinded. Tears and light.

'They found Oscar.'

Chapter Forty

It was 4 a.m. by the time they got to the Hayat residence in Knightsbridge. The place was full of bodies. John, Lara, Victor and Spencer. All awake. Tired, but awake. Stress, fear. The air was thick with it. A middle-aged man introduced himself as the family doctor, Gerald Sandler. Ari was there too. Sarah avoided looking at him. Yet all she wanted was answers from him. About Rachel. It took every fibre in her body, to stay on track. She would have her moment with Ari. He would have to answer her.

'Is this really necessary now?' John was saying. 'Can it not wait until the morning?'

'No, it really can't. We need to see him.'

'He's not well. Gerald, please tell them.' Lara pleading.

'My patient has suffered immense trauma after the events of this past week. I don't think it's wise for him to be subjected to your interrogations...'

'Listen, mate, his wife's dead, murdered, and he's just turned up. Unless he's in a coma we are talking to him, okay?'

'Really, you come into my home with this attitude,' John blustered at Moomy. Wrong move.

'We came here because your son has been missing for a week. We busted our asses trying to find him, trying to stop him ending up like Millie. Now, if he's back, we want to know where the hell he's been all week. And we need to know what he can tell us so we can find the fucking scum that killed Millie.'

'DS Khan, please,' said Sarah. 'John, this has to happen. None of us want to make this unpleasant.'

Lara scoffed at this. The Hayat clan gathered around them. A wall to prevent them getting to Oscar.

'The sooner we speak to him, the quicker we'll be out of here. If Millie's killers are still out there, we need to find them. Before they get away. Don't you want us to find them? Give your son closure over who killed his wife?'

John muttered in Arabic, turning away from them. Sarah could tell he was swearing from the tone of his voice. Ari was staring at her from where he was seated. She wished Scott was here. He had simply called to tell her that Oscar had come home and he needed her there to speak to him. That was all he had been told. Scott's presence would make this more official than they wanted it to be at this moment.

'My son has been through hell.' It was Lara's turn now. 'And I cannot believe you will deny him a few hours of rest. Have you no heart?'

The beseeching mother, but Sarah was immune to it. Paying Millie off to not marry Oscar and then what? Killing her if she reneged on the deal? Oscar was home. For Sarah it opened everything up again. The family getting rid of the stray Millie, while their own son was protected. Or were Paul and Oscar behind this? Was Moomy right about the whole heartbroken widower act so they could carry on and make a life together? Keep John's money in the process.

'And what about Bill? Don't you think he deserves answers?' exclaimed Moomy.

No one responded. They had forgotten about Bill and Angie, it seemed, the parents who had lost their only child.

'Come on,' Sarah said, addressing Moomy. 'Let's come back in the morning. With a warrant. And who knows, the press might hear about all of this by then. So we might have an audience too.'

Sarah turned to go but John stopped her.

'Thirty minutes. That is all I give you.'

It was a start and it would be enough to at least get some answers. Sarah was not enthralled by the way the Hayats were behaving, it was textbook shifty. Ari was still watching her. His text message played in her head. What did he know about her sister Rachel? She looked away from him, she couldn't get distracted like this.

That would have to wait. For now she needed to speak to Oscar and find out exactly what had happened to him and Millie.

—

Doctor Gerald Sandler sat by Oscar's side. It was a condition of the interview. Or chat. Whatever they were going to say to Oscar would be done in front of the doctor. Sarah took a seat on the other side of the bed. Moomy was calling Romesh; he had messaged to say he needed to speak to them urgently. Sarah urged her to make the call. It was a necessity as well as an excuse. Sarah hated herself for it, but she thought Moomy might be too abrupt and end up potentially sabotaging the interview.

Oscar looked a lot better than Millie. Not just because he was alive. He was wearing a T-shirt, his body hidden under the bedsheet. His forearms and hands were visible to Sarah, but there were no tell-tale signs of struggle or damage. None of the trauma that Millie had suffered. Maybe he was just showered and clean, but he didn't look like he'd been subjected to the same trauma that Millie had been.

His face looked concerned. He kept staring at the doctor, trying to make sense of who Sarah was and why she wanted to speak to him.

'Where are my parents?' he asked.

'They are just outside,' said Doctor Sandler. 'The detective here wants to ask you some questions about Millie.'

At the sound of her name Oscar became agitated, trying to get out of bed, but wincing in pain.

'Millie...' he said, strangled voice and sobs colliding to make it sound almost animalistic.

'I'm sorry for your loss,' Sarah said, giving him a few moments to compose himself.

'I still don't believe it,' he said. 'I can't believe she's gone.'

'When did you last see Millie? Alive?' Sarah asked.

Oscar looked at her, his eyes almost childlike, then he looked at Doctor Sandler. The doctor shook his head, his voice low when he spoke.

'He doesn't remember anything,' he said.

'What do you mean?'

'He remembers the wedding, but that's it. After that, the kidnapping, what happened to him this week. He doesn't recall any of it.'

Sarah didn't trust herself to speak. Was this a joke? How very convenient.

'Please, I don't know what's happened to me. I only remember the wedding day. Millie and me at the altar. After that, it's all gone. All of it.'

'Where were you this past week?'

'I don't know,' he said, sounding more and more distressed.

'How did you get home tonight, Oscar?'

'We found him outside,' Doctor Sandler said. 'He was ringing the bell, confused, hallucinating.'

'What are you saying to me? How did he get here? Who dropped you off, Oscar?'

'I don't know.'

'What do you remember? Tell me.' She tried not to raise her voice but she didn't believe this charade. He didn't remember anything of this last week and then turns up at home?

'I remember the wedding. And then I remember being on the street, outside the house. That's all.'

'How did you get to the street?'

'I can't remember. Oh God, I can't remember. Please. Millie, what happened to her?'

'We were hoping you might be able to tell us,' Sarah said exasperatedly.

'I don't know. I can't remember anything.' He started to emit sounds as if he were in pain. Doctor Sandler calmed him down and told Sarah they should let Oscar rest.

–

Sarah was in an empty room at the Hayat's, Scott on the line. This room was decorated in the same Versailles style.

'His doctor is claiming he's had some sort of trauma. It's affected his memory. Apparently that can happen short term. He doesn't remember anything.'

'You don't believe him?' Scott yawned on the other end, tired from being awake all night, just like her.

'No, I bloody well don't. It's so unbelievably convenient, he just happens to forget the last week where his wife was murdered and he was kidnapped. All of it gone, but then he turns up outside his family home, able to remember everything else. Come on, Scott, things like that don't happen. You don't just have such perfect memory loss.'

'His doctor believes him?'

'His family doctor? Are you kidding me? We can't trust someone so close to the Hayat family. He's got to be hiding something for them. The whole thing is a convenient joke.'

'Calm down, Sarah…'

'Don't, Scott, just don't. This isn't me overreacting or being difficult. This is them trying to cover up the murder of a young woman.'

'What can we do? If he doesn't remember being kidnapped, what can we do?'

'We treat him like a victim and we process him like we would anyone else. Do not let Jane Haslam or any other political a–hole get in the way of this. I want a forensics team here now. And I want our own medical expert.'

Scott sighed into the phone. She knew she was asking a lot, him having to face up to the likes of Jane Haslam, the Foreign Secretary. She would end his career if she could. And probably hers. Still, there was no way she was going to let this play out any other way.

'Okay, hang tight. I'll see what I can do.'

Moomy came in when she was done.

'What's the craic'

Sarah filled her in, watching the anger she felt on Moomy's face.

'No fucking way, that is utter bullshit.'

'Keep your voice down.'

'This is just… bullshit. He did this. I swear to you he did this so he could live his secret life with Paul Chandran. He arranged this, I know he did. There's nothing wrong with him, he's a fucking liar. His whole life is a lie and this is just one more.'

Sarah felt the same, but she was also aware that they were at an impasse. How could they prove he was lying?

'I doubt he just materialised on the street,' Sarah said. 'He must have taken transport here. I want every CCTV camera link on this road checked, and the pricey properties around here; I can guarantee you that he will have been caught on camera somewhere. I have forensics coming, we can take blood samples to see if he was under the influence of something, check for any foreign bodies on him.'

'He's had a shower, you said, it's all probably gone.'

'Not all of it ever really goes that quickly. Along with forensics, I've asked DCI Blake to send through some psych support. I want a full evaluation done on him. There must be a way to tell if he's lying.'

'Let me punch the truth out of him.'

'Yes because torture works, doesn't it?'

'It does on 24.'

'This isn't a TV show. We just have to hope we find a way to get the truth from him somehow. He is faking his memory loss, and I want to know why. I will not let this family get away with a cover-up.'

She stared hard at Moomy, both of them silently aware that money could let you do anything. Even let you get away with murder.

Chapter Forty-One

It was 7 a.m. The sun had hidden itself behind thick clouds, which were spitting rain.

Sarah had drunk a cup of lukewarm coffee earlier, something she hardly ever chose. Moomy had insisted, saying it had been too long a night and they couldn't make mistakes. Moomy was probably still feeling the effects of the vodka.

Moomy had left for the office early, said she needed to check something with Romesh before they reported back to Sarah. Curious, but Sarah had enough going on in Knightsbridge, trying to marshal a whole team of specialists.

John had, as expected, gone ballistic, Lara had kicked it up a gear, then Spencer. Surprisingly, it was Victor who had stepped in, said they should let the police do what they needed. That Oscar might not be able to remember but there might be other ways he could help. Victor had the maids bag up what he claimed were the clothes Oscar had been wearing when he came to the house. Forensics had then taken samples from Oscar in places that a shower might not completely clean. Under the nails and the blood in his veins.

Doctor Ramone, normally dealing with the dead, was for once dealing with the living. He reminded Sarah he was a doctor first and foremost. He examined Oscar physically, making notes of any bruising and trying to determine where the pain was coming from. He even took X-rays with a mobile AI device that was being trialled.

Finally, a Doctor Farah Naz had arrived, ready to assess Oscar's psychological condition. She had an hour's session with him and then left without feeding back to Sarah, saying she would send her report and discuss it at HQ later in the day.

All the while John stood stoically outside Oscar's room, giving Sarah the sort of look that said she was finished. That she would pay for this violation of his home. Lara had taken herself off to her bedroom with Spencer when she realised she was powerless to stop what was happening. Victor aided the investigation making it unnecessary to get an official warrant to do anything.

Helpful. Too helpful. Maybe Victor was hoping they would find something on his brother, still hoping his own journey to the Hayat billions was possible.

As she got ready to leave the flat, she caught sight of Ari. He had stayed throughout the process, watching and making mental notes no doubt. Sarah wanted to pull him aside, question him about the message he had sent her, about Rachel, all night. The opportunity had never arisen. Until now. They were alone in the lounge, as the family had retired after the last of Sarah's team had left. Ari stood up to go as well, but she stopped him.

'What happened here tonight, Ari?'

'What they said.' He was cold, distant. The sort of coolness you got when someone was pissed off with you. Pissed off because they cared.

'You believe him?'

'Yes. But you don't believe me, so what does it matter?'

'It's a little convenient, isn't it?'

'Life is like that. The truth always seems inconvenient and a lie.' She knew he was referring to his own truth. About his father being the reason he hadn't contacted her. The reason they hadn't moved forward with their relationship, when she had thought it was something else. That Ari was just adding her to the list of women he had slept with.

'Ari, what is happening here? What are they hiding? Because I know they are hiding something.'

He ignored her and started walking away, clearly not willing to speak to her about the Hayat family.

'Rachel,' she said, a quiver in her voice.

He stopped, his back still to her. That wide back, she remembered the feel of its hardness, the muscles and bones under his skin. Resting her head against it, feeling reassurance. She wanted to hold him again now. But she couldn't. Her faith, hers and Ari's respective choices, the distance and life. They weren't the same people they had been then. And yet, she knew they were exactly the same at some point. When Ari and Sarah had seen reflections of something in each other. That something might have been love. She blinked it away, she had to focus on this instead. On Oscar Hayat. And on Ari Newman and the message he had sent.

'You said you knew about my sister. What do you know, Ari?'

Was there hope in the sound of her words? Desperation? Because those were the things she was feeling. Years since Rachel had left, years of searching and trying to find out what happened to her. The blame her father laid at her door. The blame she felt herself. She needed it to end. She needed Rachel back. Alive and safe and hers.

'Not here,' he said.

She didn't ask him where, just silently followed him out of the Hayat residence. She didn't bother with her own car; instead, getting into the Lexus that Ari had parked up. They drove in silence, the London rush hour enveloping them, until they reached a small mews in Gloucester Road. Ari parked his car outside one of the houses. He had obviously done well for himself, she thought. Private security certainly paid better than any of his past roles.

He led her into the small mews house. It was chilly inside, the air stale. As though no one had been there for a while. He probably hadn't, she realised. He showed her to the open-plan lounge kitchen, switched on a kettle and the heating. He left her alone while he headed upstairs to change, coming back down in jeans and a jumper. His feet bare.

They sat in the lounge, which was heating up, drinking the tea he had made them. There was silence. No clock, no neighbours, no traffic. Just silence. Neither of them felt the urge to fill it until their cups were empty. They needed the downtime, the switching off, until Sarah had to finally ask again:

'What do you know, Ari?'

Chapter Forty-Two

Romesh looked rough. He was hardly the fashionista of the office but today he looked as though he had just rolled out of bed. Or not gone home at all, she guessed.

'Don't let Saint Sarah catch you, she'll give you a right bollocking,' Moomy said, taking space in the empty chair next to him. Bizarre world. Screens, keyboards, numerous laptops, servers, wires. He looked like he was playing an American crime show version of himself. Moomy never got why he worked for the Met.

'You want me to get you some coffee?' Moomy offered.

'No, I'm buzzing already,' he said, shaking a giant plastic cup at her, not revealing the contents. Probably an energy drink of some sort.

'Got any food?'

'Nah, mum's cooking something. They'll drop it off later.' He had no intention of going home then, or sleeping. They had showers and lockers at least at the office. 'How did you get on with Oscar?' he asked.

'Bullshit that's how. Remembers everything apart from the bits that we really need him to remember, the last week basically. Doesn't even know how he got back into the country let alone home.'

'We're checking the CCTV across London using face recognition. You know how that pans out sometimes.'

'I thought they fixed the glitch?' The software had been developed by some of the most intelligent brains in the world. It worked great. Unless you weren't white. Or male. They had developed the intelligence pointers based on images of largely white men, so when the software tried to recognise ethnic minority faces, or female ones, it failed to register them as even being human.

'They did, we have a patch, but how well it works… I don't know.'

'Luckily for you, Oscar Hayat is a Caucasian male.'

'Tru dat.'

'Anyway, the street they live on is one of the most exclusive in London; they have hundreds of CCTV cameras. We'll pick up something,' said Moomy.

'Most of them are trained on the expensive properties around there, not the street. So far we only have Oscar coming to the front door and collapsing.'

Moomy bit her lower lip, licking the back of her bottom teeth. It was an unconscious tick she had picked up when under particular stress.

'Tell me then, what else did you find? The calls to Sarah? She said you wanted to speak to her urgently.'

Romesh dragged his fingers across screens.

'She was convinced that Millie must have got back to the country via private jet, so she tasked me with trying to find anything odd,' he said.

'Nice.'

'Yeah, there are well over a hundred thousand private flights a year to the UK, the majority of them to London.'

'Fuck.'

'So you can imagine. Just this last week there have been two thousand three hundred and thirty-one registered private flight journeys, for business or pleasure. From all over the world. I did an algorithm search and eliminated most of them.'

'How?'

'Frequent flyers, celebrities, families. Still left me with a hefty list. So I checked any that had unknown passengers on board, plus anyone who brought over cargo.'

'Can't you limit it to jets from Istanbul?'

'No. It's too easy to travel without needing to fly between Istanbul and neighbouring countries like Bulgaria. She was gone a week. You can get far in a week.'

He was right. The risk that they had been taken out of Turkey was low, but it was in those risky areas that mistakes happened.

'There were several flights that arrived with unidentified passengers,' he continued. 'So I'm having those checked out. And plenty with cargo on board. The search is still on.'

'Okay. That sounds like it's a work in progress. So why the urgent messaging for Sarah to get back to you?'

They were looking for a needle in a haystack, she knew.

'Because supposing that we assume Millie and Oscar were kept in Istanbul, then it narrows down the potentials significantly. There were only thirty-two private jet flights from Istanbul last week. Of those, only two had unidentified passengers. And of the thirty-two, only one also had cargo.'

Moomy stared at the screens trying to work out where the pattern was, which one would lead them to the answer. Romesh had seen it, but she was looking too, trying to get to the conclusion before she was told. She didn't manage it.

'That flight was a special flight, chartered by one Kamal Michaelides. He was the only passenger and his cargo was put directly into a waiting van at Southend airport.'

'That name means nothing to me. Who is he?'

'Kamal Michaelides is a Cypriot businessman, works for the Cypriot Embassy, so had diplomatic immunity. More than that, though, he is rumoured to be one of the biggest gangsters in Europe.'

Moomy sat up straighter. 'Any link to the Hayat family? Or to Dimitri Popov?'

'Yes. That's why I was calling. Not with Dimitri but with his father. Michaelides' family is notorious for being major people traffickers across Europe. Their specialty is refugees from conflict zones.'

'How the hell does someone like Kamal get to work for the Cypriot government if that's the case?'

'Much like Dimitri, Kamal has gone legitimate. He's now just a rich businessman doing import and export of goods from China.'

'And yet?'

'Well, the coincidence is massive. A known associate of Dimitri Popov turns up in London with a box, the very week that John Hayat's daughter-in-law is killed and his son turns up alive.'

Moomy didn't tell Romesh what she knew. How Sarah had been told in not so many words that Dimitri Popov had been eliminated at the say of John Hayat. Also, if it was related to Popov, then revenge would only be achieved by the death of Oscar. If he was alive, then what did that mean? Was Popov really behind this, was Oscar a victim rather than the husband who had killed his wife? Whatever was going on, Oscar being alive was the key to explain why Millie had died.

Chapter Forty-Three

'You start,' he said. 'Tell me about your half-sister Rachel.' His voice was smooth, aside from a slight accent in which *half* sounded like *halve*. What did that even mean? She didn't just half love her sister.

'Asking me that is like stealing my watch and then telling me the time,' she said. 'You said you had information for me?'

'I do. She's on a watch list. And she got out. Out of Raqqa.'

There it was. The key that meant he knew just what had happened. Just what she had been battling. The loneliness of it all. Still, she wouldn't tell him everything. Not why Rachel left her father's house or what drove her to do the things she did. Sarah would protect her sister from that, at least.

'When did she convert?' Ari asked.

'Shortly after I did.'

'Did she say why?'

'Not the same reasons as me. I did it after my mother, because I needed it. I was falling to pieces, Ari. This saved me.'

'And Rachel? How did she get it so badly wrong?'

'I took Rachel with me. She cared about my mother, but she wasn't as affected by her death. I think she was more worried about me, the effect it had on me. With our father being such a disappointment, she looked to me, I guess.'

'What about her own mother.'

'Long story. Anyway, so when I became Muslim, she saw the change in me. She saw me calm down and begin to live in some semblance of peace. I took her with me to the mosque once, thought she might be able to battle her own demons.'

'That worked,' he scoffed.

'That's not how it happened. It didn't happen in my mosque or at college or through friends. It happened in her bedroom, alone, through her computer. I had no idea what was happening. She didn't show any outward signs; she didn't start covering her head or praying. Afterwards, oh God, yes, I saw it all. But then I was so busy I lost myself in work and my prayers and I took my eye off her. And then it was too late.'

He took the mug of tea that had gone cold from her hands. She leaned back on the sofa, unable to look at him as she spoke.

'She left one day. The usual thing. Flight to Istanbul. From there to Bodrum. Immigration saw this blonde-haired blue-eyed girl going for a party holiday. And in Bodrum...'

'She disappeared.'

'Yes.' It was why the Millie case had brought her emotions to the fore. The disappearance in Turkey, turning up dead. It was all too reminiscent of Rachel.

'Did you hear from her? After she left?' Ari asked.

'No,' she lied.

She had, but it wasn't for her to tell Ari that part. That conversation was the one thing she had that would help her find Rachel if she was alive. Find her and even save her.

'Nothing? No call, no message?'

'No.'

'That is odd. Normally there is a goodbye message, so the family can alert the media and give ISIL publicity. That's their modus operandi for girls like Rachel.'

'We had no contact from her, or those bastards in ISIL.'

'How did you know where she went?'

'She disappeared; I had her computer checked. There was enough on there for me to know. We found her travel bookings to Turkey. CCTV of her boarding the flight at Stansted. Arriving in Istanbul, taking the bus to Bodrum.'

'And after that? How did you know she was alive?'

'MI5 traced a social media account to her.'

She didn't go into the details. There was a picture. She knew it was Rachel. Dressed like some jihadi bride. Trying to encourage others. Sarah had denied it was Rachel at the time, said just someone who looked like her maybe. The account was her social media though; it was being operated by her, according to the security forces.

'That's it? That is the only evidence of her living?' said Ari.

'Yes. And I cling on to that. Hoping it meant she was alive at least.'

'She is. Or rather she was.'

Sarah looked at him coolly, trying to still the emotions crashing inside her.Ari got his laptop and sat close to her. She could smell his familiar scent as he uploaded images and documents.

'She was in a refugee camp.'

'How did you know it was her?' Sarah asked.

'She gave your name as her next of kin.'

'To who?'

'To camp registration. They didn't act on it, but like I said, I kept an eye on you. Your name turning up in a refugee camp where known ISIL members were verified to be hiding. I couldn't just let that go.'

'So what happened to her? Where is she, Ari?' Sarah said, the emotion clear in her voice.

Too many years with nothing and now proof that her baby sister was alive at least. She didn't want to think beyond that, not about what condition she was in or what she had done. Just that she needed rescuing and Sarah hadn't stopped her leaving, hadn't saved her before.

'I don't know. The last I can tell she was at this camp. After she registered, she disappeared. There are thousands of people in that camp. She never made herself known again.'

Sarah listened as he told her the camp's location, and she knew she had to go and find her. Ari held her gaze as though he could read her mind.

'They are killing them off, most of the ISIL members. In the camps when they are exposed, they are being silenced and killed. So don't hold out hope. And don't do anything that will get you into trouble. She made her choices, she has to live with them.'

'I can't just abandon her, Ari.'

'Yes, you can. Because she abandoned you to follow that fucked-up life. How can you even still be a Muslim after everything she ended up doing?'

This wasn't the time to explain to him what the difference was between her and ISIL. He was lashing out, being provocative, she knew. He was trying to get her to react. She wouldn't. Instead she was thinking what she had to do to find Rachel. First she needed to solve this case and then she would be gone.

She got up to leave, checking her phone, looking away from him, as she headed to the door. He stopped her, jamming himself against it as she tried to open it. He looked hard at her, reading her.

'Don't do it. Please.'

She gently pushed him aside and left, closing the door behind her. Her mind in turmoil. She owed Rachel this.

Chapter Forty-Four

Kamal Michaelides lived in a detached house in Barking riverside. It was a strange location, Moomy thought, to live if you were raking it in through illegal means. Then again, it was miles away from the sort of people looking for you. Easy to hide, lots of privacy.

His background was one that was becoming all too familiar. International gangster family. New generation going clean. Not so easy to do. Truth and lies? The fact was he had an operation big enough to smuggle two people into the country. How well would his cargo have been checked?

The house had mock Tudor panelling. SUVs, two BMWs parked up outside. There were security cameras but no patrolmen. She didn't think it looked like a mafia don's home. Until she knocked on the door. Video Entry-phone security, who told her that Kamal was not at home, especially not for the police. She asked where he was: no answer back. She made a show of giving up, went back to her car and drove off. She parked up around the corner, before heading back on foot, down a parallel road. The houses, even though spacious, were fairly close together, and she could see the front door to Kamal's house from the gardens of the houses opposite. She cut through an alleyway, then another, until she had positioned herself at the side of a house that looked empty. She was well hidden by bins, and from there she crouched, waited and watched.

–

Two hours nearly. Not a good amount of time to be in that position. Then the front door opened and Kamal came out. Moomy dashed her aching body across the road, surprising him and his entourage, which included his wife and kids.

'I need to speak to you, Mr Michaelides,' she said. 'It won't take long.'

His security guards came towards her, ready to send her packing, no doubt. Kamal halted them, spoke to them in what she assumed was Greek. They stopped, didn't quite back away, but didn't come towards her either.

Kamal spoke to his wife and children next, who got into the SUV with two of his guards. The car drove off. He didn't invite Moomy in, but he got into the back of a BMW and she followed him.

'We are due at a lunch event at the embassy.' He didn't specify which one, his accent thick but polished. 'I have sent my family on ahead. I will follow them in ten minutes.'

'This won't take long. If you're honest.'

He was shocked at the way she spoke to him. probably used to deference and fear.

'I just need to speak to you about a journey you took. Three days ago. From Istanbul. I'm sure you remember it.'

His eyes were cool and grey and didn't give anything away.

'What about it? It was a business trip.'

'What type of business?'

'We are looking to start manufacturing in Turkey. I was meeting with my contacts there.'

'Manufacturing what exactly?'

'Jeans.'

'Jeans?'

'Yes.'

She laughed. She didn't mean to. That wasn't what she expected.

'I act as third party transport at present. We import a lot of goods in bulk from the Chinese mainland that smaller businesses cannot afford to do. Now we are going to start making our own products and bring them.'

Moomy didn't ask what those goods were. Had he really replaced selling girls and boys into slavery and prostitution, selling drugs and weapons, with jeans? She thought then of his children, all three had looked under the age of ten. His wife, she looked very sophisticated. Worried look on her face as she got into the SUV. Maybe those things mattered and changed a man?

Maybe.

'And what was in the cargo container you brought with you that day?'

'The cargo was checked and signed off at both Ataturk Airport and Southend. It was jeans.'

'Can I see the container? It was loaded into a van, I believe.' She didn't say that Romesh had got her the registration of the vehicle from airport records.

'We don't keep our goods here.'

'Then?'

'There is a warehouse twenty miles from here. That is where our cargo goes.'

'Would you like to take me?'

'If you have a warrant, then yes.'

'I'll get a warrant, all right. Take me about fifteen minutes to get it sent via e-mail. Then no doubt your lawyers will have to get involved. A whole team of officers will want to search the warehouse. Your family will expect you at the embassy. All very embarrassing and time-consuming.'

'What do you want?'

'I want to see the van and the box that was brought over. You don't have to come. Send one of your henchmen with me.'

Kamal looked at her as if he wanted to punch her. Moomy knew self-defence. She could block his punch and hit him back much harder. She wasn't intimidated. He broke eye contact first, spoke in Greek to one of his security. He was well over six foot and had a lithe, slim frame. She could take him easily.

'This is Gregory. He will drive you there, show you the van, show you the box and then all is good, yes?'

'Yes. And you know the box was stamped, don't you? So I know what I'm looking for.'

'Of course.'

Moomy said they would take her car. She could feel Kamal's eyes burning into her as she set off with Gregory. Give. A. Fuck. She laughed as she walked.

Chapter Forty-Five

Sarah was in no mood now to play nice. Not with Oscar or John or anyone else. She needed answers to close this case. She needed to go and find Rachel. Her mind was reeling from what Ari had told her. Why hadn't the camp contacted her? They should have. Incompetence. Then again with thousands of refugees... no, still, the fact that Rachel was British and Sarah was too, that should have triggered something?

Rachel disappeared, Ari had said. After registering. Was she even alive?

'Why don't you try a subtle approach?' Scott said. They were in his office back at HQ, the room feeling full and stifling. Lack of windows and Victorian plumbing combined, with some dodgy central heating, were all playing havoc together.

'Because we don't have time. The Hayats are playing with us, I can feel it. Oscar's memory loss is just too convenient, as is his return. We don't see him anywhere on CCTV until he walks into view of the house they live in.'

'Coincidence and serendipity happen in real life,' Scott said carefully.

He wasn't meeting her eye; he was thinking, disturbed by something. She knew him too well not to pick up on those signs.

'Doctor Farah Naz, the psychiatrist Doctor Ramone recommended, spoke to him at length,' said Sarah. 'Tried to work out if he was faking it. Inconclusive. She said retroactive amnesia is the hardest to expose as fake. We need to question him and trip him up.'

'Then interview him, you don't need to arrest him. There is only circumstantial evidence.'

'Let me guess, the Foreign Secretary has been on the phone?' Jane fucking Haslam, as Moomy would say.

'Yes. There is that as well. We have to be careful who we piss off.'

'Even if it means not finding a ruthless killer?'

Scott looked at her, blinking as though surprised to see her.

'Scott? What's going on?'

He smoothed back his hair and leaned back, his hands behind his head.

'Jane Haslam was very clear. I go after John Hayat and I lose my job.'

'I'm not asking you to go after him. I will. Also, she can't do that, you don't work for her.'

'Come on, Sarah, you know how it is.'

'It's not right, that's what it is.' She breathed deeply. 'Listen, let me do it. I can go rogue. You deny all knowledge if anything goes wrong. I need to speak to him and going around and doing it nicely won't work.'

'You won't get a warrant and without it they aren't compelled to speak to you.'

'Trust me, when I tell Oscar what I know, he will talk.'

Oscar was looking fresh after a few hours' sleep. As though nothing had happened. Showered, dressed in tailored khakis and shirt. He looked like a poster boy for *Made in Chelsea*. Sarah was getting more and more irritated as she looked at him, so nonchalant and calm about everything. As though he knew he had got away with it. She was also feeling the effects of running on adrenaline and lack of sleep.

They were in the same lounge in which Sarah had interviewed his mother. The same tea service. Oscar had asked to be alone, despite Lara attempting to be in the room with him.

'Luciano. A male escort. We know you and Paul visited him on two occasions. We have CCTV footage. You see you were very clever, covering your face as you entered and left, standing parallel to your friend so you couldn't be seen. You knew even then, didn't you, that you were doing something that you might regret later. Such careful strategic planning of the whole thing. Yet not as clever or as clean as you thought.'

His face remained calm, but his eyes were darts, panicked. He was probably thinking how he could deny this, but he wasn't fast enough as Sarah hammered him with everything that Paul had told Moomy. They had also checked the CCTV evidence again. What Oscar didn't realise was that there was a camera which looked towards the lifts, and when the doors opened he had lowered his hand, his reflection caught in the back of the lift. It was grainy and it probably wouldn't stand up in court, but he didn't know that. And she knew it was enough to scare him.

'You have this life, where you and Paul are exploring another side of you. Paul seems to be in love with you, in fact. And you come from a world where no-one cares about those things. So why did you have to create such an elaborate hoax as to marry Millie? I always wondered why you were so keen on the wedding shots on Instagram. Our tech lead did some digging and found that you've not only changed your hashtags for that post – to be some of Instagram's most popular ones to drive the post's traffic – but that you also commercialised those pictures. Paid to boost them in effect. Declaring to the world you had married. A woman.'

Oscar was putting up no pretence now, he gulped loudly, he was wringing his hands, sweat on his face. He was looking at her as if he was a child caught out in a lie. It reminded Sarah of his mother, the little girl lost act she pulled with her sons. Hiding the ice-cold determination that she had lashed out at Sarah with, the same that Millie had suffered.

'Was it easy to plan? Millie's death? Were you thinking of the details as you stood there, exchanging vows?'

'I didn't kill her.' Soft voice, clear words. 'We were taken.'

'I thought you couldn't remember anything?'

'It's what happened, the evidence is there, I was told.'

'How do you know you were taken? How do you know you didn't shoot the driver, kidnap Millie and then bring her to London only to kill her?'

'I didn't do that. Look at the bruises on my body.' He pulled his shirt up, revealing marks that were purple and yellow on his small frame.

'Well, of course, you had to be roughed up a little bit. To make it seem authentic.'

'It didn't happen like that.'

'Oh yes? Then how did it happen? Because supposedly you can't remember?'

'I didn't plan anything; I can remember that much.'

'Why did you marry Millie when you are in love with another man?'

'I'm not.' Anger now. 'I am *not* in love with Paul, I don't know what that fool has told you.'

'Then what was it?'

'It was nothing, just experimenting. It's always been just that. I like it, okay? Is that what you want to hear? I like having sex with men and women.'

'Then why not carry on doing that? Why entangle Millie in your mess?'

'I love her. I wanted to spend the rest of my life with her.'

'And when she found out about your sex life? Were you just going to hide it from her forever, carry on behind her back?'

'That part was all over. I just did it to try it. I would no more have cheated on Millie with another man than I would another woman.'

'I don't believe you.'

'It's what I planned to do.'

'Give it all up just like that?' Sarah clicked her fingers in his face and he jumped back. 'That doesn't happen. Those feelings, that urge wouldn't have gone away.'

'No, but the urge to sleep with other women would have been there too. I wouldn't have acted on that or…

I didn't kill Millie and please don't bring this up to my family.'

'Why? Your brother Spencer is a notorious playboy. Your mother had quite a wild time growing up, I'm sure, in London's jet set. What are you afraid of? Your father?'

Oscar looked at her with the same child-about-to-cry expression.

'Your father wouldn't understand, would he?'

'Of course not. He's not from here. He grew up in Iraq. They live differently. He quotes the Bible to me all the time, randomly. He was persecuted for being a Christian by Saddam Hussain; he holds on to his faith. There is no way he would understand. The best he and my mother do is turn a blind eye to everything that me and my brothers get up to. Just don't bring it home. Home, you bring the girl that you will marry and the children that she will produce.'

'And you chose a girl from the wrong side of the tracks. What did you think, she would be so overwhelmed by all this money that she would quietly just accept your choices? You were buying her allegiance, weren't you?'

Oscar laughed; it was forced, manic. 'If you think that, you really haven't a clue who Millie was.'

Sarah leaned forward. 'Then tell me who she was.'

'Millie, Millie, Millie. God, I loved her from the moment I saw her. First day at Oxford, she was so different. She had the weight of the world on her shoulders, so much more mature than everyone else. Really wanted to do something with her life, yet she wasn't dull. Fascinating and so alive. I wanted her.'

'But Declan was already in the picture.'

'Yes. I watched them from the sidelines, playing friend to Millie, as she wasted herself on him. Still, she always held sadness in her eyes. And when I found out about her mother, well, all I wanted to do was to take a bit of it away. That sadness.'

The theatre nights, the trips to Paris, York and Edinburgh.

'Attempting to seduce her with your money?'

'Millie didn't give a fuck about money. Not like that. She wasn't into designer crap like the girls I grew up with are. Money for her meant only one thing, that she could help her parents.'

'So how did you manage to get her onside?'

'There was nothing calculated about any of it. Not the way you're suggesting. Her and Declan broke up. He was always so self-absorbed, typical actor.'

'They had problems and you just happened to step in?'

'Yes.'

'I do wonder, though, how Millie found out about Declan cheating on her?'

Oscar couldn't meet her eyes.

'You told her, didn't you?'

'No.'

'Then?'

'I told a common friend. That's how it got back to Millie. The girl involved confirmed it to Millie when Millie confronted her.'

'You didn't feel guilty that your friend – as Millie was back then – who you cared about so much, who had so much going on in her life, was being destroyed? No, you only cared about creating your chance, your opportunity.'

Oscar flashed his eyes at her, colour in his face.

'Declan didn't deserve her, after what he did. She deserved something better.'

'A husband who was going to marry her and then sleep with God knows who?'

Again the anger. He had a temper on him for all his little-lost-boy act earlier.

'I told you, no. For Millie that was all going to stop.'

'Or maybe Millie was your ticket to have it all. The perfect wedding, keep your father happy, then an accident that meant she wouldn't be an issue any more? And you could go ahead and play the devastated widower. Isn't that what happened?'

'No. I wanted her.'

'Really? Even after your mother told you about the money Millie had taken? The bribe she'd accepted to not marry you?'

Oscar looked shocked, finally realising just how much Sarah knew, and just how precarious his situation was.

Chapter Forty-Six

Gregory smelt funny. Like he hadn't washed in soap but some sort of cleaner fluid and then added a splash of after-shave on as an afterthought. He didn't say much either. Moomy put on some music as she followed the satnav to where the warehouse was, in some place outside of Battlesbridge.

'This says it's twenty-eight miles not twenty. Are you sure it's the right place?'

Moomy had let Sarah know already where she was going, making sure she spoke loudly into the phone, so Gregory heard her. Just in case. Not scared. Careful though. Gregory looked like he would gladly break her neck. She also knew Kamal wouldn't send someone with her unless it was someone he trusted.

The sun was bright as they arrived at the warehouse. Moomy felt like she did after a night out. No sleep and too much action. Her body clock was off-kilter. It wasn't even 5 p.m. yet.

The warehouse had been built on farmland, away from any neighbouring buildings. There was barbed wire around it, security cameras and lots of security guards. Concealing weapons? She couldn't tell but they were wearing jackets, not the usual security guard uniform. They looked lackadaisical, eyeing Moomy's Mazda, until

Gregory stepped out. The effect was instant; they all stood to attention, shouting orders to each other. Confirming to Moomy exactly what she had thought.

'Power,' she said.

Gregory still ignored her. He issued instructions in Greek as he led her into the complex. Moomy looked back at her car wondering if she could climb the fence and bypass the barbed wire if she needed to. No, she would have to fight her way out. She felt excited by the prospect.

Gregory didn't waste time, though, or take her to some torture chamber. He took her straight to where the vans were parked. Moomy checked the licence plate she had on her phone. It was a white SUV, looked like a lot of the others in the lot. Moomy checked to see there was no damage on the plate area, signs it had been replaced recently. She then combed the entire vehicle, taking pictures as she did so. She even took a scraping from the inside and dropped it into a plastic bag. There wasn't much to see though. She jumped out, Gregory standing to one side, smoking and talking into his phone. He ended the call and snapped to attention when he saw her.

'Finished, now take me to the box that Kamal brought with him that day.'

Gregory didn't flinch, just kept his immobile face and aloof attitude in check. Probably pissed off that some girl was ordering him around.

The crate was in one of the warehouses, in a space the size of a hangar. It was surrounded by dozens of other similar crates. Again, like the van, easy to fake and show Moomy what they wanted her to see. She checked that the customs stamps on the crate matched the ones that Stansted airport had sent through. There was that much, at least. But the crate had been placed in the centre of the warehouse, ready for her to inspect. Why had that happened if the security at the front had been surprised to see Gregory? Something was off, she knew it.

Moomy checked the outside of the crate carefully, asking Gregory if he could open it. It was full of jeans, as Kamal had said it would be. She fingered some of them, the material coarse under her touch. She rifled through some of the contents of the crate, her hands reaching down. She asked Gregory to help her empty the crate. He did so, not reluctantly, making her more suspicious. The jeans piled on the floor of the warehouse; she knocked inside the empty crate. There were no hidden shelves or parts to it, nowhere you could stow bodies. Packing the crate up again she checked the label on one of the jeans. *Made in China.* She didn't let Gregory see she had clocked on. The jeans were supposed to have been made in Turkey. That was the whole premise of Kamal's new business. They had managed to fake the outside of the crate, even put on a show for her with the panicking security guards as the big boss arrived. And yet were too dumb to fill the crate with the right make of jeans. Problem was there were hundreds of crates in the warehouse. How could she possibly search them all without a warrant?

'Let's go,' she said to Gregory.

He followed her out to the entrance of the compound, but she didn't offer him a lift home. He could find his own way.

Moomy drove away, making a phone call to ask for a team and a warrant. Scott was barely listening to why, he seemed more interested in his meeting with the chief superintendent and the Met Commissioner. Meeting? Golf and a drink at a private club more like. Privileged assholes. She didn't buy Sarah's whole sob story about Scott being raised on her council estate. He was so far up his own arse.

Moomy didn't have time though. She wanted to be sure. Now. The impatience. She parked up in an empty field about ten minutes' drive from the compound and waited.

Chapter Forty-Seven

Sarah needed honesty from Oscar. If he was guilty, that was the last thing she would get from him, she knew. Still, she hoped her knowledge would floor him, make him realise his secrets and lies were not so easily hidden.

His reddened eyes were staring into space, sweat forming in obvious drops. His heart must have been racing like crazy. She thought she could hear it, although it might just have been her own.

'I confronted Millie about the money, when my mother told me. I thought it was callous of my mum. Right after we had exchanged vows. What exactly was she trying to prove? That Millie was some dirty little gold digger? I hated her at that moment.'

'Millie?'

'My mother. She took the happiest moment of my life away from me. All for what? Her own selfish notion of what she thought would fit into our family. Even though she tells everyone she married for love, picked my father, her rough diamond. So why couldn't I? Love.' He scoffed. 'As if she knows what that is. She married my father for his money.'

'Did it make you angry when your mother told you? Towards Millie?'

'Yes. I was livid. I don't deny it. I asked why she did it. I screamed at her. Right before we went on honeymoon. I swore and shouted and asked her why.'

'Did she tell you?'

'Yes. She said she had to. For her parents. For her mother. It was all for them. She knew it was wrong, but also she knew that the very fact it was offered proved to her that she would never be a part of this family. She knew our marriage was a mistake.'

'The marriage? Or had she found out something else? About you?'

'No.'

'Are you sure you didn't make her an offer of your own? You would stay with her if she let you live the way you always had? That she kept your secrets? Did you offer her even more money than your mother did? And she refused. So you…'

He stood up, it was a swift, agile movement. For someone who was supposed to have been tortured for days, he didn't seem to be in much pain. Very different from the wincing the night before.

'Is that what happened, Oscar? You tried to buy her to play a role, and when it failed, you had to get rid of her?'

'I loved her. I loved her. I loved her!'

'Did you arrange to kill her?'

'No.'

'No? Or can't you remember?'

He shook his head. 'I know without remembering. I would never have killed her.'

Sarah stood up, watching the assertive, fixed young man. The alive young man. She didn't believe him, that was her truth and the one that was guiding her. She needed to trace his financials and see if there were any clues. Transactions that might point to what he had done. Payments for Millie's death, his own safe passage home. She knew she wouldn't get the warrant signed off with what she had so far, with the connections the Hayats had. She needed more.

'Sit down,' she commanded. He looked at her as though he was about to spit, then did as she had asked. 'Tell me, what do you remember about the honeymoon? Do you remember Istanbul at all?'

He shook his head. Sarah unlocked her phone, swiped on the screen until she found what she was looking for. It was a video showing Oscar and Millie arriving in Istanbul by private jet. It was a shot from far away, their faces visible but blurry. What was obvious, though, was the distance between them. Oscar stomped ahead of Millie off the airplane, she behind him. He didn't bother to help her off the moving stairway; instead, got into his car. No love there, just anger. Millie looked towards Oscar's side of the car, running her fingers through her hair and wiping away at her eyes before she got into the car and disappeared from view. The last known shot of her alive.

'What were you angry about?'

'I wasn't angry, we had just taken a flight. I was tired.'

'That looks like anger to me. The sort that might lead someone to kill another person.'

'I told you I wasn't angry, just tired. We both were. I just wanted to get to the house and…' He stopped, reading the expression on Sarah's face.

'You remember, then? So tell me, what happened before you got to the villa? Who kidnapped you and shot your driver, Oscar?'

His words tumbled out of his mouth, explanations, lies, confusion, anger.

'I don't know. I was just saying that's what it looks like. I didn't say I remembered; you're trying to trap me.'

'You were very clear, Oscar, you said you remembered exactly how you felt when you got to Istanbul. So then you must remember how you felt after you left the airport, how you felt all that week, a week in which Millie was tortured and then killed.'

'I don't.'

'I don't believe you.'

She left him, feeling the adrenaline. This might just be enough to get the warrant she needed.

Chapter Forty-Eight

The team arrived with fanfare. Moomy had failed to disclose that Gregory worked for Kamal, a man with diplomatic immunity. It would have caused an issue she was sure. Then again, fuck it, there was no way a cargo-full warehouse was a diplomatic safe space. Although Gregory had tried to say it was.

'This is the property of the Cypriot Embassy,' he was insisting.

'Show me your papers,' Moomy said.

She felt more confident now with ten officers behind her, ready to do their search of the premises. Although, she could still take Gregory in a fight if needed. A kick to the balls, very hard, and all men went down crying like babies begging for their mamas.

'Because I have bona fide papers showing this is just a commercial warehouse and we are going to search it,' Moomy added. 'Get in the way and you will all be arrested.'

The papers said no such thing, they were just a warrant to search the premises. But he wouldn't know and she said it with so much authority he believed her. No fucking way would he start a gunfight or risk harming Kamal Michaelides and the embassy. She strode past him, issuing orders to the team. They put on their gloves and boots, and spread out, hunting down the swapped crate. She knew it was here and she would find it.

Gregory and his henchmen looked on, before he started making frantic phone calls. Kamal would not be happy. He would contact his friends in the police, she knew. They didn't have long.

Moomy asked her team to follow her to the warehouse in which the fake crate had been. She told them all what serial number they were looking for, anything that looked tampered with and damaged, containing jeans made in Turkey.

Standing in the darkened warehouse she realised what a task she was asking. Still, they had to do it. This was it, she knew they would find it here: the method in which Millie and Oscar had been smuggled into the country.

After an hour of fruitless searching, Moomy was getting pissed off. They had looked in nearly every crate in the warehouse, checking it for double fitted hidden areas. There were mainly clothes and plastic goods, cheap tat that you might find in a pound shop. Nothing that was manufactured in Turkey. No crate that might have been the one.

She was swearing, shouting. It was meant to be motivational but she knew she was probably irritating the hell out of everyone. Transferring because she was irritated herself. Had she miscalculated? Fucking hell. The fallout would be epic from this one.

Another hour. Nothing.

'Fuck, fuck, fuck,' she exclaimed.

Gregory was staring at her, absolute hatred on his face. Her phone rang. Scott.

'You need to leave. Apologise and leave. Now.'

Like fuck she would.

'We searched nearly every crate on the complex, ma'am. I don't think there is anything here.'

'Keep looking,' she said, not even knowing the name of the officer she was talking to. What was the point? Keep everyone impersonal so she could order them around. Getting involved in people just screwed you up. 'It's here. We have half an hour.'

They went crazy. Searching every little corner, even doing body searches on the guards in case they held keys for locked doors. Nothing. Nothing at all. She had a hunch that they wouldn't have had time to hide the crate properly, but they hadn't found anything. It still didn't explain what the fake jeans were doing in the crate.

'Fuck!' she shouted. She walked out of the complex, ignoring Gregory.

Scott would yell her ass down into nothing, she knew. She needed to avoid him until Sarah was back.

–

The story broke. He knew who the woman was now. The one they had moved from his van to the car. Her name. Millie Beaumont. The press conference with her father. He watched it with his own daughters in his arms, asleep, safe. This man, his daughter would never be safe. His heart broke. What could he do?

It wasn't right. They had tricked him. He had signed up for something else, not this.

As his daughters snored lightly next to him the way that children do, his mind circled with his options.

Tired and stressed there was only one way. A way that meant he would be safe and his family. But the people who took Millie wouldn't be.

Chapter Forty-Nine

Scott looked at them both. His face was red. As though he'd been drinking all day, only it was absolute, spitting anger.

'What the hell were you thinking?' he directed at Moomy.

'I thought I had them. It all fit. They had the plane, the cargo and more than that, the fake jeans.'

'Why did you keep all of this from me?'

'Because I knew you wouldn't sign off on it.'

'And what exactly did this little foray of yours achieve?'

Sarah flinched as she heard the polish in Scott's voice, knowing Moomy was giving her a look. *See, he is fucking posh*, she was probably thinking. Sarah kept her eye on Scott. She needed him to agree to her request to arrest Oscar, to be able to investigate his finances. She could have kicked Moomy; she hadn't even cleared her mad search idea with Sarah. There was going off script with Scott, that was always fine, but going off script with Sarah, that was a no-no. They were never meant to do that with one another. Ever.

'I thought—'

'I asked you what you had achieved,' Scott interrupted. 'Did you find what you were looking for? This imaginary crate?'

'Then why were the jeans from China?' Moomy exclaimed.

'Because Kamal Michaelides is a smart businessman,' said Scott. 'He knew he could charge more for goods made in Turkey. The cargo was a ruse. He imported Chinese jeans from Istanbul into London so he could mark them up with fake Turkish labels and sell them on.'

'Like fuck he was. And that's still fraud.'

'That's business, and quite frankly we have bigger problems than worrying about some labels on jeans.'

Moomy looked at Sarah, but she didn't react. Why was Scott buying what someone like Kamal had told him? The man's family were notorious. Moomy might have been onto something big; if they had found trafficked individuals or drugs, then Scott would have been in a very different mood.

Sarah knew Scott's anger was the result of Jane Haslam getting into his head, twisting the knife and putting the pressure on him. She knew Scott the way only someone who had spent their life with you could. She had seen him stressed, could only imagine the sort of constraints he was in.

'You really think that's true?' Moomy said. 'Come on, the man's an international asshole, no way is he just doing a bit of label swapping.'

'You spent three hours in that place, thoroughly searching every little corner from what I've been told. The apologies and arse kissing I am going to have to do tomorrow to iron this one out, have you any idea?'

'You might enjoy it,' Moomy muttered.

'Tell me, DS Khan, why I shouldn't just suspend you right now?'

'Because I'm one of the best you fucking well have,' she said.

Sarah wanted to laugh, but the look on Scott's face.

Moomy got up and quietly walked out.

'Save me the speech,' Sarah said, trying to lighten the mood. 'I know the drill. Why is she here? Why don't you just fire her? She only has a job because I vouch for her.'

'She went totally off-grid today. Did you know what she was up to?'

'Yes,' Sarah lied.

She knew it was the one thing that would protect Moomy now.

'How could you be so incompetent and let her do that?' He didn't believe her, she knew, but she also knew he wouldn't openly call her out on it.

'She had a hunch, a good hunch. She followed the trail from the evidence Romesh had and she followed her instincts when she saw there was something not right.'

'International incident over some mislabelled jeans. For Christ's sake.'

'Don't blaspheme,' she said, stern voice. He couldn't help himself, relaxing an inch at that. 'It backfired, and I'm sorry you have to deal with the fallout. Sometimes we follow things that don't lead us to the right place.'

'The amount of time and money she wasted.'

'We all learn from our mistakes. Moomy will learn from hers. That's the way it is. Give her time. She's good.'

'Is she?'

'Yes. She's tough, she intimidates people, especially those who have things to hide. We need people who are passionate and have spine.'

He was quiet, looking at his fingers.

'Tell me about Oscar.'

'Moomy found out about his private life. Gay escorts, a best friend with benefits. He had something major to cover up, Scott. Millie dying is very convenient for him. As much as his memory loss is.'

She laid her phone on the table between them, played him Oscar's interview. Scott's face was neutral, the blue eyes placid. She knew he was turning over all options in his head though.

And she knew she had to push him. She needed to resolve this, before it was too late. Before Rachel was lost to her forever. And before the Hayat family covered their tracks. That was if they hadn't already. After all, Oscar had come back. So he must have known it was safe.

Was it too late already?

Chapter Fifty

Moomy let the vodka hit her system. She knew even Sarah couldn't save her from this one. And then all her hard work to make it in this world, change her life and turn it around would just be gone. She would just end up being the same girl that Harry had driven over the edge.

—

When Haroon saw her again she had her trademark shorter hair, falling just below the ears, full make-up, wearing a leather miniskirt, high heels and a black velvet jacket. He walked right past her.

Moomy recognised him though. His hair was longer, floppier, falling into his face. That face she had touched, tasted, held, dreamed about, cursed. Loved.

She called his name.

'Who are you?' he asked, looking at her for a moment, surprised.

'You said you would die for me… and yet in a few years you'd forget about me? What loyalty.'

'Mumtaz?' He couldn't say anything else. He just held her.

The anger subsided in her. She hadn't been held with affection in so many years.

'I wrote to you.' Moomy raised the betrayal that was eating at her.

'I never got a single letter. I swear.' Haroon seemed sincere.

'Your parents must have burnt them. Explains why your mum gave me such a cold shoulder when I saw her.'

'They caught me that night, running away. Of course they knew. Dad… well he had a heart attack. He hasn't been the same since. My brother J got beat for it, for causing it. He became a nightmare after that. I think I've fucked up all their lives. My dad looks so old.'

'I saw them both,' said Moomy. 'Your dad. And J.'

'He's gone totally bonkers. Dad misplaced his anger into him. He was beating J for not chaperoning you and me when he had the heart attack. J blames himself, blames me. He made my life hell these last few years. Him and his dickhead friends.'

'My heart bleeds. Was he forcing himself on you every night? Threatening to beat you unless you applied for a visa? I think not.'

'Okay Moomy, you win in the misery stakes. I'm sorry. I had no choice.'

'You could have saved me.'

'I couldn't. My dad was so ill, my mother in tears. I was sixteen, I had no money, nothing. I had to do my A levels, get to uni. What would I have done? Walked in guns blazing into your village and demanded they hand you over? Then what? Where would we have lived, what would we have subsisted on? Love? Love doesn't fill an empty stomach.'

'Well, I did just that, walked away from everything and I've been living alone for the last four years. I'm alive, never starved. You're a coward. There, I said it. You are a spineless shit. Fucking coward.'

'Yes, I am. And? This is who I am. I'm sorry.'

'So you keep saying. Well, sorry isn't going to fucking cut it this time.'

'What do you want from me?' he said.

'Nothing. You have nothing you can give me.'

She turned to walk out of his dorm room. He asked her not to go. She faltered, caved.

'Technically you're still my wife,' he said.

They went to sharing their world again, sharing their beds, their lives, their friends. They tried to capture the time before. They failed miserably.

—

Moomy was drinking, smoking, getting high. Haroon was trying to stay true to his faith. They clashed continuously.

They went out with their friends. He got angry as Moomy got pissed. They fought in public. Screaming matches, accusations like weapons, thrown glasses, punches. They broke up every weekend, only to crawl crying into each other's arms again.

Haroon told Moomy to dress properly. Moomy told him to go fuck himself. Her dresses got shorter, her heels higher. She had her breasts on display in lectures, in the canteen. He burned with embarrassment as his Islamic Society friends passed him by.

One night, Moomy got so drunk she passed out on Charing Cross Road, the traffic swerving to avoid her collapsed form. He left her there. She broke up with him the next day.

Only to get back together again when he had come to her at night, his hormones raging.

They made angry, desperate, violent love. There was no affection there, no memory of the first time, the trepidation, the newness, the tenderness. They were hungry, raw, passionate.

It was as though the love had turned to hate, soured for both of them. Finally it went too far and Moomy had told him.

'I was pregnant. That's what I wrote to you. I was pregnant with your child when I went to Pakistan, when I was forced into that sham marriage. You go on about me driving you crazy? I fucking carried our child for nine months.'

'What are you saying? Where is it?'

'*Dead*. That's where. Fucking dead. He lived for ten minutes. I named him after you. I held his cold, still body in these fucking hands. But no matter how much I cried nothing brought him to life.'

She reached into her wardrobe, took out a jar full of dirt and shoved it into his hands.

'That's from his grave.'

'Moomy?' He held the jar, he fell to his knees, he keened, the tragedy of it all knocking the wind from him.

They could never be together after that.

–

Moomy turned her rage into her work. She got a rep for being a shark, the woman you went to when colleagues who couldn't hack it any more complained.

She played just as hard: drinking and men. She went out clubbing every weekend, bars every night practically. She had her little band of girlfriends, exotic beauties; they, all four of them, cut an image that made men ga-ga whenever they walked into a room.

Moomy, though, didn't care. She had two aims: get drunk and get laid. The pain numbed for another night.

She cut back on her drinking only when Sarah told her to go to rehab.

The pain didn't seem to go away through any other method though. It was there, cavernous, real, dark. It was gnawing at her, just like the memory of her baby did.

How could you plug that with alcohol and drugs and men?

She woke up one day and didn't know where she was, who the man in bed with her was or what she had done. Moomy didn't go over that night too many times, but it was the lowest point after Haroon. She felt ashamed.

She cut back. And time played out its course.

She got herself together, until one night she saw Haroon, his arms wrapped around a pretty brunette, exchanging words of affection.

They seemed… they reminded her… they were more than…

She had vomited, unable to control her body, the knowledge that Haroon had moved on so easily like a death blow.

Moomy went home, got dressed in a red cocktail number, called up her girls, hit the bars and clubs in Chelsea, and got drunker than she had in a long time.

So drunk she had lost her shoes…

Chapter Fifty-One

Sarah felt the chill of the morning, her body aching in the position in which she had slept. The flat was dark, empty, freezing. It was barely 2 a.m. and she forgot she had set her alarm for the *Tahajjud* prayers. The prayers for the committed. For those in desperate need. When the walls between worlds were thinner than threads. She was tired, in pain, thirsty. Still, it was a big day. It would be a big day. Her sleep was stilted anyway, putting in markers for prayers didn't do much to alter that. She made the best of it.

She would pray now, go to sleep, then wake up to pray the dawn prayer, then sleep again before waking for work. That was a normal day when a case didn't mess with her schedule.

Moomy's words: *you use your prayer like a crutch. Like most people use alcohol and drugs.* Always that accusation, this was just a thing, a phase, something she would get over when she realised it was replacing one dependency with another.

Though this one had fewer side-effects. Bar the tiredness. Then again all dedicated officers had that problem. She was no different.

Usually, she and Moomy worked separately, their cases sometimes intertwining. It had been good working closely with her. Sarah knew she was using Moomy as a Rachel replacement, playing older sister to the girl who had lost her way. And Sarah knew Moomy was alone in ways that only those who had been cut off from their families could be. Sarah tried to be a kind of family to her in return.

It worked. For both of them.

Sarah running towards a world Moomy had run from.

One day, maybe they would reach a crossing point, where they could no longer run the same lane. For now, they were okay.

-

Scott was still playing politics, trying to manage the situation. He had made a polite phone call to John Hayat, asked him to bring his son Oscar to the police station. John had, of course, kicked off, slammed down the phone, called Jane Haslam, called his contacts at No. 10. None of them answered the phone. Things had shifted a gear. Scott had an official warrant signed off, and it had to be enacted. Nobody wanted to get their hands soiled by what was heading John's way. Scott gave him thirty minutes to realise his friends had abandoned him, called John again, told him by law they needed Oscar in the station for questioning. He needed to give access to his bank accounts and phone records willingly. They could do this in a low-key, civilised manner. Or do it with a press orchestra for company.

By 9.30 a.m. Oscar had arrived at the station. His lawyer was with him. No sign of John.

Sarah showed Oscar and his lawyer into a waiting room. The lawyer seemed to be old school, probably one of Lara's family friends, all steel hair and steel eyes.

Tailored suit, handkerchief in pocket, tie pin, waistcoat. You could tell the type. Max Stevenson. He looked like an undertaker more than a brief. She knew not to under-estimate him though; John's money would buy the best. The quiet ones who kept their clients quiet as well. The evidence had to be strong. Sarah knew hers wasn't, she was hoping Romesh would back it up with something he might find. She knew Oscar was too clever to leave a paper trail, but Romesh would find one even if it was well hidden.

'Oscar, we spoke yesterday. And as part of the interview you seemed to recall an incident that had taken place in Istanbul. When you and your wife landed, the day on which your driver was shot dead and you and your wife disappeared. Prior to this point you had claimed that you had no recall of events after the day of your wedding to Millie Beaumont. Yet this event happened some days later when you were on honeymoon. Can you explain the discrepancy?'

Oscar stoic, no comments. Nothing at all. Just tension on his face. Like he was trapped into coming. His father probably forcing him to be here.

'I believe this perfect recall of what you were both feeling at the time, suggests that your memory loss is not real. I have spoken to Doctor Farah Naz, do you remember her? She gave you a psych evaluation the day you came home?'

No acknowledgment of the question.

'She thinks the recall is evidence that she would testify to in a court of law that suggests you are deliberately withholding details of where you were this past week. The week in which you and your wife disappeared. A week in which she was brutally murdered.'

Sarah placed photos of Millie's dead body on the table between them. She then took out photos of Paul and Luciano.

'This man on the left is your best friend, Paul Chandran. The man on the right is an escort who calls himself Luciano. He has testified to the fact that you and Paul met on two occasions in order to have sadomasochistic sex that included verbal humiliation using racist and foul language.'

He was clenching his jaw, his eyes were giving away his embarrassment. Stevenson was his father's friend, probably friends with their entire circle. Sarah was exposing Oscar's secrets to him. Stevenson didn't seem too bothered though. Maybe he had been briefed already?

'I believe you married Mille Beaumont in order to hide this secret life. Furthermore we have evidence of money being transferred to her account from your mother. Sums of money to act as bribes to keep her from marrying you.'

Sarah put copies of bank statements on the table, her fingers jabbing at the offending transfers into Millie's account.

'When she failed to do this, your mother disclosed this fact to you. I believe you struck a deal with Millie, to stay married to you, as long as she accepted the life you were leading. When she refused, you planned to kill her as the only way out of this.'

She felt her breath quicken; she was speaking way too fast. She stayed quiet for a couple of minutes. Neither Oscar nor his lawyer felt the need to fill in the silence.

'I believe you smuggled your way into this country, with Millie, from Istanbul after staging a kidnapping in which your driver was killed as collateral damage. When you arrived back in London, by means which we will discover, Millie was killed at your request. When you felt safe enough to do so, you came back to your family home, feigning memory loss.'

Oscar was like stone. Nothing moved, he blinked, he didn't fidget, he swallowed, the nervous ticks in his face had settled. His hands were clasped tightly in his lap. Stevenson stared at Sarah. Not intimidating, not angry, almost curious.

'Do you have anything at all to say?'

Oscar didn't reply.

–

Disaster. Fucking disaster. What the hell. Sarah was just telling him everything they knew, everything he knew. Had to get it on official record, Moomy knew. Still. There was nothing: no hammy confession or breakdown. Just silence.

She was watching and listening on her phone, video transmitting live from the interview room. She was with Romesh. Did he sleep there? He was rifling through Oscar's financial history, phone history, Internet history. Blank, blank, blank. The guy was clean. Too clean.

'Shite,' she said. 'What about CCTV, anything at all? This guy did not just teleport outside his family home like Harry bleeding Potter, okay. He physically had to get there.'

'I'm checking but the CCTV angles down that street really don't show the traffic that well. There are too many vehicles, none of the ones on surrounding roads have hit anything suspicious. Seriously, Moomy, I can't find it, how he got home.'

'There needs to be something, there has to be. Show me all the vehicles that were on any of the surrounding roads at the time Oscar came home.'

Moomy got sent a file in three minutes by Romesh. She saw the density of the traffic. It was horrendous even at that time around there. Too many cars speeding around those roads. They could all have stashed Oscar in them.

'No links to Michaelides?'

'Nope. We checked every licence plate. Nothing related to the Hayats or any of his cronies.'

'Maybe he got an Uber? Or a normal cab?'

'Uber would show on his finances.'

She listened again to Sarah repeating the evidence she had against Oscar. Hoping he would grow tired and irritated and say something to give himself away. Nothing. And Moomy had failed her. She hadn't got anything to deliver back to her, to help her.

'You've checked anyone connected to Paul as well?'

'Yep. Nothing. Checked all his friends, family, the lot.'

Moomy hated this: when they thought they had found the answers, and they opened the back of the truck, only to reveal it didn't contain anything illegal after all. Just empty space and dust.

She jumped as Romesh swore. 'What?'

'Look at this.'

Moomy stared, not registering, then registering.

'You have got to be kidding me,' she said.

Chapter Fifty-Two

Victor stared out at the view. Canary Wharf. Like some tech city from the future. Fright lights and glass windows, reflections of darkness and greed. His world. He had the knack for this. The real heir to the throne. And now, it was in sight, in touching distance. He had won.

He picked up his phone. Dialled. Spoke quickly but softly.

'It's done.'

He stared again out of his windows. His view. His future.

It hadn't been easy to achieve, and even now he felt torn about the results and the sacrifices. Yet he knew that he had done the right thing. He had stepped up and proved himself. The legacy of the Wickhams and the Hayats was safe at last. In his hands.

Victor pulled the piece of paper from his desk drawer again. His fingers tracing the words, the signature of his parents. The document that made him first choice, first preference. That put him ahead of Oscar and Spencer.

Yes, he had played dirty, then again he had the mental strength to do that. And that's what winning should be about; being the best. Not some retarded inheritance idea. Well, he hadn't let that happen. He had done it his own way.

He thought of Oscar stewing in some prison interview room. His sordid sexual history being paraded before everyone. His poor parents. The look on their faces. Then he had played videos of Spencer snorting everything under the tables of every club in London. The hookers, the drunken rants. Especially the rants in which he claimed he wanted Oscar dead and hated his father. One rant he had even slated their mother, his biggest ally. She would forgive him, his father wouldn't. So Victor had acted, quickly and decisively. Before it was too late, used his father's anger to rewrite their company's future.

Poor John Hayat. Looking around the room his father had been left with one choice. The youngest choice. Victor.

–

Lara hadn't moved since John had left with Victor. Staring ahead. Spencer sat curled up in the sofa opposite her. He had no words of his own. What was he meant to say?

Lara's tears crawled down her cheeks.

Spencer started to tremble. Was he craving something, he wondered? Had he become so addicted he couldn't even go a few hours now? It was the strain, he knew. Victor. Fucking arsehole. Played a blinder, he had to give him that. Desperate for it all. He hoped he rotted along with his wealth. Ended up lonely and pathetic and ruined.

And what would happen to them? Maybe there was a way to fight it? No. Victor was too clever for that. Nothing would change.

The clock marked off time. Its chimes ringing through his mother, her very core shaking. She closed her eyes and reached for her phone.

John stood on Waterloo Bridge. His favourite. Westminster, Canary Wharf, St Paul's. The old and the new, all visible to him. He dragged on his cigar, taking it in deeply. In his left hand, his favourite drink in a tumbler. Ari had parked off the bridge, waiting for him. Not knowing his task for John. His final task.

John gulped back the liquid. This was it. Cigar, burning alcohol in the throat, London in his view.

He had gambled and he had lost. He thought of Oscar. How he had played him, played them all in a way. Ruined them. The shame of it. And Spencer. The product of Lara's mismanagement. Her indulgence for her golden boy. The prettiest of her sons; the one who resembled her and her Aryan-looking friends the most. He was not worthy of being John's heir.

And then Victor. Sly, determined, dishonourable Victor. The worst in some sense. The best in others. John had chosen. He had a vision and he knew Victor would at least see it through.

He finished his cigar, put it out into the empty glass and made his way to the waiting Mercedes.

'Where to?' Ari said.

John told him; Ari didn't question it. If only he knew, John thought. If only he knew.

Chapter Fifty-Three

Sarah looked at their faces.

'I don't understand this, Romesh.'

His hands moved across his touchscreens, pulling images into her view. Stacked up against each other, a story unfolding before her eyes.

'Who is that?' she whispered.

'This is Rupert Cooper. He was a playboy and showjumper back in the eighties. Not a household name, but from one of those old English families. Country estate, crumbling by the time he inherited it, devoted his life to his horses and animals.'

Sarah stared at the image before her. The resemblance was remarkable.

'Where are these pictures from?'

'*Hello!* and *Tatler* mainly, some from *Horse & Hound*. All online now. I'm telling you this new store we have for us has the best search algies on it. Any press clipping going back to when the Victorians kicked it all off, it's all so easy now.'

Sarah studied the pictures. Rupert looking posh, spoilt, impeccable, devastating. Any woman would have fallen for him..

Romesh swiped the images in front of her, different women. And then one woman. Constantly by his side, at different events. Charity galas, show jumping meets, the Olympics. Arm in arm. The golden couple. They cut a handsome pairing with their matching blond hair and blue eyes. So carefree, so in love. It looked obvious.

Sarah stared at the conclusions that had been formed in Moomy's and Romesh's eyes.

'Come on, guys, it doesn't mean anything. Not really. It was thirty years ago.'

'And yet the result of that time is still with us?'

Sarah looked at Moomy. She couldn't let them run away with this theory. But what they were saying was true. Rupert Cooper and Lara Wickham. The hot couple in their social circle. Destined to be together. Until her family had stepped in and forced her to marry into the Hayat fortune. Yet the resemblance between Rupert and Spencer was incredible.

'Spencer was born a couple of years after the Hayats came back to London,' Romesh added.

'She must have shacked up with her ex,' said Moomy. 'Dirty mare.'

Romesh sniggered at the equine reference.

'So, you're saying that Lara had Millie killed and Oscar kidnapped because she wanted Spencer to inherit everything? The son she had as a supposed result of her affair with the man she really loved? Come on both of you. How did she do it? Why would she? No mother would choose between her children like that. Where is Rupert now?'

'That's just it, he died. Last year in a freak horse-riding accident.'

'He never married or had kids,' Moomy added. 'Maybe Spencer was his: the only one?'

'You're just conjecturing now. Scott would kill us if he could hear us. We base evidence on DNA not facial characteristics. That's what eugenics was based on and look what happened there.'

She couldn't let them sway her, not just by a shallow resemblance. Okay a strong resemblance, but still. Oscar was here and the fake amnesia was a real indication that he was behind this. Not some far-fetched notion about Lara Hayat and an ex-lover who might be the reason for her harming her own children.

She wouldn't do that. Maybe to Millie, but not to her own children. Sarah had seen how cut up she was over Oscar's disappearance, when she thought he might have come to harm. And how would Lara even know how to arrange something as messed up as this? It didn't sit with her precious princess nature.

'We need to pursue Oscar Hayat, not this,' Sarah said.

'Listen, that's not all,' said Romesh. 'I think this is an endgame. I picked up some movement. John Hayat is heading off to Higham Airbase. I've been monitoring private jet information.'

'That doesn't make any sense. His son is in custody.'

'Yes, and we're perfectly placed to ask him exactly what the fuck is up with this family. Millie is dead, John is about to leave the country, Oscar gave himself up for questioning even though he claims he's lost his memory. And we think Lara is protecting the last memory of her ex-lover I'm telling you, rich people are fucked up.'

-

He planned it meticulously. He had taken a snapshot of the car as soon as he had his wits about him. His dashcam, which took the picture without any interference from the lights of the vehicle. He knew the number plate, the car that had taken Millie. He knew it by heart now, he had stared so many times at it. Waiting and deciding. What was the right thing to do? There was always only one thing. But how could he do it without exposing himself?

Truth was he still needed the cash. He still needed to do the drop offs and the pick-ups. So he was going to use an old telephone box he had spotted on his travels. Those random empty roads. He would call, and it would be anonymous and it would all be okay. He would absolve himself of this.

The police needed to know. Millie needed justice. He had unwittingly led her to her death, and now it was time to make people pay.

–

The traffic was on their side, as they sped through the London streets towards Higham Airbase. Sarah knew the way but she let Moomy drive, aware that in this state, at this stage, it was better Moomy was kept busy.

Back at base she knew Scott was about to get bollocked by Jane Haslam and possibly even Jane's boss. But Scott had nerves of steel, he could hack a telling off. Especially if Sarah and Moomy managed to get him an explanation about exactly what had happened.

'Look, I know you think there's nothing to this Rupert angle, but I think there is. Imagine if there is one son you love the most because he reminds you of the love of your life. Because he is the last piece of that sacred history. Wouldn't you do anything to protect him?'

Sarah didn't respond.

'And imagine if Oscar and Millie had had children. The money would have ended up there, not to her beloved Spencer. This way she gets rid of Millie, so no baby mama, and also damages Oscar in such a way that he can no longer function enough to run the family business. Too far-fetched?'

'Yes. And no. Because people do all sorts of random things when they're in love.'

'How would you know? Who've you been in love with?'

Sarah just smiled and looked out of the window.

–

Rob Thorp greeted Sarah and Moomy outside the perimeter fence of Higham Airbase. They didn't want to give the game away. A fleet of police cars were parked up behind scrubland, not visible from the runway. It would take officers just minutes to get to where they were needed.

'What's their status?' Sarah asked Rob. He nodded at Sarah, looked at Moomy suspiciously. The above-the-knee dress and boots always did make people question her abilities. Result achieved as far as Moomy was concerned.

'They've boarded. No problems. As you asked, I simply checked their documents and wished them a pleasant flight.'

'And the runway?'

'The decoy plane is on the runway as you asked. The pilot is waiting for take-off. And the emergency ambulance you ordered is parked up next to it.'

'How long have they been waiting?'

'It's been about forty minutes now.'

'Okay. Any longer and I think they might start to get suspicious.'

'I doubt it. We normally have multiple flights every day, especially at busy times. These private jet users are used to it.'

Sarah hoped the façade was working.

'Okay, let's go,' she said to Moomy.

The two women headed off on foot through the perimeter fencing and onto the airbase. The sun was bright, hurting their eyes. Moomy took out shades, Sarah just used her hand. They came up to the parked jet from behind the tail, walking under its body, and then round the side to the aircraft door. Rob released the stairs of the jet for them.

Sarah rushed up, Moomy waiting on the tarmac. They weren't armed. Sarah was confident they wouldn't need to be, that they wouldn't be faced with guns.

She was wrong.

John Hayat sat holding a Glock, pointed directly at her.

Chapter Fifty-Four

Sarah took a seat opposite John. She wasn't betraying how nervous she felt, facing this man with determination. Playing out the final acts of something she didn't understand. She had pressed the emergency on her phone already. Everything they said would be broadcast to Moomy outside; meaning, hopefully, she could get some help and end this.

'I need to take off,' he said. 'Please.'

Sarah stared at him. Pulling a gun on an officer was not going to get you clearance to go anywhere.

'You have the gun, John, you get to make the decisions.'

'It's got to be done. If I don't leave now, it will all be over. For all of us.'

'You're not making sense, John.'

He looked up at her, as though surprised she was there. Lost and unfocussed. Then snapping back, he seemed to grip the gun harder.

'If I don't go, everyone dies. What happened to Millie happens to Oscar, to Victor and Spencer. One by one they all die.'

'Why?' Sarah said.

'Revenge.'

'Is this related to Dimitri Popov?'

John nodded, the gun shaking in his hands.

'I thought I could handle that situation. It would be war, yes, but it would be dealt with. I have my ways.' Ari, she thought. 'But this has become something else. This is something only I can do. I must pay for my sins, detective.'

'Whatever you think you have to do, John, let's just relax, put the gun down and talk about this. There are always other ways. If you explain to me what happened, we can discuss it.'

'There is nothing to discuss. I have tried everything to save my family and my money. Now I must go and not look back.'

'John, let me help you. Please.'

'Millie was killed on your streets, detective. They took her from another country and they brought her into your city and they killed her. You didn't protect her. How will you protect me or anybody else?'

'That was different. We didn't know who we were dealing with or that she needed saving. If you're honest with me now, we can make sure that you are protected, John.'

He had tears in his eyes when he spoke, his voice thick with passion and grief.

'The men who took them, they released Oscar only because they wanted me in return.'

'Which men?'

'I'm not sure. They are Russian, I can tell you this much. Which means they are related to Popov. How, I don't know. But they are. If I don't go, everyone dies, just like Millie did.'

-

Moomy felt the adrenaline burning through her. She wanted to get out of there, knock some heads around. She didn't dare though. Keeping the plane in her line of vision meant Sarah was still on British soil and there was still a chance all of this would end up okay. It had to. She was trying to co-ordinate the officers on the ground, all of them shouting and asking for instructions. She didn't ever think she would be glad to see Scott turn up. He organised the Met presence, set up armed officers in a perimeter around the plane, got a negotiating team onsite. Someone had clamped a giant yellow metal block onto the plane wheel, so it wouldn't be able to move and take off. Scott had also brought Oscar with him.

Moomy was in Rob Thorp's office with Oscar and his lawyer. Stevenson looked as though he was enjoying his day out of a stuffy office.

Moomy sat across from Oscar asking him for an explanation.

'This is a mess now,' Moomy told him. 'Whatever your father planned, whatever scheme he was going to pull off, none of it is going to happen. Do you understand that? What I need from you, now, is the truth. Why exactly is your father leaving?'

Oscar looked at her, unsure, but he no longer seemed to be the closed book he had been at the station. Seeing the plane and the armed officers surrounding it, he probably realised shit had hit the fan. It was time to give up and stop his foolish act. But he was clinging on to something, unsure, a script he had been told to follow.

'Oscar. Your wife died horribly. The men we think did it are about to take your father. What the hell happened?'

'Please,' Oscar said, his voice hoarse and as if in pain. 'I can't do it. Let it be, let him go.'

'Go where, Oscar?'

'Wherever he has to.'

'He has to? Why does he have to do anything?'

'Don't you see? He doesn't have a choice. He needs to go. If he doesn't, then...'

'Then what? Oscar tell me. Dammit tell me, my colleague is on that plane with a gun pointed at her head. Who killed Millie?'

Oscar clamped down.

'Oscar I will not let Sarah die. None of us will. If she doesn't get off that plane your father is likely to die here too. So whatever he was going to do, it won't happen.'

This scared him. He looked up at her, panicked. *Yes, dickhead, that's rattled you.*

'So, why don't you quit the games and the act, and tell me what the fuck happened to you and Millie so I can stop this blowing up in everyone's face.'

Oscar looked over at Stevenson. The man seemed passive. Oscar looked at Moomy, weighing up the situation.

He banged his head on the table in frustration, groaned like an animal, then started talking. Telling her exactly what had happened to him and Millie and why John Hayat, his father, was willing to be kidnapped and taken abroad.

Scott listened to Moomy without his usual judgement and condescension. She had just got him an important part of the puzzle.

'Oscar and Millie were captured by masked men on their way to the villa in Istanbul. We know those men shot the driver. They were just thugs for hire, Oscar said, local Turkish men. They handed Millie and Oscar over to another set of men. These ones seemed more organised, Oscar said. Their clothes, weapons, vehicles. All very polished. Hired guns, he's thinking. They drove Millie and Oscar for hours, he said, maybe half a day; he's not sure. He said they were then held in some outhouse, where Millie was tortured in front of him. He said he didn't understand what they wanted; he kept begging them to stop, told them he would pay them whatever they wanted. They filmed what they did. What happened to that film… he guessed it was sent to his father.'

'Here in London? With a request for what? Money?'

'No, Oscar doesn't think so. He said after a few days they were then taken to another location. Both of them were sedated. That was how they got into London. He remembers waking up in some type of holding cell. No windows, one light. They were held separately, he and Millie. He doesn't remember how long he was kept there, but after a few days, he thinks, they released him. They put a bag over his head and took him home.'

'Just like that?'

'Yes.'

'So, why didn't he call the police and tell them all this? Why didn't he tell us when we were questioning him? Why lie?'

'He says it was his father's request. They had told Oscar about Millie having been killed, and told him that unless he complied with the silence they needed, the rest of his family would end up like that. There was no protection.

So his father asked him to feign the memory loss. Before his brothers arrived, or their medical doctor, or our team.'

'And he went along with it?'

'He'd just been through a pretty horrendous ordeal. I think he was ready to go along with anything his father asked if it meant it was over.'

Scott looked at her carefully, evaluating all the information.

'What are you thinking?' he said.

'Someone hatched this plot against John. That Oscar was taken as a threat; Millie was killed to show John what would happen to his child unless he agreed to pay up. I think John probably has to physically be there to do some sort of weird money transfer thing; that's why he needs to go.'

'So, what now? Oscar has no idea what his father was doing?'

'No.'

Moomy breathed out in frustration. Sarah was on that plane. She felt like rushing it and rescuing her, even if she got shot doing it.

Chapter Fifty-Five

Sarah stayed as calm as she could. John looked at her, unsure of what to do. Her phone wasn't close, but she knew her voice was being carried. She and John had been through enough today, this week. He seemed resigned though; more tired than he had been since she had met him. This man who had battled the odds to build himself a future. And then risked it all to pay a price to protect his loved ones.

'Tell me, John. It's time for the truth. So that I can help you.'

He took a long sip from a cup that held black coffee. Sarah hated the taste so had never become addicted, unlike so many others in her profession who seemed to thrive on it.

'They are clever, these people. Whoever they are. They did not call or write. No threats or demands for a ransom. They sent Millie as a warning, of what they could do.'

Sarah felt a gut punch. Millie, a life wasted and for what? To scare the Hayats?

'They then sent Oscar. He was allowed to leave and return home so that I could go in his place. A message he delivered.'

'Go where?'

'I don't know. I am to go to Istanbul and from there…
I put all of my world in order. I rewrote my will. Victor
is now to take over the company. After Lara, of course.'

A jolt.

'Lara's now head of the business?'

'Yes. You know how hard it was for me to build all of
this? The things that I had to do?'

Sarah knew the official version, the one he had already
told her.

'My parents were doctors, in Iraq. That is all true. They
were also opponents of Saddam Hussein. They saw his
genocide and his oppression and they made a choice. They
became spies, hoping that they could help bring down his
government. They reported back to the CIA on Saddam's
activities, locations of his troops, the Republican Guards,
and his armaments. It wasn't a successful ruse though.
They were captured and killed.'

Sarah could imagine what that would do to someone
like John. A young man losing his parents. What sort of
thirst for revenge it would give him.

'I went crazy after their death. By then I had already
built my business, a fast food and supermarket empire
across America, I had met and married Lara. I had the
American dream, still it meant nothing. I had begged my
parents to leave and come live with me when I first made it
to America. They refused. Said their fates were written in
Iraq and they would not abandon their people. When the
First Gulf War started, I decided it was time for revenge.
I went back and I spied for the CIA. Giving them vital
intel on what was happening on the ground.'

'And in return?'

'In return I was given insider knowledge that helped launch my gas and steel business.'

'Sounds perfect,' Sarah said, hoping she didn't sound sarcastic. She had a difficult relationship with spies. She knew the value they provided, and how important they were. Yet she didn't know how she felt about assets that betrayed their own nations.

'It was. Except, that bastard was still in power and I wanted revenge for the death of my parents. But life goes on. Then the Second Gulf War began. And there was my chance. Once again I headed back to Iraq and once again gave vital intelligence to the CIA. This time Saddam fell and finally I felt that my parents' deaths were dealt with. That I had the vengeance that I needed.'

John was sweating, desperately trying to get his story out. A truth hidden for so long that he needed to exorcise it from himself.

'I thought then it was all over. My children were growing up, Lara and I had everything. Nothing could touch me. And then things went very wrong very quickly after Oscar disappeared.'

'John, I understand the pressure, but unless we know who these men are we can't help you.'

'That is it, detective, there is nothing to tell. Oscar barely remembers who they are. He is their only calling card. They are invisible. But if I don't go then what happens to my family?'

Sarah offered him assurances of protection, but this was beyond anything even she had come across in her twenty odd years of police work. The important thing now was to get John off the plane and try to make sense of what had happened to Oscar. And to Millie.

Chapter Fifty-Six

There was an anticlimactic feeling in the room. They had stopped John from leaving; Turkish police had been informed about his rendezvous. Oscar had been out of it, drugged, he didn't remember much about the Turkey ordeal.

'So what now?' said Moomy. 'Millie is still dead. Do you think they're all just bullshitting? That this really never happened in the first place? I mean it's so far-fetched. Maybe John was playing a part to save Oscar? Maybe he really was behind all of this?'

The theories and possibilities were numerous, but Moomy did have a point. There was, in the end, only Oscar's word that he had been kidnapped with Millie, that he had been drugged and then dropped off at home with a message for his father. John Hayat was to willingly, secretly, give himself up to save his family.

'The people behind it are clever though. Using humans as their messengers. They don't trust the tech. Everything can be traced, so they use assets that can't be traced easily.'

Moomy seemed to be dejected. Scott was less so.

'I'm guessing the Foreign Secretary is off your case now?' Sarah said, sounding more acidic than she wanted.

He grunted in response. It was true, it just didn't matter anymore. Jane Haslam was only interested in herself and her own spin and lies. She had saved the Hayats from a public scandal, that's all she cared about. And Millie?

Sarah remembered seeing Millie on Hampstead Heath. Dead. Cold. Gone. It was not right and it felt worse that it was on her watch that Millie wouldn't get the justice she deserved. She would not let this be a cold case; she was determined to find out what happened to Millie. The only issue she had was there was nowhere to go now. They had run out of options. John pointed the finger at Dimitri Popov, even though Ari claimed that Popov's entire network had gone down. So who was left to exact revenge on his behalf? It didn't make sense.

International gangsters and international kidnappings and people trafficking. It seemed too big for her and this room. That on the streets of a city she loved and worked in, someone could lose their life and there would be no comeback.

'I think you should both go home, have a break,' Scott said. 'There isn't much to do for now.'

'There are still a few threads left,' Sarah said. 'We had so many tip-offs after Bill's public interview. I think we should follow those through.'

'Please, mostly from weirdos and trolls with nothing better to do. The same sort of twunts that mouth off on Twitter and Facebook from their armchairs.'

'Maybe, but I'm not ready to give up,' said Sarah.

'For today, it's done. That's an order.' Scott didn't seem to convey any force behind the order, but still, Sarah could do with a break. Maybe it would give some kind of clarity.

Chapter Fifty-Seven

She was hoping Ari wouldn't be at home. He was, though, and she was seated in his lounge drinking tea within minutes. She wasn't in the mood, it just meant it gave her some time to clear her head before she had to speak to him.

'How is John?' she asked.

'Tired. He was given some tablets by the medics to help him rest. I've sat down with him and arranged a security detail, how we are going to protect him and his family.'

'It is just so odd. The sort of revenge that has been taken against John. I mean that takes passion. It's not something random, it's been meticulously planned.'

'And that doesn't sit well with you?'

'No. Because I am sure that the network Popov ran doesn't have the organisational skills left. More than that, it doesn't have the people left that would hate John and his family enough to carry out this action.'

Sarah understood what he was saying. She had been thinking the same all day. Still, that wasn't why she was here. She looked at him expectantly, hoping he would sense what she wanted.

'And you?' he said at last. 'What now?'

'That's why I'm here. I need your help.'

Ari stretched on the sofa next to her. His body lithe and muscular. He looked at her, considering.

'Sarah, please.'

'I said when this was over that I would find her. I just think having you with me will be better than going it alone.'

'Okay. If you insist. But we plan this properly and we do it when I say it is okay. When I know where Rachel is for sure. Is that a deal?'

'Yes,' she said.

He was right; she couldn't go out there blind. Ari would make sure it was as painless as possible. Painless. It was unlikely to be that.

'Thank you,' she added. 'But please, Ari, I need to go quickly. I don't want it to be too late.'

'I will try.'

They sat in silence before she got up to leave.

'What about us?' he said softly.

'Not now,' she said. 'Probably not ever. Does that change things? Will you still help me?'

'Of course. What do you think I am?'

'Good night, Ari,' she said. 'I need to go and pray.'

'Well, that's a first in terms of excuses girls have made,' he said, laughing as she left him.

—

Sarah had prayed, was in bed, unable to sleep when the doorbell rang. It was Moomy.

'I thought you had a hot date?' she said, as Moomy walked in without apology.

'I did. I just, well, I got used to sleeping here. Also, I think staying the night with someone so soon sends the wrong message.'

Moomy made up the sofa bed, and crashed out soon enough. Sarah sat in the sofa chair, dozing. It was funny; the wide-awake feeling had seemed to ease with Moomy there.

'I don't know,' Moomy said looking at Sarah. 'It feels like we haven't really caught who did it. I mean the person that put the gun to Millie's head. That sort of ending.'

'Yes. I know what you mean. That's our world though. That's life though. Nothing really ends.'

'You sound like *The Lion King*. Get a grip, mate.'

They lay in silence for a while.

'John's probably going to worry for the rest of his life,' Moomy said quietly.

'Yes. We all have our demons though. Not much we can do about it, except learn to live with them. And, you know, lots of the time you realise that what you feared the most isn't quite as bad as you first thought.'

'Lecture much, it's the middle of the night. Keep that shite to yourself.'

'Sorry.'

'It's okay. Glad you care.'

'I wouldn't go that far. Anyway get some sleep. Tomorrow there will be a whole load of new crap to deal with.'

Sarah knew her own peace was going to be short-lived.

Chapter Fifty-Eight

Moomy wasn't ready to give up. No way. Bill deserved closure. So she was doing what she never did. She was trawling through the crazies list. You always got them in any investigation, especially when you made a public appeal for information. This ranged from Millie being some sort of teleporting savant, seen all over the country, doing everything from Elvis impersonations to having possessed someone's cat. Allow that shit. People really were trolls. And social media had just given a free pass to people who should have Internet ASBOs as far as she was concerned.

It took Moomy three days of nonsense and false leads. Then finally, she had something more than just a crackpot and their hunch. She had a lead that felt real.

Moomy played back the voice message. It was a man who was covering the phone mouthpiece and it wasn't very clear what he was saying.

'The girl, Millie Beaumont. I know who took her. It was two blokes, they had accents sounded, you know, East European, maybe Russian. I can't say for sure.'

At first she thought it was just a Brexit nutjob, blame everything on the East Europeans and get us out of Europe.

'*They took her in a car.*' He gave the registration. And that was the interesting bit. He slowed down and carefully read out the registration number. Twice. As though they needed to get that if nothing else. And that was it. The call ended.

Moomy felt disconcerted. She played the message again. No details of where it had happened or by who. It was possible that it was someone trying to get revenge or set up an enemy. Or there might be something else to it. She had followed enough dead ends already, so why not this one? Luckily for her the admin team had sifted through a number of tip-offs already. She had about thirty that they thought might be worth following up. And this was one of those.

Romesh was at his screens, working on other cases.

'That's what happens when you're too good at what you do,' Moomy said. 'Take a leaf out of my book and take the piss, no one bothers you much.'

'I wish I could but it's like an addiction, my hands start itching if I'm not at a computer screen trying to work something out.'

'Yeah, well we all have our demons.' She had spent enough time with hers. Maybe that was it. She wanted to help Bill because her own memories had reminded her just how bad some people were to their kids. And she had seen even worse during her time with the popo. So when there was a blameless man whose life had basically gone to shit, she felt as though he deserved some sort of closure. And she was the one who would give him that.

'I'm in the middle of something, though, so whatever it is, it will have to wait.'

Moomy glared at him.

'Listen, brown boy, don't give me that attitude. Look around here, I mess up and they will never give an Asian girl a job again. So you better help me for the cause, okay?'

He just laughed at her.

'The cause with you is always Moomy.'

'Come on, Romesh, this is easy stuff. Car reg.'

'Why don't you run it?'

'Because you will not only get me the who but there might be follow-up questions I have. And if it's of any interest I need you to start attaching your algies to it. Let them grow. See, I do pay attention.'

Lies. Sarah had explained how Romesh saw algorithms in his mind. Like little creatures he had nurtured, used to attach and feed off little bits of information to grab more information until they were monstrous and had everything you wanted to know. He really did need to go and see his girlfriend.

'What is it?' Moomy asked, seeing the change in his demeanour.

Romesh had already tapped the registration into his keyboard and started a run. Within seconds he had a name. And then in a few more seconds he had a file.

–

It had only been three days since they had been at Higham Airbase and yet it had felt like weeks. In that time they had been tying up the Hayat case, trying to close it down. Sarah felt empty inside, typing away, trying to make sense of her notes. This was always the bit she enjoyed the least, the note writing. Words on paper to try and make sense of a life.

Then Moomy turned up. Practically bore down in Sarah's face. There was energy coming off her, excitement in her eyes. Sarah sat up, nothing other than men or drink got Moomy this animated.

'What's going on?' Sarah asked.

'Listen, I know my last hunch with the Michaelides was a bit of a mishap. But check this out. We had a tip-off.'

'We had hundreds.'

'Yes, and the team have sifted through them. They sent me about twenty strong leads and that's what I've been working on over the last three days. Just following up, seeing if there is anything that might help.'

'What, even the one that said they saw Millie up in Scotland? After she was dead?'

'Well, you're the one that believes in life after death.'

'So, anything of interest?'

'Yes. We had a tip-off, made from some out of the way phone booth apparently, so you know, not easy to trace. That's what got me interested in the first place. Anyway, this call said that Millie was taken by two men, with accents. It was the night before she was killed.'

'Sounds a bit vague?'

'No, it's more than that. The caller gave us number plates for this car.'

Sarah sat up in her chair, interested.

'I ran a check. And they come back to Arkady Dohan.'

The name meant nothing to Sarah.

'Romesh ran his magic and he got me some more details. Arkady is an Albanian national, came here years ago, settled. Never been arrested, married with kids.'

'So this is interesting to us how?'

'It's because of who he works for.'

'What do you mean?'

'He works for a man called Leo Salter.'

'Again, means nothing to me.'

Moomy put the printout down on Sarah's desk. Leo Salter was an oligarch from one of the former Soviet republics. He had holdings in Azerbaijan and Georgia mainly, dealing in natural gas and oil. He wasn't Abramovich wealthy, but he had money. Lots of it. The sort of man who came to London to hide his wealth from Putin. Wealth that wasn't necessarily clean and so could be hidden in assets across the capital. But Salter didn't have a criminal record and was one of many mid-level rich guys from that part of the world who had made London their home. Sure Oscar claimed he was held by Russians, but really, did Oscar even know any Russian to corroborate this?

'Are we going to just arrest every Russian in London?' Sarah said. 'I'm not seeing the bigger picture yet.'

Moomy asked Sarah to turn the paper over. Sarah scanned the sheet. And there it was. Something at least. The key piece of information that explained why it seemed Moomy was ready to explode.

Chapter Fifty-Nine

Victor sat at his desk, anger like acid in his veins. How had this happened? One moment he was at the very top, everything he had ever wanted his. And the next, it had all gone the other way. When John had left in some sort of reverse sacrifice, he had made Victor his heir. But that hadn't lasted. As soon as John had left the townhouse, his mother had stepped in. John had left her in charge until her death. Which also meant she had the power to change his will. Why did John believe that his self-serving wife would ever be suitable to head up the company?

Victor took a paperweight from his desk and slammed it at his office door. Neither damaged. Only him.

His mother had contacted the lawyers and had them create a new edict. One which saw Spencer as the one to inherit everything. Why not Oscar? Because he had been through enough and he was too damaged. Why not Victor? Because Spencer was older. Sure, he had made some mistakes, and the videos were not pleasant viewing. But forget all of that. *It's in the past, we can make sure he will be okay. And I don't believe in your father's nonsense. While he was here he got his own way, but he's not here now. So it's a different future for all of us. I'm not going to just give you a token.*

So what did he have? They gave him a couple of smaller freeholdings, companies that dealt in logistics and provided consultancy to other businesses. Soft stuff. Not the actual wealth that comes out of the ground that made the Hayats rich. A few properties as well, but not the key, expensive stuff that made the Wickhams a powerful force in the capital. Still, at least it wasn't just shares and money. His mother didn't see the business as some sort of title that couldn't be split up. She had divided it.

Given most of it to Spencer. Some to him. And Oscar? She gave him the money, told him to live his life. Victor didn't care though, one less asshole to get in his way.

John couldn't believe what his wife had done in just hours. He was livid. That was worth watching, at least. Only, then she took him to their bedroom. And when he came back he agreed. Oscar was too fragile, been through too much. Spencer was the next in line.

Victor felt his world crumble. Everything he wanted and everything he believed in and had worked for. All of it just gone. Millie died for nothing. Oscar was taken for nothing. None of it mattered any more, because it didn't change anything for him or his family.

The anger took hold of him again and he wanted to break something. Or someone.

–

They were in Scott's office. It was late and they were all tired. But the most pressing thing was to find who had killed Millie and who had held Oscar in London.

'So, we think we've found what we're looking for,' Sarah said. 'We tracked down the vehicle that belongs to Arkady, the one the tip-off said took Millie. From where she was taken we still don't know. The car's been cleaned thoroughly, no surprises. We didn't bring it in, though, and we haven't approached Arkady yet. We don't want to scare him or have him send warning signals through the chain.'

Moomy was feeling energised. She had thought that whole exercise was a waste of time, looking through the tip-offs, but it had led them here. They were looking at a possible breakthrough. Sarah just had to convince Scott one more time.

'We tracked the car's movements as much as we could. It doesn't really hit CCTV or traffic monitoring cams until the day of Millie's death. But even then it's innocuous and goes nowhere near Hampstead Heath.'

'Why are we discussing it then?' said Scott.

'Because the car crossed paths with another vehicle the night of Millie's death. Arkady met someone at about 3 a.m. that night. It was just a brief meeting, but both vehicles were seen in Seven Sisters. They parked up outside a snooker hall that's frequented by guys with nothing better to do. It's not even a real snooker hall by all accounts, more a networking hub.'

'Probably full of police informants, which is why it's still open,' Moomy said.

'We have the two men on CCTV,' Sarah continued. 'They both exit the second vehicle. Arkady's car was parked at the snooker club from about 8 p.m. that night. He must have taken public transport to wherever he met this second man, and after the fact, the man gave Arkady a lift back to Seven Sisters.'

'Do we have a name for Arkady's friend?' asked Scott.

'Yes. It's a Rudy Borisovsky. From Georgia, again settled here for years and no known criminal record. Again works for Leo Salter.'

Scott seemed to take in what they were saying. Sarah herself had taken a while to get her head around everything. Here were two men who, until a few hours before, had no connection to Millie or the Hayat family. Now they were being looked at as their prime suspects.

'How does this tie in to Millie's death though? If the two men were meeting miles away?'

'We tracked Rudy's vehicle as well. They used that one because Millie had been seen by someone getting into Arkady's car. The man who gave us the tip-off in the first place. So they probably thought Rudy's car was safer.'

'Was it?'

'Yes. When we did a search of vehicles in and around Hampstead Heath, his car did flag up. But it was one of dozens around there, and they marked their route carefully. We saw it arriving but we didn't see it leave and there was no coverage of where they parked or moved the body.'

'Have you looked for Rudy's car?'

'Yes.'

'Can we not trace the car? It might lead us to where Millie was killed?'

'Romesh is trying. He's also done a search of their mobile phones, but nothing is giving them away,' Moomy added. 'Burner phones probably.'

'So what do you want me to do now?' Scott asked.

'Arrest and search warrants for the two vehicles and any properties associated to both Arkady and Rudy. And we need to follow through Leo Salter's link to the Hayats.'

Scott cursed, rubbing his face. The Hayats. He obviously didn't want to go there again and risk pissing off Jane Haslam.

'Before we go near the Hayats I need more evidence,' he said.

'I understand, it's just if we arrest these guys, then the flares are up. We will lose the element of surprise and give the Hayats and Salter a chance to protect themselves. We need to act on everyone at the same time.' Sarah tried to sound convincing.

'Then I need more before I authorise this.'

Moomy and Sarah exchanged glances.

'Romesh couldn't find anything on the phones of Arkady and Rudy,' Moomy began hesitantly. This was going to go one of two ways with Scott. 'He did, however, check phone calls made to Leo Salter.'

'And who signed that off?' Scott's face was tense.

'We can do a historic check if this is right,' Moomy said. 'Say we did it after we got sign off.'

'For fuck's sake,' Scott muttered.

'Anyway we found this.'

Moomy slid a paper across the desk for Scott to read. His eyes gave nothing away.

'It's not going to stick unless we have some evidence, you know that?' he said.

'Yes,' Sarah said. 'We will work on getting that. I'd like to do the interview first at the Knightsbridge address though. If that's okay. So it's not under caution or an official interview. I'm not expecting a grand confession, but it will at least rattle some cages.'

She knew this was all that might happen, the interview. The Hayats were too clever to get their hands dirty. When the evidence was found, Arkady and Rudy would take the fall. Leo Salter would not be implicated. Sarah had worked on cases like this before. Men worked for the Salters of the world because they had family connections or some sense of affiliation. It worked both ways usually. They would cover the tracks of these wicked individuals and in return their families would be looked after.

But if this was all the justice Sarah was going to get for Millie, she would have to accept that.

Chapter Sixty

Moomy was always surprised when she hit places like this. It was only an hour's drive from Hampstead Heath, but it was pure countryside. In fact it was the Chiltern Hills range according to her satnav. Rural hideaway, perfect for carrying out the evil that men do. Fucking men. No, that wasn't true. Not all men. She parked up outside what looked like a dilapidated building made of bricks and a tin roof. It was the only structure out here, the rest was agricultural land and storage units. Moomy and the local force had already scanned them, doing searches which were reminiscent of her time at the Michaelides stores.

She knew that this would be it though; it had the right feel about it. The sort of place you could hide someone.

Romesh had found evidence of Rudy's car being seen in the area. And this place was registered to Leo Salter. After that it was about getting a warrant. Unlike the Michaelides storage units, this place wasn't heavily guarded. It seemed to barely be used for anything other than growing crops. And she had no doubt the outhouse was the go-to place for anything that needed to be done that was really under the radar. Like kill a girl.

Doctor Marcello Ramone tapped her on her shoulder. He really was hot.

'Are you ready?' he said, handing her boot covers and gloves. He had given up trying to get cops into full body suits; they never complied and usually ended up ripping them off or discarding them inappropriately.

'Yes, I think so.'

She followed him inside, two of his team had already started their work. They were using dull lights to inch their way in, as Moomy carefully followed them. They had developed new kit which highlighted any substance of interest like blood or fluid, evidence to be collected. It was all digitally stored so that the rest of the team would have an easier job of coming behind them and collecting it. There was no brilliant marker, like the Luminol they'd used back in the day, but it was efficient and meant they didn't miss evidence.

The inside of the building under the lights of the CSIs revealed a simple structure. The outside brick and tin roof were reflected inside, with wooden slots holding the roof up. She could see daylight in places; it wasn't well maintained, nothing of value would be kept here. There was an old tractor, rusted shovels and barrows. A ladder, some tools. The old steel industrial-style shelves, but nothing that looked fresh or as though it was functioning.

They crept forward, the four of them, scanning the place. Marcello was walking close to her, his face now covered in the CSI hood, only his eyes showing through protective glasses.

They carried on walking through the empty space, the darkness and damp oppressive. Moomy imagined what Millie had been going through. Was Oscar also held here? They would have to bring him and ask him to identify this place later. For now they needed to know it was the right place.

The CSIs came to a halt against a far wall. Moomy and Marcello stopped behind them and she saw what they had. It was clean, the floor of the building was a cheap lino. But there was a bottle of bleach and a rag. It was just one rag but it was from a packet of ten. The plastic wrapper had been left behind. Moomy looked at the space; it was between two wooden support structures that held up the roof. They were sturdy and had metal chains around them. Somewhere you could handcuff a person? There would have been a lot of blood, and some of it would still be here.

'Can your systems detect anything?' she asked.

'Yes,' said one of the CSIs. 'Definitely blood.'

Moomy nodded even though they couldn't see her. So this was it. The place Millie died. She was sure of it. Moomy wanted to cry, her insides raging. But she wouldn't, not yet anyway. They didn't know anything for sure.

'Anything else showing up?' she asked.

'There are fragments here of metal and wood; bone even, I suspect,' said the CSI. 'That's what the images are reflecting back to us but until we collect and analyse we won't know for sure.'

'Fucking bastards,' Moomy fumed.

There was no fucking way these guys were going to get away with it. She just hoped Sarah knew what she was doing. Their best shot was to at least get the assholes who had killed Millie. And at the moment it seemed to be Arkady and Rudy. Why they did it, well that was for

Sarah to confirm. If she could. Moomy didn't hold out much hope.

She left the CSIs inside to collect the data and the blood and DNA they might find. Bleach could only eradicate so much, and she didn't know how thorough a job Arkady and Rudy would have done. Bleach was only effective to a point.

The CSIs outside were scanning the surrounding area, tyre marks in the mud, any dropped cigarettes. One of them saw her and called her over. They pointed to the charred remains of a substantial fire. It had caught and spread, and the CSI confirmed it seemed recent. It was probably where the used rags had been destroyed.

It would be a long day, but it would also be a good day. They would find the truth buried here somewhere. And the answers, which were so few sometimes in the work they did. That was what mattered in the end.

Chapter Sixty-One

John greeted Sarah in the lounge. He looked half the man she had met only a few days before, the man with zeal in his eyes as he searched for his son. The man who was terrified his son would meet the same end as his daughter-in-law. The man who was ready to sacrifice himself for his family. The fire had gone from him. He had been running for so long, from so many different shadows, that he was tired now. Even his clothes, once sharp suits, were now casual attire. He looked a pair of slippers and a pipe away from being her grandfather.

'Do you feel any better?' she asked him.

'No. I fear an unknown. I think all the time where my wife and children might be harmed. I am keeping Ari busy. So much security at every place. I don't feel safe anywhere. Not even here at home. And I did this.'

John looked surprised when Sarah made her request. He gave Sarah the privacy she wanted though. The privacy to speak to his wife alone.. Sarah watched as Lara casually sauntered in, wearing slacks and a blouse, her face bare of make-up and still striking.

'Detective, how are you?' she said, while ringing the bell for tea and sitting opposite her. Lara Hayat in all her cool glamour. Oblivious to her truths being found out.

'I'm well. And yourself?'

'John said you wanted to check in on us. That is very kind of you.' Could she be any more patronising? 'The children are getting on with it, settling into their new roles. John is struggling but I am sure he will recover.'

'New roles?'

'Yes. Spencer is now head of Hayat and Wickham. Victor is acting as a type of deputy. It is as it should be. Problem with people like John is they always want to be like the establishment.'

'People like John?' Sarah hoped her stare was icy and direct.

'People not from here, you know. They want to fit in so adopt all sorts of ridiculous customs.'

'Yes. Like arranged marriages.'

Lara seemed unsure what the reference was to, so just tilted her head, her eyebrows crossed. Tea came in and was poured. Sarah didn't touch it. Not today.

'And Oscar?' she asked. 'What role does he play in this new dynasty?'

'Oscar is just broken. I want him to heal and then I've told him he will be back in the company. He said he didn't want to be the one responsible anymore and that's understandable.'

'Poor Oscar. Although not as poor and black as Millie, right?'

This pissed Lara off. Pissed off people always made mistakes.

'I really don't like this tone of yours. I am not racist. My issue with Millie was never about colour; I mean look at who I...'

'Yes, I know, the man you married, who could easily pass off as European. Very different to Millie.'

'Why are you here?' Steel in her eyes now.

'Let's talk about your marriage, shall we?'

'That's none of your business quite frankly…'

'And how this great love story of yours is nothing but a fabrication. How it was never your desire to marry John Hayat. How you did it to save the Wickham family business.'

'I don't know what you mean.'

'Press reports from back then, all talking about how Wickham Estates was about to go into receivership. You must have panicked, your whole family must have panicked. I mean imagine losing all this.'

Sarah gestured towards the wealth around them with her arms.

'There were rumours and some issues, all exaggerated. We are still here thirty years later.'

'Yes, thanks to John Hayat's money. How did it feel? When your father said you would be marrying him?'

Lara was quiet. Planning or shutting up? Sarah didn't care. She was just starting.

'Being forced to marry John to save your family. Very noble. Very unromantic.'

'I loved him,' she whispered.

'No. You loved another man. Rupert Cooper. The darling of the posh set. You were both captured by the camera numerous times, ready to announce your engagement one article said. And then things went wrong financially and you had to marry John. How did that make you feel?'

'Rupert was just a dear friend; the press exaggerate everything. You really should know better. Now, are we done dissecting matters that have nothing to do with you?'

'It must have been heartbreaking. Having to play happy families with John, all the while knowing that Rupert would be suffering your loss and having to watch you play wife to another man. Is that why you moved to America?'

Lara was still and cold.

'Then what happened? You decided you wanted to be near Rupert again? Did John know about your relationship with him? Before you were married? I doubt it. He's hardly the sort that reads *Tatler*. I'm sure your father said the same to you, John wouldn't be aware. But what about afterwards? How did you keep your relationship a secret then?'

A wry smile, a shrug, a challenge. Is this all you have? She wasn't denying it though. Sarah drank some of the tea after all. It did taste nice, and what the hell, she was probably never getting invited around here anytime soon.

'I doubt you even introduced Rupert to John. Because if you had, I'm sure he would have realised. Especially after Spencer was born. The child, a mirror image of his father. No?'

Now there was anger.

'How dare you come into my house and accuse me of these things.'

'I'm glad you're angry, because this isn't the end of it.'

'I want you to leave. Right now.'

'No. Not until I'm done. This isn't an official interview; you are not under arrest and I am here in my own capacity, not as an officer. So you can try and remove me, but I will scream this house down, and if John doesn't know it yet, he will know that Spencer is not his child. I will even offer to do the DNA test for him.'

Lara stood up, her composure gone. 'You bitch,' she spat. There it was. The vicious woman who had hounded Millie. The woman who was only interested in those she loved. And that did not extend to Millie not even to her own husband.

'Sit down. Or I swear to you, today I will open your secrets for the whole house to hear.'

Lara sat down heavily, her hand dangerously close to the tea tray. She wouldn't attack Sarah. Then again who knows what she was capable of?

'It must have killed you, knowing your golden child would not be your heir. Yet you went along with it, telling John you agreed. What were you waiting for? John to die so you could reverse his will and make Spencer the head of the business? And then Millie came along to ruin your long game. Millie who might give Oscar a family, and that would really screw things up. Because then you would have a fight on your hands. Oscar might agree to share the business with his brothers, especially if certain aspects of his private life were used against him. But would Millie give up the right to her children's futures so easily?'

'She wouldn't have a choice. I would have control anyway.'

'Yes. If your husband died. Then you could deal with Oscar. Oscar and his family? That complicated matters. Millie was an unknown who could ruin your plans for your son. Were you so lost in your love for Rupert that you forgot your other two children? Using one son to betray your others? What were you thinking?'

Silence.

'You thought you had time on your hands. But Millie took that away from you. And so what did you do? I'll tell you what you did. Leo Salter.'

Lara finally looked worried.

'Yes. We did wonder why he would get involved. Why he would help to kill an innocent girl who had walked into your filthy rich world, the outsider to your sickness. And then we found out. One wicked turn deserves another, right?'

Lara's hands were itching, her eyes sharp and scared, colour in her cheeks.

'You helped him launder his money. It was a personal transaction; you still hold power at Wickham Estates, we know. He bought property through you, and you allowed him to turn his smuggled and illegal millions into assets. Quite the trick, isn't it? Turning rich immigrants into members of the inner English circle? And yet a woman of colour? With no money?'

Lara was crumbling before her.

'So you called in your favour early. I'm guessing the favour would have been called in for your husband; instead, you decided Millie needed to be stopped. She had to be silenced. And so you put your plans into place. We have phone calls between yourself and Leo. And we have more than that. Leo's men. The ones who killed Millie. We have them too. And we have the evidence of where it happened. Oscar should be able to confirm that. You should have killed him too. Although I guess you're not so rotten that you would kill one of your children. So he survived, broken and ready to do your bidding. To allow Spencer, the remnant of your relationship with Rupert, to get everything. And yet it wasn't enough, was it? Because there was Victor. And he played his own game, more ruthless than you. He really is your son, isn't he? He messed things up for Spencer and he made himself heir apparent. So you had to act again. And how? You used Oscar as a messenger. You told John he needed to leave and sacrifice himself for his family. And he was going to do just that, until I stopped him. You must hate me.'

Lara stared at her coldly.

'So there you have it, Lara Hayat. This is who you are. And I am here to tell you that all your money and power and game playing, none of it will work. Once we have Leo Salter's men in custody I will make sure that your reality is exposed for the world to see.'

'You have no proof and that would be libel.'

Sarah got up and made to leave, but turned around to give Lara one last threat. She knew Lara would never be convicted: there just wasn't the evidence, and her money really would protect her.

'Shit sticks. And I am willing to go down for that. So you just watch and wait, because one day I will make sure that the truth of who you are is there for the world to see.'

Epilogue

Moomy was on the sofa bed, adrenaline and vodka in her veins. Sarah was in the rocking chair.

'You know you should just move in and save on your extortionate rent,' Sarah joked.

'You got a spare room?'

Sarah looked towards Rachel's room. No, she couldn't give that away yet. She and Ari had unfinished business over Rachel. Giving her room away would mean Sarah had given up on her. Logically, she knew there was no way Rachel could come back. After the things she had done. But if she could get her to a British prison, maybe she could talk to her, make her see the gravity of what she had done and let her serve her punishment here properly.

'No, I don't.'

'Well, I'm not paying for your sofa bed.'

'Isn't it time you stopped escaping your past, Moomy? Give up that studio flat nonsense and move somewhere more reasonable?'

'Fuck you, Dad.'

'Ouch.'

'Well, I don't tell you who to date, do I?'

'I don't date anyone.'

'Exactly that's the issue. You should though; it might do you good. Or are you dating your prayer mat still?'

Sarah didn't reply. She was drinking the hot chocolate she had made at home. It tasted foul. Too much cocoa powder.

'I spoke to Bill today,' Moomy said. 'Don't have a go at me about protocol and shit. He's alone, poor guy, won't do him or me any harm to have a chat now and then.'

'I didn't say a word. It's a nice thing to do. Very out of character for you, though.'

'Bitch.'

'How is he holding up?'

'He's a mess. But at least we got him some sort of justice.'

'Did we?'

'Yes, we did.'

The blood found at the Chiltern outhouse matched to Millie, along with her DNA. There were also remnants in both vehicles belonging to Arkady and Rudy. The gun used was found at a garage that Rudy used out of London, after warrants were issued and any address Rudy or Arkady had used was searched. They had kept the jackets they wore that night as well, confident they would not be caught. And it turned out the way Sarah thought it would.

'I wish we had broken the bastards,' Moomy said. 'They refused to implicate fucking Leo Salter at all.'

They knew better than to put their families at risk. They didn't give a reason for killing Millie and there was no paper trail anywhere. A house purchase made by Leo from Lara back in the eighties was hardly damning evidence.

And Lara Hayat herself had got away with the worst of it. Except, it seemed that maybe her plans hadn't quite worked out. Spencer was no longer running Wickham and Hayat. His incompetency had forced the board to remove him. They couldn't take the company from the legal owners, but they did not want him operating. His removal seemed to give John his chutzpah back, and he was back in charge. With Victor as his second.

So, she had failed completely, despite her cruel plans. Despite what she did to Millie.

'I want to rip her skin off,' said Moomy, as if reading Sarah's thoughts. 'It pisses me off that she's going to get away with it.'

'Yeah, well, she won't forever.'

'I want to see her suffer now, not in some hell I don't believe in.'

'Patience, one day that woman will fall. And we will be there to see it.'

'I fucking hope so. See this is why I would never live here. I need a fag and a drink.'

'Go to sleep.'

—

Moomy headed back to her own place in the morning. She wondered if she might see her hot neighbour Jake again. It had been a one off, just to feel better after seeing fucking Haroon. Nothing wrong with a bit of TLC now and then.

She didn't see the guy until he practically collided into her. What was this? Attack Moomy outside her apartment block week?

'Watch it,' she said. No place for niceness when you could get stabbed or all sorts. Show you don't mess around.

She turned to walk off. Asshole.

'Mumtaz. It's me.'

Moomy froze. Mumtaz. What the actual fuck? In a second her past had slammed into her. No, no, no. This wasn't happening. Who the hell had found her? Moomy's heart battered her ribcage, her throat dry. The fight stance she normally took had stopped dead inside her. Just like that. Who was it? She knew though. She didn't even need to see.

'I need your help,' he said.

Moomy turned around, staring into eyes she had never wanted to see again . This man from her past, the past she thought she'd left long behind.

'How did you find me?' she said.

But she knew, and she didn't like what was going to happen next.

–

The graveyard was full of the usual suspects. There were the old ladies visiting their husbands and friends. A young woman who had lost her partner; she always came with a baby who must have only been a year old. They always broke Sarah's heart. She should talk to them really. The staff that tended to the graves, made sure they looked flat and clean. De-weeding and watering plants and flowers. There was a peaceful hum to the place even though it was freezing.

Sarah stood at her mother's grave. She said a prayer for her and told her what was happening in her life.

'I miss you so much, Mum. And I really hope one day we are together somewhere again.'

There was no reply, of course. That's not how it worked.

'I found Rachel. I promised you I would. So I'm going to bring her home.'

A faint breeze ruffled her headscarf, and twirled the pink plastic windmills on a grave nearby. A child, the grave so small. There was no guarantee of a long life. You had your time and you had no idea what it would hold.

'I love you, Mum, and I will miss you for the rest of my life.'

It was always what she said when she visited.

She walked back to her car, where Ari was waiting for her.

'Are you ready?' he said.

'As ready as I'll ever be.'

A LETTER FROM ALEX

Thank you so much for reading *The Unbroken*. It's the start of a new series for me, going back to my police procedural/crime roots that I started with *Cut to the Bone*.

There are so many novels out there that follow this format, so I didn't want to write just another run of the mill story or introduce characters that were imitations of those that already exist. I wanted to really create characters that were raw, fresh and totally kick-ass.

At first, I thought of using a male/female dynamic as in my first two novels, but then thought actually, why not create a female duo? Hera is a testament to how well two women at the top can work. I also wanted to say something important with both my characters. All my favourite detective series from Patricia Cornwell to Angela Marsons are about the leads for me, as well as the story.

Moomy was an important character I wanted to write for many years. Her background is very similar to my own, but the way her life shapes up and the choices she makes, are areas I really wanted to discuss. Moomy, the 'bad' Asian girl who has gone off the rails, has been portrayed many times. But I rail against the idea that someone simply wakes up one day and turns their back on everything they know simply because they want to get drunk or laid. I wanted to explore a story that was too common when

I was growing up and give a voice to those women, to explain how they survived and thrived. She is also great fun to write-saying and doing everything I don't have the guts to.

Sarah was another character I was fascinated by. I always wondered why women such as her, born and brought up in the West, who had all the freedom that comes with that, would choose a world that was restrictive. I also wanted to really understand how someone like Sarah would be received, the challenges she would face. And I hope I get to continue her voice, because she is very much of the moment.

The story of the novel itself is one that has been festering in my head for a while too. I love writing about the rich and powerful, and how they have different rules applied to them. And how decent police officers don't care about special privileges and buck the system to bring them to justice. I also wanted to show what happens when an ordinary girl dares to marry into a family that is worth billions. The pressure, expectations and ultimately the sacrifice.

I have had so much support since the publication of my first crime novel, especially from the blogging and writing community. You welcomed me in no questions asked and really cheered me on, and I have made some lifelong friendships from it. For an author like myself who is new, that support is crucial, without that backing and help there is no way I would even be writing today. So thank you, and I really hope I can receive the same love and backing for *The Unbroken* that you showed my earlier novels.

I really hope you enjoy reading this novel, and it would mean the world to me if you would write a review if you do. Reviews and recommendations are so important for an author like me, and every single one is gratefully appreciated. I love reading, it's my passion, and I hope I can make other people escape into a different world the way I do when I read.

I would love to hear your feedback, I am active on Twitter, so please do get in touch. And thank you again for reading *The Unbroken* and your support, it's greatly appreciated.

Alex

Twitter:
https://twitter.com/alexkhanauthor

Facebook:
https://www.facebook.com/alexkhanauthorpage

ACKNOWLEDGMENTS

I forget all the people that were kind to me this last year-it was one of the worst after the death of my mother, so just thank you for every kind word and thought and gesture. It was hugely appreciated and I want to thank you all.

Alison Bonomi for being my go to when I have issues with the world. Thank you - and all the team at LBA.

Keshini Naidoo for letting me follow my path in writing without compromise.

Lindsey Mooney for knocking on every door trying to get people to read my work.

MKAZORHZZI – I wish only the best for you always.

God, my family and friends – still here, still there. Thank you.